SHAUKAT OSMAN was b̲
home in the village of Sabal̲
He studied Economics at St̲
a Master's degree in Bengal̲
Calcutta University. In 194̲
Institute of Commerce and i̲
he taught in Chittagong Government College of Commerce and at
Dhaka College until he retired in 1977.

He has published over sixty volumes of fiction, drama, poetry
and essays. His fiction includes *Adam's Children* (1945), *Janani*
(serialised in 1945–46 and published in 1961), *The Slave's Laugh*
(1962), *The Wolf Forest* (1980), *The Insect Cage* (1983), *The State
Witness* (1985) and several volumes of short stories.

Uniquely among the Bengali Muslim writers who emerged in
the forties, Shaukat Osman uses the lives of peasants and the
urban poor as his themes. He became increasingly involved in his
nation's struggle against cultural oppression, bigotry and
obscurantism and this is reflected in his literature. Ironically, *The
Slave's Laugh*, a fictional allegory critical of the cultural policies of
General Ayub Khan (the military dictator who took power in
1958), won him a prestigious literary prize which was presented by
the president himself.

OSMAN JAMAL has an M.Phil. in English Literature from
Leeds University. He has taught and lectured widely on the
subject in Dhaka College, the University of Chittagong and in
Bradford schools. He has been translating Shaukat Osman's fiction
since 1962 when they were colleagues at Dhaka College. Osman
was one of the subjects of a lecture he gave on the literature of
Bangladesh at the Commonwealth Institute in London in 1986.

SHAUKAT OSMAN

JANANI

Translated from the Bengali by
Osman Jamal

HEINEMANN

Heinemann Educational
A Division of Heinemann Publishers (Oxford) Ltd
Halley Court, Jordan Hill, Oxford OX2 8EJ

Heinemann: A Division of Reed Publishing (USA) Inc.
361 Hanover Street, Portsmouth, NH 03801-3912, USA

Heinemann Educational Books (Nigeria) Ltd
PMB 5205, Ibadan
Heinemann Educational Boleswa
PO Box 10103, Village Post Office, Gaborone, Botswana

FLORENCE   PRAGUE   PARIS   MADRID
ATHENS   MELBOURNE   JOHANNESBURG
AUCKLAND   SINGAPORE   TOKYO
CHICAGO   SAO PAULO

First published in Bengali by Student Ways, Dhaka in 1961
© Shaukat Osman 1961
This translation © Osman Jamal 1993
First published by Heinemann Educational in 1993

Series Editor: Ranjana Sidhanta Ash

British Library Cataloguing in Publication Data
A catalogue record for this book is available from the British Library.

Cover design by Touchpaper
Cover illustration by Mark Edwards

ISBN 0435 95083 5

Phototypeset by Wilmaset Ltd, Birkenhead Wirral
Printed and bound in Great Britain
by Cox & Wyman Ltd, Reading, Berkshire

93 94 10 9 8 7 6 5 4 3 2 1

Introduction to the Asian Writers Series

Heinemann's new Asian Writers Series, aided by the Arts Council of Great Britain, intends to introduce English language readers to some of the interesting fiction written in languages that most will neither know nor study.

For too long popular acclaim for Asian writing in the West has been confined to the handful of authors who choose to write in English rather than in the language of their own cultures. Heinemann's entry into the field should dispel this narrow perspective and place modern Asian writing within the broad spectrum of contemporary world literature.

The first six works selected for the series are translations of novels from five languages: Bengali, Hindi, Malayalam, Tamil and Urdu. The six novels span seventy-five years of change in the subcontinent. *Quartet*, one of Rabindranath Tagore's most skilfully constructed and lively classics, was first published in 1916, whereas the most recent work chosen, *The Fire Sacrifice*, was written by the up-and-coming Hindi novelist Susham Bedi and first published in 1989.

These first six titles face the normal problems affecting literature in translation, not least the difficulty of establishing an exact parallel of the thought or verbal utterance of the original in the target language. When the source text is in a non-European language and embodies a culture and literary style quite alien to English language readers, the translator's task is made even more difficult.

Susan Bassnett in her invaluable work on translation studies describes the typical colonial attitude to the literature of the colonised as a 'master and servant' relationship, with the European translator attempting to 'improve' and 'civilise' the source text. At the other end of the scale she describes a kind of 'cannibalism' in which the translator almost 'devours' the text to disgorge a totally new product. Fortunately, the translators of this series fall into neither category but manage to retain a balanced view of their craft.

While it is very important to produce a translation that uses a style both readable and engaging to an English language readership, it must not obscure the particularities of literary devices, figures of speech, and aesthetic detail that the author uses to convey his or her sensibility, imagination and verbal artistry. Should such faithfulness to the original produce in the English version a greater degree of sentiment or charged imagery than the reader might expect, one hopes that he or she will be ready to accept the novelty of writing from an unfamiliar source.

In publishing the Asian Writers Series, Heinemann is taking a bold step into an area which has been neglected for too long. It is our hope that readers will respond with interest and enthusiasm as they discover the outstanding quality of these novels.

RANJANA SIDHANTA ASH, SERIES EDITOR, 1993

Introduction to Janani

At the heart of *Janani* is the tragedy of a poverty-stricken mother, crushed between the conflicting claims of her devotion to her children and her honour. Hence the title *Janani*, the Bengali word for mother. *Janani*, Shaukat Osman's first novel, was partially serialised in 1945–46 in a Calcutta literary magazine, and the book was published in Dhaka fifteen years later, in 1961, by which time Shaukat Osman had established himself as a major writer in East Pakistan (Bangladesh since 1971).

In *Janani*, Moheshdanga, the archetypal Bengal village created by the author, is distanced from the city giving it a timeless quality. The novel's perspective is implicitly that of a child and Osman's method, in the early chapters, is one of building up, through a simple narrative, the details, often cinematically conceived, in the life of a peasant family. Azhar Khan is an orthodox Muslim, descended from a Pathan warrior, who settled in Moheshdanga as a fugitive from the revolt of 1857. His wife, Dariabibi, energetic and proud, has a natural dignity to which everybody defers. However, the world of Moheshdanga, like that of Greek tragedy, is governed by unquestionable imperatives and Dariabibi is to become a victim of these imperatives.

The inter-relationships of the characters hold Moheshdanga in a stasis until the coming of the seducers from a more urban world in the shape of Yakoob and Rajendra. A word must be said about the historical background to the novel, especially because Moheshdanga, so remote from the city, the playground of history, would seem to be untouched by history. The early forties was a time of great turmoil in Bengal. The anti-imperialist struggle reached its peak in 1942 and 1943 saw the great Bengal famine. What was of even greater significance for years to come was the ascendency of religion-based politics. In 1940 the Muslim League demanded the partition of India. The actual partition, of 1947, following a series of inter-religious conflicts and blood-lettings, was still a few years away when Shaukat Osman started writing *Janani*. A quarter of a century later, the break-up of Pakistan would reveal the vacuity of the solution sought by the partition. But the politics of religion refuses to die and today in the wake of worldwide crisis of modernity, of the enlightenment tradition, it is once again raising its 'reptile head'. The history we have failed to transcend remains a contemporary nightmare and the questions Shaukat Osman poses and tries to answer in *Janani* remain unresolved.

What he tries to do can be put in terms of three questions. What is at the root of religion-based politics? What is the nature of intra-religious or sectarian conflict? Is it not possible for Hindus and Muslims to live together in harmony as they have done for centuries? Osman answers the first question in Chapter 22 where the *zamindars*, Hatem Bakhsh Khan and Rohini Choudhury, in their selfish interest over the possession of a marshland throw the two religious communities against one another. In Chapter 25, the author gives a droll account of a quarrel between two Muslim sects – the Hanafis and the Majhabis. Osman explores the third question through the relationship between Azhar Khan, an orthodox Wahabi Muslim, and Chandra Kotal, a low-caste Hindu. In this experiment in the possibility of civilisation within the microcosm of Moheshdanga, the author does not make things easy for himself. Azhar and Chandra are by no means kindred souls. Temperamentally, Chandra is the opposite of stolid Azhar; Chandra's joy of life enlivens the novel like an electric impulse. In their attitudes to life, they are poles apart. Azhar does not approve of his friend's irreverence, his cavalier attitude to conventional morality, or his addiction to home-brewed toddy. Chandra dislikes Azhar's timidity, his spirit of seriousness (in the Sartrian sense of the expression) and agrees with Dariabibi that he is 'a quiet devil'. Yet we find their friendship entirely convincing, and more so for its occasional hurdles. Azhar feels isolated when Rajendra teams up with Chandra to set up a folk theatre. Their friendship is further threatened when the *zamindars* incite communal frenzy. Even Chandra falls under its spell. It is a pity that, during this period, Azhar goes into self-imposed exile. When he returns, Chandra refuses to talk to him, but only temporarily. For Chandra has no closer friend, and Azhar returns from his last exile to put himself 'in Chandra's hands'. After Azhar's death Chandra remains a friend of the family. Dariabibi, in purdah, never appears before Chandra, but it is to him she turns in need, and when she sends Amjad demanding his presence, even a drunken Chandra will hoist the boy on his shoulders and totter off across the fields.

Shaukat Osman has devoted an increasing amount of his writing to the nation's struggle against religious bigotry, social obscurantism and political oppression, taking on what he considers to be a writer's inalienable responsibility. This has not always had a salutary effect on his fiction. *Janani*, however, written earlier and free from any proselytising zeal, remains his most powerful novel to date, achieving something of the status of a modern classic.

OSMAN JAMAL, 1993

Chapter One

It was past twilight.

The kitchen in the courtyard had no roof on it. Only the silhouettes of the bamboo posts and canes occasionally became visible in the flames of the fireplace. There was another kitchen to the south of the courtyard, but it was uncomfortable working inside a covered hut in summer, so Azhar had built a roofless kitchen for Dariabibi in the courtyard.

Dariabibi was making up a fire in the oven. The pot crackled, and with each gust of wind flames leapt out. You could see Dariabibi's face; beads of perspiration stood out on her temple.

Amjad was sitting beside his mother watching her cook. In another corner Azhar Khan, his father, was chopping bundles of hay.

'I've looked everywhere for the calf, *Abba**,' Amjad said. 'He's very naughty! And so is his mother. Losing her calf like that.'

Azhar was putting the chopped hay into a wicker basket. Suddenly the wind knocked the nearly full basket on its side and the chopped hay started blowing away. Azhar cried, 'Amu, catch 'em, son, catch 'em.'

Dariabibi moved to help her husband. She was about thirty, slim, her round face grave.

Amjad ran about chasing bits of chopped hay.

'Look, *Abba*, they're flying away.'

Bits of hay blew upward with the wind.

Tired, Dariabibi exclaimed, 'The way you work!' and looked at her husband.

Azhar replied quietly, 'It was so sudden. Hasn't happened before, has it?'

---

*Abba: Daddy. For a note on Muslim/Hindu terminology for family relationships, see page 216.

1

Her hair dishevelled, clutching a fistful of hay, she called out, 'Amu, come here, son, see what's fallen in my eye.'

Dariabibi had sat down. Amjad ran up to his mother.

'Put these into the basket.'

Amjad immediately obeyed his mother's order.

'My eye hurts.'

Dariabibi rolled the corner of her sari into a little bundle and held it to her open mouth to blow on it; she then applied the warm compress to the eye.

'Is it better, Ma?'

'Hang on, son.'

Amjad was wearing an unsewn *lungi*. Imitating his mother, he put the corner of the *lungi* into his mouth.

'The curry's burning!'

Dariabibi rushed to the oven.

'Amu, get me a little water.'

But it was no use asking Amjad to help. Dariabibi ran to the other kitchen, where the pitcher was.

Pouring a bowl of water into the pot, she said, 'Father and son did it. The eye still hurts.'

Azhar was sitting on a bale of hay, holding a coconut hookah.

'Dariabibi, is there enough fire in the oven?'

Sitting beside the oven, Dariabibi was tidying her dishevelled hair.

'Why not? We're burning pricey firewood, aren't we?'

Azhar looked at Dariabibi; a shadow of fatigue had fallen across her fair face. His enthusiasm crushed, Azhar twirled the pipe on the ground.

'You know we're burning leaves. What sort of fire can leaves make? Allah hasn't written in our fate we'd burn firewood, has he?'

'Keep using them.'

'That's what I'm doing. Sweeping up leaves isn't easy. The other day Zaker's mother said, "Don't sweep up leaves from our tree, dear . . ." Have you sold all the hay?'

Azhar smoked a great deal. Now the spell induced by tobacco was nearly broken and he lost his patience. Holding his hookah pipe, he stood in front of Dariabibi.

'How else did I pay the land tax?'

'The cattle would have survived on it if you hadn't . . .'

Looking up at her husband, Dariabibi pulled the corner of her sari over her head and quietly took the pipe from Azhar's hand.

'Amu, get a potsherd.'

'What's a potsherd for?' Azhar asked.

Dariabibi's voice was very smooth now.

'If the wind comes gusting, flying sparks from the pipe could start a fire.'

When she had lit the pipe, she carefully covered it with the potsherd.

His eyes closed, Azhar smoked his hookah to the sound of bubbles passing through water.

'There are some trees by the pond; how about cutting them down? You won't have to worry about fuel for a few months,' he said.

'No, if you cut them down, what then? What'll you do when you need them? There's the children's marriages to think of.'

Amjad was sitting by his mother. He said, 'Who's getting married, Ma?'

'Me!' Dariabibi smiled, an electric impulse charging her serious face.

Then, looking at Azhar, she said, 'The boy won't let us talk. Your father's getting married, Amu.'

Azhar smoked away silently. He had ploughed a few *bighas* of land; Dariabibi's words didn't reach him. He felt sleepy in the tobacco haze.

Like someone just waking up, he said, 'Who's getting married?'

'You, me, the whole village.'

Dariabibi laughed. Azhar simply cast a glance at her before getting back to the hookah. Azhar Khan was a timorous sort, untouched by anything except the daily struggle.

Dariabibi said to her son, who was sitting beside her, 'Call your father. See if he's awake.'

'*Babaji.*'

'What is it, Amu?'

Dariabibi addressed her husband. 'I'll finish cooking now. Talk to the boy.'

'Ma.'

'What?'

'Look in the cowshed and see if the calf's got back.'

'Good job you remembered.'

She told Azhar, 'Go and see if the calf's got back.'

Azhar had no doubt that the calf was safe.

'He'll be back tomorrow morning, you'll see.'

Amjad quietly said, 'Tell him to go and look in the cowshed, Ma.'

'Why don't you go and look in the cowshed?'

'Leave it for tomorrow.'

The white calf was Amjad's favourite; there was no other reason for his complaint to his mother.

'Ma, if a fox gets the calf?'

'How can a fox touch such a big calf?' Azhar said.

'Well, the foxes these days!' Amjad said.

'Well, the foxes these days, so why don't you go?' Dariabibi said to her husband in mock anger. And, to her son, 'How far did you go to look for the calf, Amu?'

'As far as the graveyard.'

Dariabibi took a pot and walked off to the other kitchen. To the west there was a thatched hut with two rooms where they lived and slept, its walls made of plaited bamboo. Next to it there was this kitchen, where pots and pans were stored.

Leaving the pot in the kitchen, Dariabibi returned.

'Did you go to the old graveyard?'

The old graveyard was where the martyrs were buried. There was a new graveyard for recent deaths.

'I keep telling you never to go there and you won't listen.'

'I wasn't scared, Ma.'

'Never you mind. I'll get the holy water of the elder *pir*.'

Dariabibi got a bottle of water and a clay bowl.

Azhar, who wasn't very well, was dozing; he hadn't noticed what mother and son were up to.

'What did you get, Dariabou?'

'Holy water for the boy.'

Azhar rushed to them with the speed of an arrow.

'What are you doing? What's this?'

'Why, what's wrong?'

'Holy water! Such heresy in the home of a Wahabi? What'll people say?'

'Sit down!' Dariabibi cried in a hoarse voice. 'You keep your "heresy".'

'It's no good, Dariabou,' Azhar quietly replied.

'Why do you make trouble over this? Children fall ill and things. I'm not drinking it, am I?'

By then holy water from the bowl had drenched Amjad's throat.

A man of few words, Azhar stood sullenly for a while.

But Dariabibi would not be prevailed upon. So, hookah in hand, Azhar went back to his place.

Dariabibi felt her husband was annoyed. The atmosphere had to be brought back to normal.

'Go and talk to your father,' she told her son. 'I'll go and stoke up the fire.'

Amjad hesitated.

Although Azhar was silent, there was the sound of the hookah. Amjad went and sat down on the mud floor beside his father.

Azhar now spoke: 'You're sitting on the mud floor. Come and sit on my knee.'

'May I come as well?' Dariabibi called out.

'Come on, Ma.'

With his son perched on his knee, Azhar puffed away.

'Leave it, son,' Dariabibi said. 'It's no use my coming.'

Azhar saw Dariabibi stretching out her palm to taste the salt in the curry, a smile making lines on her face.

The fire was dying; cooking was over. Dariabibi was not visible any more but her laugh could be heard.

Then a shadow fell across the courtyard, followed by somebody. A naked three-year-old girl was walking up, her hair uncombed and her eyes so full of pus she could not open them properly. She appeared as if she had come out to supervise the courtyard.

Azhar's eyes first fell on her.

'Come here, dear, come. Where have you been?'

'Here comes the ghost woman,' cried Amjad.

Dariabibi laughed as she looked over her shoulder: 'Old woman, so you've woken up at last.'

Naima, Dariabibi's three-year-old daughter, got in the way in the evenings when she had work to do, and often cried. So Dariabibi had put her to sleep.

Naima didn't go to Azhar; she went straight to her mother.

'Hang on, dear.'

Dariabibi removed a pot from the oven and made Naima sit on her lap. She wiped the pus from her eyes.

Naima did not speak at all; she yawned as if she hadn't slept well.

'What, you want to sleep more?'

Naima didn't speak; she snuggled her face against her mother's breast.

'Hang on a bit. Then I'll serve your *Abba*, Amu'll eat, you'll eat.'

5

At the talk of food Naima moved restlessly in her mother's lap.

Dariabibi said, addressing Azhar Khan: 'Finish with your night prayers. No use delaying any further. She's still sleepy.'

'Amu's snoring,' said Azhar.

Seated on a bale of hay, Amu swayed; a whole kingdom's sleep had come to his eyes.

Dariabibi fetched water in a *bodna*, a water jar with a spout.

'Listen,' she said, 'I sowed some gourd seeds there to the south. They've sprouted. I water them every day. Go and do your ablutions there. Let a little ablution water fall on them too. The water from the washed feet of the master.'

Without a word Azhar went to the south of the yard for his ablutions. He didn't like Dariabibi laughing about these matters.

Now that cooking was over, Dariabibi placed a pot on the mouth of the oven to prevent the burning leaves from scattering in the wind. She had finished work for the night.

She fetched another jar of water and spattered it on dozing Amjad's face.

'Now wake up. We'll have our meal. You didn't read at all this evening.'

Naima was still grumbling.

'Just hang on a bit. I'll go and wash my face in the pond.'

Azhar Khan, who had finished saying prayers, rolled up the tattered prayer mat.

Dariabibi said, 'A new prayer mat will never be bought. Cheating God in every thing.'

'They asked for one and a half rupee for a prayer mat at the fair.'

That ought to have been the end of the argument, but Dariabibi wouldn't let go.

'Tattered mat. Let the head keep hitting the ground. When people see the calloused forehead, they'll say, Here's a pious man.'

After he had rolled up the prayer mat, Azhar Khan opened his mouth: 'Azhar Khan doesn't say his prayers to deceive Allah,' he announced. 'Everybody knows of my great-grandfather Ali Asjad Khan. I belong to that family.'

'My great-grandfather is an educated *moulvi*, do I have to learn to read?' Dariabibi taunted.

Azhar Khan could not bear to hear his family denigrated; he usually stopped being a nice man. But today he held his peace.

'You say your prayers on the mat as well,' Azhar said. 'Do you fancy being pious too?'

'Our paradise lies beneath your feet. If you can use it, how can it be wrong for me?'

For a moment Azhar Khan gave vent to his anger.

'Don't ask for anything else then. It's just a mat, I'll get one no matter how costly.'

'You don't have to be so angry. The forehead's worn out on that mat; Allah hasn't given us the means to buy a new one, has he?'

Azhar kept quiet. Dariabibi's words caused a turbulence in his breast. She was becoming so disobedient. Standing sullenly, Azhar Khan said 'God forbid!' three times.

'Keep a watch on the children. I'm going to the pond.'

She had this moment of rest after the whole day. A *Chaitra* breeze was blowing; unnamed flowers had bloomed somewhere in the vegetation.

She got back soon. Azhar, who was sitting on the veranda with the children, said, 'That was quick.'

'Perhaps the goat'll give birth. It's not that late; go and fetch her in here.'

'No, no, she won't give birth yet.'

'She's calling out every now and then. If she gives birth at night, that calf's so naughty, he'll kick the kids to death.'

The pond lay beyond a little abandoned house. To the north-west of the pond was the cowshed, where cattle and goats were housed. Snakes thrived in the long grass on the sides of the pond. So Azhar felt no urge to get on with the job.

Without another word, Dariabibi entered the kitchen. She kept her ears open as she ladled out the curry into a bowl, listening to the goat calling out.

Naima did not eat with her own fingers, so when others had finished eating, Dariabibi put the girl on her lap. Not fully awake, she quietly ate from her mother's fingers.

Dariabibi's ears were ever alert to the call of the goat. These dumb animals were an asset to this indigent family. Two kids had been born in the cowshed last year and gored to death by the cows. It should not be allowed to happen again. If those kids were still alive, they could be sold at a good price now. Only the other day the traders had come to make enquiries.

Rest did not automatically follow the evening meal. The sky was

7

overcast. If it rained at night, cowpats in the courtyard would get wet and there would be no fire in the oven tomorrow. Women quarrelled over dead leaves. Dariabibi ran out to collect the cowpats in a basket. She had already washed; now she had to touch the cowpats. She did not easily get tired, but she felt bad today.

Amjad did not sleep near his mother; he slept elsewhere. Azhar Khan had an old aunt, a distant relation, called Ashekjan, who did not see well and was also deaf. She stayed here because she had nowhere else to go and somehow survived on the charity and *zakat* given by well-to-do Muslims of the village on the days of Eid, Muharram and other feasts. She went into her room before dark and did not go out again; and she didn't eat in the house. Amjad slept curled up beside her. Ashekjan, a light sleeper, couldn't keep watch on the boy, being short-sighted; so Dariabibi got up late at night and walked through the inner door into this room to see if he was all right. Amjad slept badly; he often rolled out to lie on the mud floor. Holding up a lamp, Dariabibi went in to have a look at Amjad; no, he was sleeping like a good boy.

Ashekjan was awakened by the sound of her footsteps.

'Is that Azhar?'

'No, it's Daria, *Khala*.'

'What is it, Dariabou?'

'I just came.'

'You work all day. Now go and sleep.'

'Right.'

'Dariabou,' Ashekjan spoke again. 'Now you're here, get me a little water, dear. It'll save me groping about in the dark.'

Actually, Ashekjan was not much troubled by the dark. Lighting two lamps was beyond the means of this family and Ashekjan didn't make demands. She had tamed everything to her habit. She could even make her way to the pond in the dark.

Dariabibi poured out some water from the pitcher.

'Dariabou, tomorrow I'll go to the other village to see if anybody'll give me a piece of cloth. Muslim Munshi gave me one last Eid, may Allah be good to him.'

Dariabibi could be pretty harsh with the old woman. She had to start gossiping so late at night. With Dariabibi's departure, the room again filled with darkness. Being deaf, Ashekjan could not keep her voice in balance; she shouted, 'What's the matter with the damned times? People haven't got the charity to give away a piece of cheap

8

cloth. It must be the end of times. It's not long before Dazzal the Devourer appears. It's the fourteenth century; the Holy Book can't be wrong, can it?'

After a while Ashekjan realised that there was nobody in the room and fell silent. Picking lice from her white hair, she heaved a sigh.

Dariabibi's fear was not without foundation. The continuous call of the goat was heard again in the silence of the night.

It was difficult for Dariabibi to keep lying in bed. If the goat had delivered, she would not be able to cope on her own; so she had to wake Azhar.

'Listen, the goat's restless.'

Azhar sat up.

'I'll go and see. Light the lamp.'

Dariabibi obeyed her husband. Azhar opened the door to find clouds gathering in the sky and a wind rising.

'Dariabou, can you carry the lamp? It's very windy.'

There was a clay pot in the corner of the room. Dariabibi placed the lamp in it.

'Let's go. I'll try and avoid the wind.'

One had to step carefully along the footpath beside the pond with its dense undergrowth on both sides. The damp light inside the clay pot failed to spread out. The goat's cry wouldn't stop.

A storm could start any time. The trees along the banks of the pond seemed to be crashing down, as if the spirit of the nocturnal jungle was engaged in a mad dance, laughing wildly. There was a sound of groaning all around.

Carrying the lamp, Dariabibi stepped carefully ahead.

'I could move the cowshed closer to the house,' Azhar said. 'But then where are we going to find the space? It's good of the Rays to allow us to put up the cowshed by the pond.'

Dariabibi was busy protecting the lamp; Azhar's words did not enter her ears. A wild plum bush lay across the bank; Azhar pushed it out of the way with a stick. They had to step carefully, as the footpath was cluttered with thorny twigs.

Standing in front of the cowshed, they sighed with relief. The cry of the mother goat could no longer be heard.

As soon as they opened the door of the cowshed, a white calf came running from a cluster of palm trees in front.

'Where were you at dusk, you unlucky one?'

Standing close to Azhar, the calf shook his tail, as if scolding from humans was an early symptom of affection to follow. Dariabibi put a rope round its neck; it would otherwise finish off all the milk of its mother.

First there was the cattle stall; the goat stall was in another corner, where it was darker. The wind hit the cowshed less violently as it could not easily penetrate the fortress of palm trees surrounding it.

Carrying the lamp, Dariabibi entered the goat stall and her eyes lit up with happiness. The helpless mother goat stood licking the two black kids in front of her.

The placenta had not come out yet. Dariabibi said, 'I'll get it out. What if she eats it up? Have we got the money to buy milk for the kids to survive?'

Without further delay, Dariabibi silently performed the midwife's job.

'Let's go. There could be more wind. You carry the goat, I'll take the kids and the lamp.'

Azhar hesitated; he did not like the touch of a goat which had just delivered.

'Well, if you behave like a *babu* . . .'

'Leave her here for the night,' Azhar said. 'Let's take the kids.'

Dariabibi's voice rang out: 'You take the kids, I'll carry the goat.'

Dariabibi had a good constitution; she easily lifted the goat. Happiness made her even more active.

After a while the trouble started with the lamp. The kids were held close to Azhar's chest. The lamp too had to be carefully protected inside the clay pot; if the hand trembled it could be blown out by the wind.

Dariabibi was furious when just past the wild plum bush, a gust of wind put out the lamp.

'That's not your job, is it? Why didn't you give me the kids?' Azhar did not respond. The two somehow made their way in the dark.

Black clouds came crashing down on the village. Rains would bring no end of misery.

In the dark Dariabibi repeatedly called upon Allah. Naima was sleeping alone in the room with its walls of rotting crushed bamboo. All Dariabibi's rage fell on Azhar as tears came to her eyes; she had to live with such a man.

'Not much further to go, Dariabou,' Azhar said.

10

A flash of lightning revealed the footpath; they had reached the end of the pond.

Now the rains poured down. Azhar ran along the familiar path, but Dariabibi, carrying the heavy goat, walked carefully under the rain and storm.

Getting on to the veranda, Dariabibi found the door blown open and leaves and other rubbish sweeping into the room. Naima had started howling. Ashekjan was shouting, though nothing could be made of her words.

Putting down the goat on the ground, Dariabibi sat on the mud floor. She wasn't choosy about where she sat; she was much too tired.

Azhar had lighted a lamp and sat down on the mat. Blackened cotton had come out of the corner of an oil-stained pillow. Azhar lay down.

Tired Dariabibi, with pity in her eyes, kept looking at her husband's face.

Chapter Two

There had been a shower of rain at night. In the morning Azhar went to the field carrying the plough on his shoulder. The field was a mile away and it was possible to go home for his midday meal, but then it was a waste of labour getting back to the field afterwards. So Amjad took his lunch to the field. Dariabibi didn't like that – Amjad missed school, his education suffered – but there was no alternative. Dariabibi could work at home, but it was unseemly for women who observed purdah to go to the field.

Amjad, however, liked the job. It was excruciating sitting on the floor of the *maktab* for hours on end. He would get a headache, he would yawn, yet the *moulvi* wouldn't talk of dismissing school. But here he could walk about in the fields at will; what else in the world could be more pleasurable?

Amjad could not get to the field on the dot at midday. Dariabibi did hurry, but Amjad had to eat after cooking was over and a little boy needed rest; so the sun slid towards the west. Of course that did not annoy Azhar. Smiling, he said, 'Why so late, son?'

'Cooking was late. And I can't walk very fast.'

Wiping the boy's young perspiring face, Azhar said, 'That's all right, I'm thirsty, go and get some water from the river.'

Amjad obeyed his father. He wasn't much less tired than his father, having walked under a midday scorching sun, but he was prepared to forget that in the happiness of being freed from the prison of the *maktab*.

Azhar sat down to eat in the shade of the *koyet-bel* trees.

Five years ago two *koyet-bel* plants had come floating down the river in flood. Azhar had with his own hands planted the flood-borne plants. Now other tired peasants too gathered in the shade of these leafy trees. There were some wild banana trees in another corner of the field; it was useless to plant good ones as the fruit got stolen at

12

night; so nobody planted good bananas in the field. In the past Azhar used to have his midday meal under the banana leaves. Some peasants had now started living in the fields; they were mostly *bagdi* or *teor* untouchables. Azhar too would have preferred to live in the field; you could keep watch over the crop and work when you wished; but Dariabibi did not agree. It was not possible to keep one's honour in the open; then there was no pond, and the near side bank of the river being high, the water receded to the far side in summer. A woman from a pious Muslim family couldn't violate purdah. The untouchables had no such difficulties; tiny naked children went with their mothers to the river to bathe at midday. Sometimes, when there was a flood, there would be no end of misery even if the homestead was built high enough. A few years ago, during a flood, two sons of Rashik Bagdi had fallen into the current and were never found again. Whenever the question of moving was raised Dariabibi retold the story with added colour until Azhar lost enthusiasm.

Putting down the *bodna* of water before his father, Amjad said, 'The *bodna* has gone hot. Bring it with you in the morning from tomorrow and put it in the shade.'

Azhar, who'd had a mouthful of rice, said, working his jaw, 'It doesn't matter. I'm starving.'

Sitting on a bale of straw, Amjad watched his father's eating style. The food wasn't so good: a little dhal and curried tiddlers.

Amjad looked around at the fields that lay shimmering under the sun. Even the seasonal crops on either side of the river looked colourless. The *Chaitra* wind lifted dust and sand off the ground which, like a piece of coloured smoke, set off for a distant village.

This year Azhar had sown only pumpkins; their long stems lay dozing intertwined like snakes in the sun. A pumpkin, lying on a clay boulder, had started ripening; a greyish yellow in the dazzling light of the sun. Amjad's eyes were repeatedly attracted to it.

'*Abba*.'

Azhar Khan raised his face, shrunken in the sun, with its black beard; a few grains of rice stuck to one corner of his mouth. Amjad felt like laughing as he looked.

'That pumpkin's ripe, *Abba*.'

'Not really.'

'You said they ripen if you store them at home.'

'Why not?' Azhar said, taking a mouthful of rice. 'Do you want to take it home?'

'Yes,' Amjad said shamefacedly, as if he had committed an offence.

'No, son,' Azhar said. 'I've got to supply a hundred pumpkins to the market next week. I've taken an advance.'

Azhar looked at his son; the brightness on the child's face had been extinguished.

Some rice lay uneaten on the plate. Azhar felt sad. It was doubtful if he would get a hundred pumpkins from his own patch; he might have to buy some from other peasants. Satisfying even the meanest fancies of his children was beyond his ability. A wholesaler had come last week; Azhar had taken an advance from him. He didn't like breaking promises. At other times pumpkins would be rotting on the ground and wholesalers wouldn't even touch them.

Azhar didn't dare look at his son. Keeping his head down, he said, 'There are water-melons in that field. Would you like one?'

Amjad looked smiling at his father, lines of happiness forming on his face and lips at the talk of water-melons.

'You wait here, son. I'll go and wash in the river.'

Azhar disappeared over the bank of the river. Amjad, who was looking at the vanishing figure of his father, now looked further off in that direction. There was a little wind that made the great heat just bearable. The cattle were grazing peacefully in the fields. Far away some children were playing under a *pakur* tree beside a hut; the noise they made reached Amjad's ear. Then, turning, he heard someone whistling. It could have been the call of a bird unknown to Amjad, for it was a strange whistle. Amjad looked around. And the whistle stopped.

'Whose son is that?'

Amjad started. A man emerged from behind the banana trees. He had long bushy hair and a pitch-black body. He held a sickle and a weeder in his hand.

A torrent of whistling flowed again. This then was the man who was whistling. The man's large eyes were deep black and he was big. Amjad was a little apprehensive.

Looking at him, the man said, 'Whose son, eh? Nicking water-melons, are you?'

Amjad shrank in fear. Azhar wasn't around; what was keeping him?

'You've come thieving, eh?'

'No, I've brought dinner.'

The man laughed out for no reason and then whistled as he sang:

'Behind the mustard field the moon flies
You have a man-trap in your eyes,
                    O listless one . . .'

The singer's long hair blew in the wind. After a few couplets, the singing stopped.

'Brought dinner, have you?'

Amjad replied timidly, '*Abba*'s eaten it all.'

'Then you've got nothing left for me, eh?'

Slightly lowering his head, the man smiled naughtily. Perhaps he's mad, Amjad thought, taken aback.

His left hand on his hip, the man stood askew. Then cupping his mouth with the other hand, he bawled, 'Ey, who's in the melon field?'

Amjad looked up at the fields around the river. Those children were still playing; there wasn't a trace of any other living thing except for the cows which, chewing the cud, were looking for shelter in the shade. Yet the man kept shouting. Perhaps at the invisible listless one of his song.

Now, with a flourish, he sat down beside Amjad in the shade. His breath smelled of *toddy*; Amjad moved away a little.

'Oh dear, you ate all the rice and for your uncle – ' He raised his thumb to indicate nought.

Azhar became visible over the bank of the river. He had finished washing.

The man discovered a fresh source of enthusiasm. Now he sang out even louder and, addressing Azhar beyond the pumpkin patch, cried, 'Oh Khanbhai – '

Azhar said, 'Who, Chunder?'

The man was Chandra Kotal of Moheshdanga who lived in the fields. He used to run a comic folk theatre group and had commissions from faraway villages during the *puja* and other festivals. He had little to do with the villagers and had left the village a few years ago following a dispute with his relatives. He could not bear the breath of neighbours but was on very good terms with everybody in the field. Many winds of misfortune had blown over him and his wife Elokeshi. Five years ago both their daughters had died of smallpox. Chandra Kotal was an open-hearted happy-go-lucky man. There were a few palm trees beside their hut; they were visible from Azhar's field. Bamboos for climbing them and earthen pitchers for collecting the sap for *toddy* remained stuck to the palm trees all the year round, but Chandra's season started in summer.

'Oh, Khan, hurry up!'

Turning to Amjad, he said, 'Who's that bearded old man?'

'My *abba*.'

'How do you know?' Chandra combed his moustache with his fingers and smiled.

'He's my *abba* and I wouldn't know?'

Their dialogue reached Azhar's ear. Coming closer, he said, 'You've had the *haram* stuff to your fill, haven't you, to sing like that? God forbid!'

'There you go, Khanbhai. You too scold me.'

Chandra respected Azhar Khan for his honesty. Besides, the old Khan family was known to everybody in the village. Chandra valued that too.

'How's fishing?'

In front of Chandra's hut was the meeting point of two canals where water stayed all the year round. In the rainy season Chandra didn't have to worry about farming; he earned enough from the fish he caught. He kept the meeting point of the canal and the river surrounded by a bamboo net.

'No, times aren't good. Give us some tobacco.'

Azhar Khan put down the plate and the *bodna* and picked up the coconut hookah he had left leaning against the tree trunk.

'I'll prepare the tobacco. Give the boy a watermelon. This year the crop on my patch is poor.'

Resting Amjad's young chin on the palm of his hand, Chandra said, 'Why didn't you tell me before, son?'

Chandra got to his feet. Walking across a couple of *bighas* of land, he started whistling:

> I'll sell my land and home
>> For the yellow-bordered sari
> Under the fig-tree who, alas,
>> Doesn't want me . . .

'Crazy Chunder!' Azhar Khan said to Amjad, who laughed at his father's remark.

'He was saying, "You've finished all the rice, haven't left any for me." '

'And what did you say?'

16

'Nothing. I was scared.'

'There's nothing to fear from crazy Chunder,' Azhar Khan laughed.

Chandra returned whistling and put down two large watermelons on the ground. Amjad's eyes shone with happiness.

'Why did you have to get two large ones?' Azhar said.

'So what?'

'Aren't you going to take them to the market?'

'No. They got nicked. I'll miss the next market day.'

Of the two large watermelons, one was dark green and other white with dark stripes like those of a tiger.

Chandra tapped the melons with his finger to test their ripeness.

'The green one's ready to eat.'

Ready to claw the watermelon with his sickle, Chandra stopped.

'What's your name, son?'

'Amjad.'

'Don't get impatient. Hang on for a bit.'

Chandra got to his feet, facing the river.

'What's the matter, Chunder?'

'They're hot. They've been under the sun all day. Could make the boy sick.'

'So what are you going to do?'

'Just leave them under the sand in knee-deep water for five minutes. They'll be ice-cold.'

Azhar didn't say another word. Chandra walked off to the river with the watermelons.

Azhar looked at his son.

'See, he's crazy.'

This time Amjad could not agree with his father. He looked in the direction of the river. He had begun to like Chandra very much.

The *koyet-bel* trees had not fruited for two successive years.

'There's not even a couple of fruit on the tree,' Azhar said in dismay.

Amjad didn't respond; he was waiting for Chandra. Time didn't seem to have an end.

With the beginning of the afternoon the sunrays had lost their burning qualities. A cool wind raised a murmur in the tree. The cows with their swinging udders were once again looking for grass.

'Who's in the melon field?'

Chandra stood on the bank of the river. He was holding the river-bathed water-melons, water dripping from them. Amjad felt reassured.

Azhar was preparing tobacco; Chandra stood close to him.

'Let's get a start.' He laughed.

'Why were you shouting for nothing? There's nobody in the field.'

'You've got to shout at night too. Now there isn't anybody, now there is; how long does it take a thief to appear?'

Taking the hookah pipe, Chandra puffed at random.

'You cut the watermelon for the boy,' he said.

Amjad was sitting on some straw spread out on the ground. Chandra sat beside him. Amjad felt uneasy at the great puffs of smell from his mouth. He moved away a little.

'Are you scared, son?'

'No.'

'What's there to be scared of?' Azhar reassured him. He's your uncle, Amu. Chunder *Kaka*.

Azhar cut the watermelon. It was very ripe.

'Tuck in, Amu.'

'Chunder, you have a little.'

'No, no. I've swallowed a lot of juices. No more,' Chandra said, releasing a puff of smoke.

'Can you eat it all, Amu *Chacha*?'

'Yes, Chandra *Kaka*.'

'He talks well.'

Chandra kept looking at Amjad's face.

'It's painful, Azharbhai.'

'What are you on about?'

'These children . . . they'll go through their lives without food or clothes like us.'

'Why?'

'Don't you see? Have we got the means to bring them up?'

Azhar could not agree; he did not hold such a pessimistic view about his son's future.

'If God's written in their fate . . .'

'You talk of fate. You remember Haran Chakkatti's son? A moron. I used to twist his ear, he was so bad at mental arithmetic. Now he's become a magistrate. And look at me. The best boy of the village primary now brews *toddy* and gets drunk.'

A shadow of apprehension passed across Azhar's mind; he didn't want Amjad to hear these words.

'His dad took him to town,' Chandra continued, 'and the thrashed donkey became a magistrate. You talk of fate! Hari Chakkatti doesn't go paying rent year after year. If my dad didn't have to pay rent, if I don't have to pay rent and my income goes up, we'll see which way the water flows and what gets written in whose fate.'

Azhar listened with attention but did not respond. Dariabibi too talked l%ike that. Azhar did not see eye to eye with her either. Amjad was avidly eating his watermelon. The future of his son flashed past Azhar's mind for a fleeting moment. He did not like this sort of talk; he got to his feet.

'Chunder, give me the pipe. I've still got about a *bigha* of land to level.'

After a couple of puffs, Azhar returned the pipe to Chunder.

Their eyes closed, the bulls tied to the trees were chewing the cud. The beasts stood up as Azhar turned to them, as if they were conscious of their duty.

Tying the ladder-leveller to them, Azhar got on to the field, where he would grow sweet potatoes this year.

Amjad finished eating the watermelon and, wiping his hands on the *gamtcha* he thanked Chandra: 'Your watermelon's very good, Chandra *Kaka*.'

'Take the other one for your mother. What did she cook today?'

Amjad was seven; he was aware that one shouldn't talk about the common poor fare to a stranger; he did not respond.

'Invite me one day.'

Amjad replied with an inarticulate, 'Right.'

'Azharbhai, let the boy come and see the melon field. You won't be going home yet.'

'All right. Don't be late, Amu.'

'I won't be late, *Abba*.'

It was a *Chaitra* afternoon. The clouds were conferring in the sky. The whole field was waking up to the hum of activity. Unless a storm brewed up, there would be no break in work in the fields, which were being prepared for seasonal crops. On this night of the seventh phase of the moon, the peasants who feared the heat of the sun would keep the fields alive.

Amjad looked about him in wonder. He had never been here except along familiar paths. Today, with Chandra *Kaka*, he braved the jungle and undergrowths.

Tobacco plants stood three feet high with their white blossoms.

19

There were chilli plants beside a *potol* patch. Amjad stood in front of a chilli plant the likes of which he had never seen before. The red chillies stood with their legs thrust up towards the sky as if doing somersaults like he would. Chandra was walking ahead of him; he looked back.

'Amu *Chacha*, what are you looking at?'

'What sort of chillies are these, Chandra *Kaka*?'

'What, you're a peasant's son and you don't know? They're called sun chillies. Pick some, go on.'

Amjad hesitated because it was somebody else's land. Chandra himself picked some and gave them to him, and he tied them away in one end of his *lungi*.

The peasants had put thorny *babla* branches around the *jhinga* field to deter thieves. Amjad was stepping carefully behind Chandra, who now turned round.

'Hang on, Amu.'

Between the two of them there was a strip of land where tobacco plants had grown thickly. Amjad could not see the whole of Chandra's body. He stopped and heard Chandra saying, 'It's Haran Maiti's land; that's why it's so thorny, just like him; I feel like chasing him off the field.'

A moment later Chandra stood beside Amjad.

'Right. You don't have to walk any more.'

Without giving him a chance to reply, Chandra promptly lifted him on to his shoulders.

In the beginning he felt uneasy, but soon he started enjoyed it. There was nothing to fear from Chandra *Kaka*. Riding on his shoulder, Amjad found the far peasant villages enchanting.

Beyond the fields lay the path through wild grass with grasshoppers and dragonflies flying all around.

'Hold on to my head, son,' Chandra said. 'Don't be afraid of falling.'

Then, holding an imaginary flute, Chandra started whistling. Amjad feared he might lose his balance. Looking down, he saw no end of wild grass and realised why Chandra *Kaka* was being so kind to him.

Amjad looked back at their field, but couldn't see his father. Everything remained hidden behind some palm trees, their leaves glistening in the waning sun.

Chandra stopped whistling.

'*Chacha*, are you all right, riding on my shoulder?'

'Yes,' Amjad replied briefly.

'That's right, *Chacha*. It's nice on the shoulders. The world takes on a different colour. Sit there like a *zamindar*, son.'

Amjad did not understand Chandra *Kaka*'s whimsy. As Chandra walked on uneven ground, Amjad held on to his long hair more firmly.

'There's my hut.'

Amjad turned to find the meeting point of two rivers – well, not rivers, but fairly big canals – and a few huts in a row on raised ground. Beyond them were miles of trysting fields on which the homes of the sons of the soil looked like so many oases.

With great curiosity Amjad looked at some noisy children in the yard. Chandra resumed his whistling and the children became noisier.

Approaching the yard, Chandra called out, 'Elokeshi! Elokeshi!'

A boy in the crowd of children said, 'Chandra *Kaka*'s got drunk again.'

A woman past her prime now emerged on the mound – a peasant woman, a little plump, with a worn-out face, in an ordinary sari.

'Whose son is that on your shoulder?'

'Mine,' Chandra said. 'Now get him some puffed rice or something, go on.'

With one hand behind Amjad's neck and the other under his knees, Chandra made a gesture of swinging a baby. Then at the end of a flourish and a whistle, Amjad found himself sitting on the ground. The crowd of children gathered round him. They came across the river to play here. They had no difficulty crossing over as even the high-tide water did not rise above one's knees.

'Child, come to me.'

Elokeshi held out her arms.

Chapter Three

The ninth-day moon had risen in the sky.

Amjad followed his father, who was walking behind the two bulls. The shadow of the plough fell on the ground.

As the world of human beings expanded, many unfortunate people were driven out of their villages to live in the fields. Amjad did not know what kind of people they were. His mother did not allow him to mix with their children. Cowherd boys went to distant fields to graze their cattle, but Amjad did not share their good fortune.

The child's innocent mind was touched with an exquisite happiness as the moon got brighter and the fields of seasonal crops brought the intimation of a dream. A dream of what? Amjad did not know. He suddenly felt aggrieved against his mother. The local children were bad, their company was not good for him, so he had to stay away from them. After school he had nothing to do except to present himself to his mother.

Amjad recalled Elokeshi and Chandra *Kaka*. They belonged to a different world. He had briefly seen their home, food and their way of life.

Elokeshi had said sadly, 'Child, you've come on a day when we've nothing to give you except puffed rice.'

Chandra *Kaka* laughed and talked, winking as he dangled his legs. Diffident Amjad, his head lowered, lifted the puffed rice to his lips.

'The Khan's child, isn't he?' Elokeshi queried.

'Yes. Why not call him ours?'

'Such stories we've heard about the family from *Dadi*!'

Amjad looked into Elokeshi's eyes and then looked down lest he got caught.

'And haven't you heard about the new Khans?' Chandra said.

Moheshdanga was now under two landlords. Hatem Bakhsh Khan and his relations who owned three-eighths of the village had settled in a new area and were known to the villagers as the new Khans.

'Who doesn't know Rahim Khan's father, that usurer?' Elokeshi said. 'Became a landlord with usury money.'

Chandra interrupted, 'Don't you know when a cow has the scab, you write down the names of nine usurers and hang it round the cow's neck and the maggots fall off? The first name they wrote was that of Rahim Khan's father. Are your cows in good health, son?' He turned to Amjad.

A hum of conversation had risen round Amjad and the air wafted in the magic of Chandra *Kaka*'s laughter.

Now it was blissful walking home despite the burden of a water-melon. The large fruit was indeed a burden for Amjad; he kept shifting it from arm to arm. Good job his father did not walk too fast.

Finally Amjad supported the watermelon on his head.

A thin strip of cloud drifted across the face of the moon, casting a faint shadow across the fields. A spidery darkness gathered on the path.

Azhar Khan was tired. Dusk had fallen by the time Chandra Kotal had brought back the boy. Azhar Khan had waited for a while. But it went against the grain for him to wait. So he had resumed work and spent some time doing odd jobs on the field. When Chandra and Amjad arrived, there was further delay. Chandra Kotal had so much to say. His drunkenness had passed. The night advanced in talk of pleasure and pain. It was a moonlit night, so Azhar was not in a hurry. And Chandra would not return home; he would spend the night in the melon field, keeping watch.

'Bring the boy to the field again, Azharbhai.'

Chandra whistled as he walked off across the field and Amjad watched his exquisite swinging gait.

The moon revealed her face as the veil of cloud slipped off and it was as if the bright light of day showered on the road. Amjad looked back at the entrance to the village. Silhouettes of bamboo poles stuck out from the vegetable patches and owls flew round and round to perch on them. One could see them hunting field rats in the moonlight. Amjad could hardly believe that those day-blind owls could hunt such clever animals as rats. Perhaps Chandra *Kaka* would tell him how.

Peasants huts lay on both sides of the narrow village street where the hum of life had not yet ceased. First there was the brick and

23

mortar outhouse of the new Khans where the children were reading raucously. Perhaps peasants had assembled at Hatem Khan's durbar and the landlord's men were engaged in some conspiracy. There were still some customers at Mahbub Mirdha's grocery. Under a dim oil lamp Mahbub sat holding up the scales. A paisa worth of cooking oil, half a paisa worth of dried chillies, a quarter worth of salt. A small grocery met the small needs of its customers. Nobody had time during the day; shopping began in the evening. As usual a lamp was still burning in Mahbub's grocery.

Azhar Khan put the plough down on the ground.

Then he sat down and fanned himself with his *gamtcha*. He was sweating.

'Hau!'

The bulls stopped in response to Azhar's call.

'Amu, son, put down the watermelon and nip into the shop.'

Amjad put the fruit down on the ground carefully; it would break into pieces if it slipped.

'Here, take these two paisa. I'll have a little rest. That plough's getting heavier every day.'

'What'll I get, *Abba*?'

'One and a half paisa worth of *bidi* and half a paisa worth of matches.'

Azhar took out an empty matchbox from the fold at the waist of his *lungi*.

'Here, take the box. He'll give you about twenty matchsticks. Count them, son.'

With the money in his hand, Amjad hesitated.

'What is it?'

'I don't want to go, *Abba*.'

'Why?'

'Half a paisa worth of matches, I feel shy.'

'That's why I think I shouldn't send you to school. This is what happens to a poor man's son when he starts mixing with the children of the rich.'

Amjad had been to the shop before to buy a paisa worth of sweets. He hadn't gone shopping for the household. His first errand felt like a burden.

'Go!' Azhar's voice was not smooth. 'One buys according to one's means, there's no shame in it.'

Amjad returned, shamefaced.

24

'He's run out of matches, *Abba*. Had only ten sticks. He said he'd give us a quarter worth of salt.'

'All right, go.'

Azhar Khan counted the matchsticks and put away the packet of salt, matches and *bidi*. 'Let's go, son,' he said.

The watermelon had become ten times heavier. The pleasure of running about in the field had vanished. Looking at his father, Amjad felt like choking, as if with those two bulls another beast was walking with a plough on his shoulder. The snake of hatred breathed angrily in his young breast. He walked po-faced behind his father.

The path to the Khans' was even narrower with overgrown cane and other bushes on both sides. Here the moonlight stepped down cautiously through the trees. The path was hardly visible. Azhar Khan walked even more slowly, lest the blade of the plough get tangled in the creepers.

'Amu, son, come right behind me.'

Amjad knew his father's voice – in it concern in the shape of affection showered down like moonlight.

Amjad was afraid. Walking up to his father, he felt relieved.

'Amu.'

'*Abba*.'

'You cross with me?'

Amjad could not reply immediately. Did his father know the movements of his mind?

'No, *Abba*.'

The blade of the plough had got tangled in the creepers. Azhar had to stop.

'Move the creeper out of the way, son.'

With great difficulty Amjad freed the plough from the creeper. Azhar now stepped even more cautiously.

Azhar Khan said, 'You shouldn't feel bad about being poor: it's all God's will. You annoy God if you do.'

Amjad did not reply. He just listened.

The crickets kept time in this sparsely populated village. In the moonlight the langur monkeys were still awake in the large *bokul* tree. One could hear the chattering of their babies.

Amjad lacked courage to walk along this path alone. There was the holy tomb of a *pir* under the *bokul* tree. On Friday evenings the villgers came here to make their offerings. After midnight the holy dervish went round the village, seated on a gigantic python. Very kind was this dead dervish, Shah Kerman Khorasani. Alone he bore the burden of everybody's misery. For minor ailments, his holy tomb, the Mazar, was the only refuge for the villagers.

Amjad could not muster enough courage to cast even a glance at the great trunk of the *bokul* tree with its circumference of thirty feet.

Between two thick branches rising from the trunk, there was a large hole, in which lived the python. It came out in the daytime now and then but did not harm anybody.

Legends abounded. Amjad had heard no end of them from Dariabibi and he had goosepimples when he did.

Here was a living saint, to whose tomb both Hindus and Muslims offered sacrifice.

The ripe fruit of the *bokul* tree kept falling in the dark. Amjad knew the sound. Very early in the morning tomorrow he would come to pick them.

They passed an abandoned house with its rain-washed walls still standing. A little more of the path and they would be on the track to their outhouse.

Amjad's mind danced in happiness. He repeatedly looked at the striped watermelon. Ma would be very happy.

The ninth-day moon slowly descended the steps of the western sky which, in the embrace of white clouds, looked like a placid lake.

On the path to the outhouse, Amjad did not stay behind his father; he overtook him. He knew the area like the back of his hand.

But in the yard in front of the outhouse he was scared when the shadow of a stranger seemed to move past him.

He did not mention it to his father, but stood still for a moment, then fell behind him again.

Azhar Khan's eyes were elsewhere; he hadn't noticed the movement.

'Wait a bit, Amu. I'll put away the plough and the bulls.'

Amjad unwillingly put down the watermelon on the veranda of the outhouse. He feared his father. Otherwise he was dying to go in and surprise his mother. Who had ever brought such a large beautiful melon to this house?

In the thatched outhouse, straw was stacked in one corner during the rains, ploughs and other farming equipment in another. If there were guests, they occupied the other two corners.

As Azhar put away the plough and turned he thought he saw a

shadow moving from one corner of the outhouse towards the veranda.

'Who's that?'

There was no reply; the shadow stood still.

'Who's that?'

Amjad was standing in the courtyard, he was frightened. A djinn had come to the outhouse. He had heard stories about djinns from his mother. There was a copy of the holy Koran in the outhouse. The djinns came to read the Koran.

Azhar Khan got angry when children were told such stories. Now even he was doubtful.

'Who's that?' he bawled and jumped in to the yard from the veranda, a switch in hand.

The shadow broke into a sob.

Azhar called out to Amjad, 'Come here, Amu. Who's that?'

It was a naked little girl. In the faint light Azhar recognised his daughter Naima.

'Namu, you here?'

She did not reply, only sobbed even more.

'What are you doing here this time of the night?' Azhar cried. 'Where's your ma?'

Dariabibi came out from inside.

'What's the row about?'

Azhar Khan confronted his wife: 'An unweaned child's out this time of the night – and you don't think you need to keep a lookout?'

'I've thought enough!'

Dariabibi advanced towards Naima, raising her hand to slap her.

'Just you wait, *haramzadi*. Three years old, yet can't say a word.'

Azhar Khan faced his belligerent wife.

'Well, what happened? Tell me.'

'A big girl like her went and lost her loincloth.'

Azhar asked, 'Which one?'

'The one you got her from the market town the other day.'

'Ah!' Azhar uttered a faint cry.

'And she's so dumb, born of a dumb one, that she can't say how she lost it.'

'So you thrashed her?'

Dariabibi bellowed: 'I know, my hand knows and her back knows.'

Azhar Khan pulled the child towards him and soothingly rubbed his hand on her back.

27

'What have you done? Weals all over!'

'I know what it means to be in want and they've got to go and do this to me.'

Azhar Khan got angry with his neighbours.

'Such a neighbourhood of thieves! A little girl can't always hang on to her clothes. She might have dropped it somewhere, and it's gone. All thieves!'

Dariabibi said: 'I've asked everybody. Nobody knows.'

'Never mind. Now hold the girl.'

Azhar tied the bulls in the shed and gave them a few bundles of straw.

Naima would not leave her father. As soon as Dariabibi picked her up, she started sobbing. Dariabibi kissed her daughter on the cheek and said: 'Who's taken the piece of cloth, child?'

Naima only cried.

'Let's go in. I'll go and wash.'

Amjad followed his mother, watermelon in hand. He was sad he had failed to attract anybody's attention so far. His anticipated pleasure in pride was entirely lost.

But in the room, when Amjad put down the watermelon in front of his mother and guiltily said: '*Ma*, melon!' a smile shot across her face like lightning.

'Ey, Amu, who gave you such a big watermelon?'

'Chandra *Kaka* of the field.'

'It's a ripe one!' Dariabibi smiled at Amjad and at last everything felt good to him.

Dariabibi said to Naima, 'There, look, you'd like to eat watermelon tomorrow, wouldn't you?' She tapped the fruit with her finger a few times.

'It's not very ripe, son. We'll have to leave it for a couple of days.'

A smile showed on Naima's face.

'*Ma*, I eat.'

'Yes, you'll eat too.'

Dariabibi sat down on a mat, stretching out her legs, and asked Amjad to sit next to her. Amjad described the events of the day in the field to his mother.

Dariabibi brought out a clay lamp and *karanja* oil. She did not always have money to buy kerosene. Early in the mornings, she went to pick *karanja* seeds, which she then turned into oil at the grinder's.

'Go and do some reading now. You go picking wild dates and *bokul* fruit. Can't you get some *karanja*?'

Naima, who had suffered much, fell asleep.

'She's had her fill of beating,' Dariabibi said.

Amjad did not like doing homework so late at night, but it was no use complaining to Ma. He sat down to read in the dim light of the clay lamp. Dariabibi got back to her household chores.

A few others in the neighbourhood had had their clothes stolen. It hurt Dariabibi. The piece of cloth cost only three quarters of a rupee, but even that, she knew, was the fruit of much labour.

After supper Azhar sat on the veranda and smoked his hookah. Amjad was lost in his own thoughts. Dariabibi removed the seeds from a pile of silk cotton.

'These thieves nick only children's clothes.'

'Who else has got their clothes stolen?' Azhar asked.

'Moti's son's lost his *dhoti*, Zaker's daughter her sari, and others.'

Azhar Khan released a great quantity of smoke.

'It's becoming a mean village. The Khans will have no honour left.'

Dariabibi's lips twisted slightly but Azhar did not notice that. He continued, 'Look at the way the upstarts behave and look at the old families.'

Dariabibi did not want to provoke her husband. She kept piling up raw cotton on a husker.

'What honour? Everybody's poor!' she said, as if making a throwaway remark.

'Money alone doesn't keep the honour of a family,' Azhar replied. 'The Khans of Moheshdanga are still well known in the region.'

'They're known,' Dariabibi agreed. 'But without money honour slips away.'

Azhar kept quiet.

Dariabibi did not like her husband's sudden silences. She continued the conversation.

'I'll catch the thief, you'll see.'

'To think of clothes bought at such cost being stolen by the theiving devils!'

Dariabibi called, 'Amu.'

'What, Ma?'

'See you don't lose your clothes, son.'

Amjad was blowing a fleck of cotton into the air.

'No, Ma, I don't lose clothes.'

Old Ashekjan usually got home before dusk. Today was no exception. She was hard of hearing, although at times she understood what others were saying so well she did not seem to be deaf at all and was known to many as wise-deaf.

The couple's conversation had reached her ear. She had gone to bed early but she could not sleep. She usually slept for a while during the last few hours of the night.

Ashekjan came out of her room unexpectedly. Seeing his aunt on the veranda, Azhar asked, 'What's the matter, *Chachi*?'

Azhar was kind to the old woman. She only occupied a room. What else did he do for her? He could hardly support his own family.

'Nothing, son.' Ashekjan sat down on the veranda. Then she thought of something to talk about.

'What a family you were in the old times!' she said. 'Dariabou is running it now. She's a good girl.'

The one on whom the praise was showered did not even raise her eyebrow.

'I can see your misery with my own eyes,' Ashekjan added.

Now Dariabibi cast an irate look at her. Husband and wife could discuss a thousand things about the state of the family, but that others should intrude in these areas was not to her liking.

Ashekjan had not finished.

'There's no faith these days,' she said. 'Nobody casts a glance at the poor. Dariabou!'

'What?' Dariabibi's response was curt.

'You're short of clothes. I've got a couple of saris.'

Ashekjan took them out from under her clothes: 'You have them. I've got enough for now.'

Dariabibi's voice was sharp: 'Where did you find them?'

'Izad Choudhury's mother died, so he feted the poor yesterday and gave away clothes for *zakat*.'

'*Zakat! Zakat!*' Dariabibi suddenly flared up. Gritting her teeth, she repeated: '*Zakat!* Now I've got to take *zakat* stuff? Isn't my husband alive? My son? Didn't the word stick in your throat?'

Dariabibi kicked the two saris off the veranda.

Azhar did not quite understand the proceedings. He went and picked up the saris from under the veranda and brought them back.

'I warn you! Never say such things again. I'll throw you out of my house if you do. I kick your *zakat* on the head seven times.'

Pious Azhar did not like the use of such harsh words.

'Dariabou, have you gone mad?' he said. 'What are you saying?'

'Shut up. Those who take *zakat* aren't human any more. I haven't turned into a beast yet. Allah's given me hands and feet. I'll never beg for this damned stomach.'

Azhar, who was remarkably placid, lost his temper too.

'Then go and plough the field from tomorrow.'

'I'd do even that.'

Azhar fell silent. Dariabibi had kept the family intact. If he had had an inept wife, Azhar would have left home to become a dervish.

'I'm telling you nicely, *Khala*, never say such things again. We are poor, we just survive, but we don't need it. Don't you see we buy your *zakat* rice off you?'

Ashekjan sat petrified, pressing the two pieces of soiled sari to her chest. Then she quietly slipped away into her room.

Amjad, who slept in Ashekjan's room, was yawning; he wanted to go to bed.

Dariabibi said, 'Don't go to that room.'

Amjad did not take another step. Azhar Khan sat quietly. It seemed as if a storm had blown over the veranda.

Dariabibi woke up at midnight. Amjad was not beside her. Where had he gone to?

She lit a lamp and very quietly entered Ashekjan's room. Amjad lay fast asleep on his familiar mat.

And Ashekjan sat on her haunches, her face resting on her knees, her hemp-like white hair dishevelled. There was the sound of a sob. Was old Ashekjan crying? Dariabibi looked in her direction. It was as if the female image of poverty had taken refuge in a corner of the room. Humans were Allah's greatest creation. What had happened to them! Dariabibi felt ill at ease. In the fire of poverty the wealth of life had turned into ashes.

For the first time the naked image of poverty revealed itself to Dariabibi. Why had she come here like a princess exiled from a golden kingdom? Why had she come here? She felt the pain of a burning wound.

Blowing out the lamp, Dariabibi moved close to Ashekjan in the dark and called: '*Khala!*'

31

Chapter Four

Naima was playing in the twilight with the kids in the courtyard. Azhar had returned from the field early. A loner, Azhar spent his spare time at home. Unlike his neighbours, he did not care to while away his leisure hours playing cards or dice. He talked to Dariabibi about the family and, when he had nothing to do, he smoked his hookah. When Amjad joined him on the veranda, he could not think of anything to start a conversation and with Naima he had nothing to talk about.

As the scarlet of the setting sun fell on the glossy black fur of the kids, they looked like moving nodules of colour. The mother goat lay resting on the straw but the kids were restless. They ran to their mother, pulled on her udder for a while and then roamed about the yard, bleating. Behind them ran Naima. If the kids refused to get caught, Naima, annoyed, went and complained to her mother. Then she played tricks with them. Pretending to look away, she made a sudden grab at a kid. After the first frightened cry, the kid melted in her affection. Naima held the kid close to her chest and fondled it with her soft hands, but when the mother goat approached, she retreated.

Azhar Khan quietly watched the playful movements of his daughter, his eyes misty with tobacco haze. No comment rose to his lips. Dariabibi was busy with household chores.

A little later Amjad arrived with a bundle of palm leaves under his arm. He had just been released from the *maktab*. The *moulvi* did not begrudge imparting knowledge as long as there was daylight. At this time the sprightly children avidly memorised the tables.

Amjad would have come home earlier, but washing the ink off the palm leaves after school was an extra job. His mother got annoyed if he kept losing his palm leaves. Ink-stains were not easily removed and the pond water was not very good. This delayed him, but out of fear he did not protest. Of late he had started comparing himself with those who wrote on paper and not on palm leaves like himself.

He was depressed so he went and sat down beside Azhar on the veranda. He had nothing to say to his mother. But he soon forgot it all as he watched Naima playing and happily joined her.

Now the kids took fright. Unable to outrun Amjad, they just bleated. Brother and sister kept the courtyard lively.

Dariabibi had a little free time, so she came and sat down in the breeze.

'Amu.'

'What, Ma?'

'Don't cling to the kids, they get spoilt.'

'No, Ma, I'm not touching them too much.'

Naima protested: 'Ma, I'm playing.'

'Yes, play.'

Evening descended slowly and darkness closed in on the court-yard. Dariabibi spread out her hair in the breeze, airing her body, tired and sweaty from the day's labour.

It was dark in the yard; a great time for Amjad and Naima. Now they could fondle the kids as much as they liked. However hard they thumped them on the back, they would not catch their mother's eye. But the kids were so naughty that if they were squeezed a little they bleated hard, bringing prompt remonstrance from Ma.

Dariabibi said, 'Stomp about a bit more quietly, you fourteen generations!'

'Ma, they're so timid they start bleating if you go anywhere near them.'

Amjad imitated their bleating. Azhar Khan quietly laughed in the dark. They had forgotten he was there. A lamp was burning on the veranda, from which a faint light reached the courtyard, now a colony of shadows. They could not see one another's faces.

Weeds grew beyond the courtyard, though not very thickly. Azhar Khan walked through them with the help of a paddle. The footpath wasn't of much use except in the rainy season when it was very convenient to get to the ponds and puddles for fishing.

The kids were tired, they were running about so much. Dariabibi was sitting quietly. Azhar Khan himself lit the charcoal for his hookah on the lamp. Had he forgotten to order people about? Dariabibi smiled in the dark.

The children's noise irked her.

'Stop screaming, you two.'

One of the kids was bleating hard in Amjad's arms. He dropped it out of fright. The kid, revived, ran to its mother in one bound.

The children went and sat quietly beside Dariabibi in the dark.

Ma was quiet, which frightened Amjad. 'Ma,' he called in an injured voice.

'What?'

Amjad put his head against Dariabibi and stretched out his legs. He had nothing to ask.

Stillness reigned in the courtyard.

Five minutes later, Dariabibi asked, 'Not sleepy, are you?'

'No, *Ma*.'

'See if your *abba*'s awake,' she whispered.

'*Abba*,' Amjad called out.

'What?'

'Are you awake?'

'Yeah.'

Dariabibi listened to their conversation.

'Ask him if he's been to Shimulia.'

'*Abba*, did you go to Shimulia?'

'No,' replied Azhar.

Now Dariabibi spoke directly to her husband: 'Do something about the kids or they may turn into billy goats. Get the vet.'

'Why should they turn into billy goats? They're strong kids.'

'Don't sell them from the fields, though. A couple of traders were looking for you.'

'No.'

His voice was without warmth. He was dozing in a tobacco haze.

Naima was falling asleep, Dariabibi noticed. The kids were still running about in the courtyard. Amjad felt drawn to them but, afraid of his mother, he simply stole a glance at her. He could have played a bit longer but for her. He curled his lip.

Suddenly, unnoticed, the kids stood still at the edge of the courtyard. The shadow of a red beast fell and everybody started at the sudden panic sound of bleating.

Surprised, Azhar shouted, 'Fox, fox!'

With all his might he called out for the village dogs. One of the kids returned to its mother.

Dariabibi could not quite comprehend what had happened in that instant, Two village dogs came running. Sniffing at the ground a few times, they disappeared into the jungle.

'A fox took a kid?' Dariabibi asked.

'Give me the stick. I'll go and look near the pond.'

There was a bamboo staff lying on the ground. Azhar disappeared into the dark.

In the light of the lamp, Dariabibi kept looking at the few drops of blood in the yard. The children joined her.

Dariabibi was annoyed: 'Move! What are you gawping at?'

Then she started grumbling, berating the ancestry of the fox. The kid which had returned to its mother was skinny. Dariabibi regretted that it was the good one which had fallen under the evil eye of the damned fox.

Azhar returned and said, 'I've looked everywhere. A small kid. The fox must have run away with it in its mouth.'

'Waste of labour,' Dariabibi said. 'It would have been worth four or five rupees next year.'

Naima started crying. Dariabibi did not even turn round to look.

'It's these children! I usually put them away early. I thought – they're playing, let them stay out for a bit.'

Dariabibi talked about imagined possibilities as tired Azhar once again sat down with his hookah.

It was a small kid, yet there was no happiness left in anybody's heart. The supper was further delayed. Dariabibi was in a bad mood. Even Amjad did not raise the question of the evening meal. Naima often went to bed without the evening meal. No exception was likely that night.

The goat started bleating. Dariabibi fed her with straw. She looked grave, her eyes invisible under her eyelids.

Amjad hung around his mother without a word. He didn't have the courage to say anything. He yawned and looked pitifully at his mother.

'Are you sleepy? Come, I'll give you your food.'

Azhar Khan found a cause for consolation: 'Praise to Allah, they haven't taken both the kids.'

'Bless your tongue!' Dariabibi said, with sarcasm in her voice.

That put him out; he did not say another word.

Despite her fatigue, Dariabibi could not sleep, but Azhar fell asleep in a short while. She could not take her mind off the kid devoured by the fox. So much labour had come to nought. A cow was being tended

35

for two years now, but she hadn't met her calf yet. What if one of these days the cow got stolen from the field? What could she do? Dariabibi wove webs of fear and luxuriated in the pleasure of drowning in boundless misery. Naima was tossing about in her sleep, her left elbow coming down on Dariabibi's breast. Any other day she would have gently moved her hand away. Tonight she forcefully pushed away the young elbow. She had no kindness left for anybody. Azhar was sleeping like a beast. Dariabibi had moved to the very edge of the bed. Unconsciusly she started stroking Naima's elbow. The child had not woken up.

Amjad had gone to sleep in Ashekjan's room. Why didn't the children of the poor grow up faster? That would have hastened the end of misery. When would Amjad finish his *maktab*? There would be no end of worries even after he had finished. There was no secondary school around. Would a child walk four miles to pick up knowledge? Naima was all growth, just what was dangerous for a poor man's daughter. There would be trouble getting her married before she had attained a marriageable age. Dariabibi built and demolished images of horror.

Out there was the anarchy of darkness. Dariabibi sat up in bed. Was Amjad sleeping well? She lay down again. There was no consolation in the dark except chewing the cud of one's memories.

Suddenly she recalled her first husband. Not just her first husband, but Monadir – had she forgotten Monadir? Monadir Hossain Khan. Her husband had chosen a big name for their son. She had not liked it at his naming ceremony, but she grew to like it in the end. Tears gathered in her tired eyes. Was Monadir being reared with affection at his uncle's? Her own son, yet she had no rights over him.

She had been a well-to-do farmer's daughter-in-law. They had three ploughs working and not a mean parcel of untaxed landed property. Want was hardly known to them. There seemed to be no end of work in this joint family, yet at the end of a day there was pleasure in rest. Her young husband's face gleamed in the dark in front of Dariabibi. Once she had had so many dreams of building a home, but now the future held nothing but darkness.

'Got any complaints, Daria?'

'No.'

'There's a lot of trouble in a farmer's family.'

'That's all right.'

'The boy sleeps a lot, doesn't he?'

'He cries when he's hungry and sleeps like his father. Nothing would wake him.'

Laughter rang out in the dark.

'Let him grow up, I'll send him to town for his education. Let him grow up into a man, I don't want anything else. I pray for him day and night.'

'Towns are so expensive.'

'That's all right. We'll cut all unnecessary expenses here.'

Such dreams over a three-year-old child!

'The problem is that you don't get on with my brother's wife.'

'She's mean. I work all day and she tells your mother I loll about like the figures on a clay pot.'

'Let her complain. It's no good quarrelling.'

Her husband's voice still rang out in the dark. That was the last night. He went to the market town the next morning. Bitten by a snake on his way home, he breathed his last in the village market before he got home. With Monadir on her breast, she had learnt to bear the loss. Her father-in-law was alive; the old man's affection for the child was another consolation. He would not let Monadir be put down on the ground. This was his way of fighting his grief. But he made a mistake, the price of which Dariabibi was still paying. There would have been no problem if her mother-in-law was alive. Her father-in-law followed his son within two months. A year later Dariabibi found herself abandoned on hard barren ground. The joint property got split between brothers, and she did not receive a blind cowrie. Her husband had died in his father's lap. According to the *Sharia*, neither she nor Monadir had any right to her father-in-law's property. Dariabibi appealed to her husband's brothers: how would Monadir survive? They paid no heed. Dariabibi cursed her father-in-law's ignorance a thousand times. If he had divided the property while he was alive, she wouldn't have turned into a street beggar now.

Dariabibi left her husband's home. The life of slavery was not for her. Her in-laws had started treating her like an untouchable. After a tempestuous row one day, she was ready to leave her husband's home with her son. She had no need for a *palki*. For one whose home had collapsed, what else but the ground was right for a bed?

She had set off with Monadir on her hip.

One of her husband's brothers came running: 'Be careful, *Bhabi*, you're tarnishing our family's honour.'

'Honour? What's honour to those who have no sense of justice?'

'You can stay here. Nobody's throwing you out.'

'Do I have to live like this? As a slave to your wives? I'd rather starve.'

'You won't starve here.'

'I've no use for charity. Get out of my way. Have I got any rights here?'

'We've done what the Koran tells us to do. Why blame us? When a son dies in his father's lifetime, his dependants don't have any rights to his property.'

'Don't throw the *Hadith* at me. Has Allah told you to turn people into beggars?'

'Give us the boy.'

'Short of servants, are you?'

'Our elder brother's wife has no children, she'll look after him.'

'Naturally you'll have to look after him. A small child won't do for a servant.'

They snatched Monadir away. Dariabibi did not look back. Let all past relationships be demolished, as if she had no more resentment.

'Family honour!' Dariabibi roared that day.

She would leave no stone unturned to tarnish their name. After five months she married the widower Azhar.

Dariabibi could not shut her eyes to the past, which, swaying its poisonous hood, cast an ugly look at her. So many faces came floating by . . . Javed Hossain . . . Ahad Hossain . . . Monadir. Monadir had a birthmark on his forehead. Had that round mark on the fair face been wiped out by kisses? Far away a group of cremators were still watching over in the burning ghat. Loud laughter echoed in the dark.

Dariabibi pressed her tear-soaked lips to Naima's young face. Her eyes burned. With an agonised heart, seeking oblivion, Dariabibi awaited a kind soul who would come and stand by her.

Chapter Five

A few days later Dariabibi entered Ashekjan's room and found the old woman sitting quietly holding the two saris she had received in charity. Dariabibi had entered silently so the old woman did not know she was there. At the call of '*Khala*', she started and promptly put away the clothes under her sari as if she had been caught stealing.

Before she could answer, Dariabibi said, '*Khala*, give me one of those saris, I'll pay you later.'

It was a ploy to reassure the old woman. Dariabibi knew she would not be able to pay up until six months later.

With a toothless smile, the old woman ferreted out the clothes.

'Take the good one, dear. The one with the better texture.'

Dariabibi sat down on the mat.

'You all right, *Khala*?'

Ashekjan sighed.

'No, dear. I've had this bad headache for the last couple of days, I can't see well.'

Dariabibi felt penitent. Her realisation that it was caused by her cruelty pained her.

'Come out on to the veranda. I'll give your head a cool wash. Don't go out today.'

'I have an invitation in the other village. I'll give it a try at around midday.'

'What invitation?'

'At Jalil Sheikh's. It's the fortieth day of his son's death.'

Dariabibi knew Jalil Sheikh's young breadwinner son had died of malaria recently. She recalled his face and said, 'Poor lad.'

'They're feeding a lot of people. Shall I take Amjad with me?'

Dariabibi felt as if someone had hit her all over with nettles. But there was no sign of anger on her face.

She quietly said, 'No, *Khala*, he needn't go. You aren't going either. Today you'll eat with us.'

Ashekjan often received invitations of this kind from the village. A variety of tasty dishes was offered at the homes of the rich. Ashekjan did not simply fill her own stomach, she sometimes brought home some of the food for Amjad and Naima to share out in the secrecy of her room. Once or twice they were caught at it and Ashekjan was scolded too.

Ashekjan felt no hesitation in bringing home the food offered at the fortieth-day ceremony of the dead, but careful Dariabibi sensed the inauspicious in everything. However, on this day a row did not ensue.

Jalil Sheikh was a jute merchant who owned three or four large boats. He was rich. One could imagine the elaborate arrangments for the feast at his place. Ashekjan felt tempted, but she feared Dariabibi and kept quiet, although the eye of her imagination was making her feel greedy.

Dariabibi compared the two saris in the semi-darkness of the room and said, 'I'm taking the one with the thin red border, *Khala*.'

'Good, good. These things don't suit me, dear. What I need is a white shroud to wear to my grave.'

'Rubbish! Can't you think of anything else so early in the morning? Come, I'll give your head a good wash.'

Together they went out on to the veranda. Dariabibi got a pot of water, which she poured on to the hemp-white hair of the old woman.

'Sit there quietly. I'll get three or four more pots of water.'

'Just as you say, dear. Rub in a little oil, Dariabou.'

Dariabibi ran her fingers through the old woman's hair as she slowly poured on the water through the spout of the *bodna*.

Ashekjan's body felt relieved of a burden. Dariabibi got some coconut oil and rubbed it in generously at the roots of the old woman's hair.

'*Khala*, worries burn my body. I can't hold back my temper. Don't know what I say to who.'

'I feel so much better, dear. May Allah bless you.'

Pretending to rub oil in, Dariabibi gave Ashekjan a massage. The new sari on the mat attracted Dariabibi's attention.

'Have you put the pot on, Dariabou?'

'Oh yes. Amu's had an upset stomach, I didn't give him the watered rice from last night. He'll have freshly cooked rice when he gets back from the *maktab*.'

40

Just then Amjad's voice could be heard. He was bawling from a distance, 'Ma. Ma!'

Dariabibi pricked up her ears, but before she had moved a step Amjad appeared in the courtyard.

'Ma!'

Holding up a hand, he cried again, 'Ma!'

The sun was in Dariabibi's eyes so she couldn't see Amjad properly.

'Raising the roof! What is it?'

'Have a look here.'

Lifting his hand, Amjad danced. As he approached Dariabibi, she saw about a dozen lobsters in Amjad's hand. Their slim red legs glistened in the sun.

A smile spilled over Dariabibi's lips.

'Where did you find them?'

'I'll tell you.' Amjad got on to the veranda in one leap. 'Chandra *Kaka* brought them. He went to the *maktab*. That's why the *moulvi* sahib let me off early.'

'Big lobsters, eh?'

Taking a large one out, Amjad said, 'This one's for me, there's such red brains in it!'

Dariabibi's happiness brimmed over. They could hardly afford good dishes for the young ones.

'*Khala*, it's good for you as well. I was afraid we might go short.'

Ashekjan was expressionless so far.

'What is it, Dariabou?'

'Amu's brought lobsters. We'll have a good dinner. Chandra Kotal's given him them.'

Passing the lobsters to his mother, Amjad said, 'Give us some *paan*, Ma. Chandra *Kaka*'s in the outhouse.'

'You didn't tell me!' Dariabibi rushed into her room, while Ashekjan gathered the details from Amjad.

'Here.' Dariabibi got back with paan. 'Does you uncle smoke?'

'Does he smoke? He smokes whole tobacco-fields.'

Dariabibi ran for the tobacco.

Chandra Kotal was sitting on a bale of hay in the outhouse. He was busy. Dariabibi had sent him whole *paan* leaves, whole betel nut and lime. He was preparing the *paan*.

Chandra had on a short *dhoti* with a sickle stuck at the waist. While preparing his *paan*, he spoke:

41

'Where's your *abba*, son?'

'Must be somewhere in the village. He hasn't gone anywhere.'

'I've got something to ask him.'

'Wait for him, *kaka*.'

Chandra Kotal looked about him. He had been here only a few times. In the rainy season his fish got sold at the river ghat. He didn't have to come into the village.

Watching strangers from a hidden position was a common female pastime. Chandra had correctly guessed from the hint of a *ghomta* near the back door that Amjad's mother had come.

Squeezing a *paan* into his mouth, he said loudly, 'Will your ma give us dinner?'

Amjad was going in. But Dariabibi was standing right behind the outhouse; she called her son with a gesture of the hand.

Standing close to his mother, Amjad said loudly, 'Is there any rice and dhal for a poor man?'

Chandra laughed and spoke even louder. 'Just rice and dhal won't do. Chandra Kotal slaughters a horse every day.'

This was followed by hearty laughter to which the whole outhouse rang.

'Son, ask your ma to give us some more tobacco before dinner. The spell's passed.'

Five minutes later, Amjad brought back the pipe heaped up with charcoal. It felt hot to Amjad's young hands.

'Give it to me quickly.'

Holding the pipe between his palms, Chandra sucked on it, his eyes closed in the tobacco haze.

Amjad looked at the man in surprise; he found it hard to suppress his laughter.

Chandra opened his eyes after a while.

Two *neem* trees swayed in the wind. A young palm tree attracted his attention. Young shoots had sprouted on it.

Putting the pipe on the floor, Chandra said, 'Is that palm tree yours, son?'

Amjad nodded.

'Ah, beautiful shoots! Have you got any bamboo trees?'

'A lot. Fifty in two clumps, *Abba* counted the other day.'

'You can make such sweet *toddy* from that tree, son! But your father's no connoisseur. To climb to the top on a bamboo pole and tie a jar around the tree is such pleasure, but your father . . .' Chandra shook his head.

'But we're not allowed to drink *toddy*,' Amjad said.

Twirling his moustache, Chandra produced a 'ho' sound through his lips.

'It's all right to drink when you grow up, son. But your father's a real – '

Amjad did not protest.

Chandra picked up the pipe and gave it a few random puffs. The smoke got into Amjad's eyes, which he shut in annoyance.

'Your father – '

Amjad opened his eyes.

'Your father won't come today.'

But Amjad didn't agree. In his childlike voice he said, '*Abba* won't go to foreign parts now. He's gone somewhere in the village – he'll get back soon.'

Chandra Kotal whistled and hummed. They said the audiences used to choke with laughter at his acts with the comic folk theatre group.

Chandra continued humming.

Amjad was curious, but he feared the man too. He quietly watched his movements.

'Son!'

'What, *Kaka*?' alerted, Amjad replied.

'You're sure your father hasn't left home?'

'Yeah. I'm telling you he hasn't gone to foreign parts.'

'Then I'll wait a bit longer. Get me another pipeful of tobacco.'

Amjad left without a word and got back as soon as possible.

Chandra was delighted. Amjad had brough him *paan* and *betel* nut as well.

When Azhar arrived, Chandra was smoking with his eyes shut. He did not see Azhar.

Amjad cried happily, 'Here comes *Abba*.'

'Come, come, Khan sahib.'

Chandra was keen on formality today; he stood up. Azhar laughed.

'What is it, Chunder.'

'I've been waiting since God knows when! No hint of the fig-blossom!'

Azhar took the pipe from Chandra and puffed at it.

'Sitting at home won't do. I've been out looking for something for the stomach.'

'Where did you go, may I know?'

'To the *zamindar* Khan sahib's house. Hatem Bakhsh wants to build a tomb for himself. He called me for an estimate.'

'Is that one going to drop dead?'

Azhar did not like this sort of disrespectful talk behind the *zamindar*'s back.

'What do you mean, "that one"? Speak with a little respect.'

Mimicking a penitent voice, Chandra said: 'Yeah, he's an elderly man, fifty-sixty years of age, sure I'll be respectful. He's really going to die then?'

'Don't make jokes. Everybody'll die. What about me?'

'Then you too should dig a grave for yourself.'

Azhar sighed. He wasn't so fortunate.

'He's going to spend a lot of money. There'll be brick on three sides of the tomb and white marble on the other.'

'Of course, he's going to spend a lot of money. We die because of having to spend while alive; even when they die they make it possible for us to spend.'

Such levity did not penetrate Azhar's skull. Like a fool he said, 'He'll spend two thousand rupees. Then there'll be a garden around it, that's another thousand.'

Chandra was surprised.

He answered wisely: 'All I need is a *maund* of firewood, that's all. And a matchstick, by the riverside. If I die accidentally, still no expenses, only the relatives will have to give us a hand.'

'Stop talking nonsense. How's fishing?'

'Well, that's why I'm here. What good is fishing? There'll be a good crop this season, but the wholesalers will take it all. Look at them. We catch fish, we don't have enough to eat – and they build mansions.'

'What do you want to do?' Azhar looked at Chandra with enquiring eyes.

'We need some capital, brother. Then I could go to the railway station and sell the fish there. It's not worth while carrying five or six *seers* of fish to the market. If we can put together the catches of a few of use to make a *maund* or two, we'd rake in a good profit.'

A dark line fell across Azhar's face.

'Capital? Talking of capital? There's the problem.'

'We don't need much. Fifty rupees will do. You give us some. Let s do business as partners.'

Chandra sounded very enthusiastic.

Azhar sat in silence for a few minutes.

'Khanbhai, you're not saying anything.'

Chandra cast a rather suspicious glance at Azhar.

'What can I say? If I had twenty-five or thirty rupees, would I go dumb? Can't you see our condition?'

Now Chandra too went quiet. He released a sigh.

'My condition's much the same.'

Azhar cut the conversation short.

'What's got into you? You're all right farming and fishing in your spare time.'

'It won't do any more. Chandramani has come back.'

Chandramani was Chandra's youngest sister.

'Is she going to stay with you?'

'Her husband's dead. She's got three children.'

Azhar didn't know this. His sympathetic eyes filled with pity.

'What happened?'

'Fever with delirium.'

'Oh!' With that brief sound, Azhar fell silent.

'Well, I'll have to find something. There isn't an extra room where they can stay. With those few rupees we can try our luck. Can't you give it a try, get it from somewhere?'

'Who'll trust us with so much money?'

'Give it a try anyway. We catch fish, the wholesalers take it to town to make money. Has all the money got to go to town?'

'That's what it seems.'

Chandra shook his head. 'It's a puzzle. We farm, we burn our bodies fishing, and everything rushes to town. We have neither money nor enough food.'

Azhar had an answer to this: 'Cloth comes from town and all those other things, don't you see? The harvest of the country goes to town and the town products come to the country.'

'That's all right. But they live well, why are we in such a state? Don't we work? If we don't send them any rice, what will town folk eat?'

Looking at agitated Chandra, Azhar said softly, 'Then you can go about naked.'

'Why should I go about naked? The country weavers will make cloth.'

'Those days are gone. There are still a few weavers left, does anybody touch their cloth? Can't you see their condition? It's all fate!'

Chandra fell silent. The dream of selling fish as a wholesaler at the railway station had not yet vanished from his mind.

'It's all in the town now. Those businessmen have more money than our *zamindars*. Look at how Taleb Choudhury's puffing up with his iron business. He can buy Hatem Bakhsh ten times over.'

Azhar nodded his agreement but did not make any comment.

Both were quiet.

Amjad was listening to their conversation; he did not dare to participate.

Chandra suddenly got to his feet and said: 'Give it a thought, Khanbhai. I must go now – it's getting late.'

Chandra Kotal sounded frustrated and in despair. Azhar did not reply.

Amjad was standing silently. Chandra pulled him by the hand: 'Come, son, see me off.'

In a pond by the narrow country path a lot of *shapla* lilies were in bloom. Putting some of these in Amjad's hand, Chandra said, 'Now go home. It's much too hot for you.'

Amjad walked homeward.

Chandra was walking across the fields. At the sound of whistling, Amjad turned round and saw Chandra ambling along (to the music of his own whistle) as if nothing in the world had happened to him.

Chapter Six

In the morning Azhar went to see his neighbour and kinsman Saker.

It didn't take long to get to this neighbourhood which lay beyond a small field of banana trees. A professional *latthi* fighter, Saker was the only one who had upheld the martial reputation of the Khans. A rough-looking man, his large round eyes above a long and thick moustache were enough to frighten a child. Azhar thought he might have some money now. Only a couple of days ago he had gone to beat up the tenants in one of Rohini Choudhury's leaseholds. Thanks to the *zamindars*, he was better off than his neighbours. He was even called upon to fight in remote villages.

Saker could be rough, but he was very docile to Azhar and spoke softly to him. Azhar's impression was that Saker respected him. He had never approached him for a loan before, so he probably wouldn't send him away.

But Saker was not at home. His mother spread out a mat on the veranda for Azhar to sit down and said, 'Such a weird child was born in my womb, son, I can't cope any more. Don't know why he had to learn to wield the *latthi*. I haven't got a moment's peace. When he goes fighting, rice doesn't go down our throats.'

'Where's he gone, *Chachi*?'

'I haven't seen him since last night.'

Anxious, Azhar said, 'Hasn't gone fighting, has he?'

'No, his *latthi*'s in his room. He doesn't go without his metalled *latthi*. Where would he go?'

Azhar was silent. Disappointed, he recalled Chandra's face.

Saker's mother started talking about the household.

'The young wife's scared to death. I keep telling her, get him to go farming, get a grip on your man, but no, she just keeps crying day and night for a baby. She's only young. She's not past it, is she, son?'

47

Like someone suddenly woken up, Azhar replied, 'Oh no, how old can our Hashubou be? Can't be over twenty.'

'But she's dying for a baby. Holy blessings, talismans, I've tried everything! These last couple of months there's been a let-up. If it's fated – '

'All Allah's wish, *Chachi*. What can sinners like you and me do?'

'No, son, Allah's been kind,' she said with a forced laugh. 'Do you know what the daughter of the unlucky one says?'

Azhar looked enquiringly at her.

'She says men like Saker won't be tamed until they see the face of a baby. Since that boy's grown up, I've lived in fear, son, day in and day out; there's no fun in living.'

Azhar listened without a comment, his eyes on the courtyard. Suddenly he had to turn his face away. Saker's wife was returning from the pond with a water pitcher on her hip. At the sight of her elder brother-in-law, she hurriedly moved behind the leaves of the hanging gourd in the courtyard, pulling the end of her sari over her head and holding it across her face.

Azhar felt a little embarrassed. Saker's wife was really very young. Her face looked pitiable. Though in the fullnesss of her youth, there was no liveliness in her face. As if the green of youth had taken leave of her after a moment's touch.

In the courtyard, the sun had not filtered down the gourd *machang*, from which hung a few gourds. Ten or twelve stems, intertwined like snakes, embraced the ground. Bits of Hashu's sari were visible through the leaves.

Azhar was ill at ease. It was not seemly to sit like that in front of a young woman. He wanted to get up, but there was no let-up on Saker's mother's natter.

'Bless her, son. Let God fulfil her wishes.'

'Allah's blessings, *Chachi*. What good are human words? I've got to get back to the field. I can't wait any more today.'

Azhar got to his feet.

'Come again, son. And tell Dariabou to come and see us. I'd like to have a word with her.'

'Please let me know when Saker gets back.'

There were bamboo fences on both sides of the path. Despite the growing strength of the sun, the shade here seemed darker because of the brightness around. Azhar's mind swayed with many doubts. His morning was wasted.

Suddenly he heard the ringing voice of Saker's mother. Pricking up his ears, he stopped.

'*Haramzadi*, if there's no money in the house, why didn't you tell him when he was at home? Has the hole of your mouth been filled up?'

There were further eruptions of abuse. Azhar knew she could not bear the sight of her daughter-in-law. But today he was not bothered about that. Azhar felt dejected because there was no money in Saker's home either.

Chandra had to be told; he'd be living in hope. It was pointless to ask anybody else in the village. Ghafur Khan's shop in the market township was expanding, but Azhar had failed to repay an earlier loan for the last two years, so that route was closed. Azhar recalled a few other well-to-do neighbours, but there were snags in each case. Dariabibi had brought a pair of ear pendants from her former in-laws; they were pawned at Podder's when Amjad and Naima fell ill last year.

It was not unlikely that astute Chandra would do well in business. But Azhar couldn't think of the little key to open the door of his own locked fate.

Walking to the field with a heavy heart, Azhar thought of other ways. Clouds had suddenly gathered in the sky; the sun had hidden behind them. It might rain any time.

He was close to Chandra's house when a gusty rain started. Azhar was not bothered about getting wet as he would bathe at about midday. He walked straight to the river. Chandra was not likely to stay indoors during the full tide. Besides, fishing was an addiction with him.

The vegetation on both sides of the canal was blurred in the rain. No men or animals were visible. Perhaps everybody had taken cover. Azhar heard the clanking of a boat and became happy. Standing on a skip, Chandra was drawing in a net. The stern of his boat was tied to a pole. The grating noise of the boat, pulled by the current against the bamboo pole, rose above the sound of rain.

Azhar called out, 'Chandra!'

The echo spread to both sides of the canal.

The rain abated; clouds rumbled.

Before the tide came in, Chandra had closed the mouth of the canal with a long fence net. Now with the tide pulling out he was drawing it

49

in. He looked calm. The muscles of his arms were visibly swollen. His eyes were on the net.

Without raising his eyes, he said, 'Khanbhai, hang on a bit.'

Having drawn in the net, he said, 'It won't pay for the labour. I've been working for a long time.'

Only a couple of *seers* of fish were hauled in. Ten or twelve *topshey* fish brushed Chandra's eyes with happiness.

'I thought I might try once with a *khie* net. Good job you came.'

The two of them walked towards Chandra's home. Chandra was shivering with cold; he'd been out in the rain for long. He was quiet, walking fast, carrying the fish basket in his hand.

'Hurry up, Khan. We need a smoke.'

Azhar stepped carefully on the slippery road. The rain hadn't stopped completely. A fine drizzle like the smoke shaken off a bird's wings fell from the sky.

Chandra called out from the veranda, 'To arms! Prepare!'

Elokeshi and Chandramani came out smiling.

'*Dada* seems to be calling out for battle.'

'Prepare what?' said Elokeshi, who knew, and, asking Chandramani to offer them seats, went out to prepare the hookah.

This was Chandramani. Azhar was surprised. He had seen this sister of Chandra before. She was slim, fair and much younger than Chandra, who had tried hard to get her married. But what had happened to her now? She looked like a human version of a jute stalk.

'My clothes are dripping, Mani,' Azhar said. 'I won't spoil the bale of hay. I'll squat. But why do you look so poorly?'

'Can the body hold when the fate's smashed?'

Azhar fell silent. She wasn't past twenty-five; what sin had this slip of a girl committed to deserve such punishment?

'Have you had fever, Mani?'

'These last two months I've been suffering from malaria. But I've been poorly before.' Chandramani sank down in one corner of the veranda. Her plain, white sari, the obligatory dress of a widow, matched well her pale, anaemic look.

Two dark, naked children came and stood close to Chandramani. Azhar hadn't seen them before.

'They're your children, aren't they, Mani?'

'Yes, *Dada*. Gopal, the older one, is five. Jogin's three. I keep burning for them. If he'd left something before he died – '

Drops of tears fell from her dull, sunken eyes. Gopal and Jogin stood close to their mother.

With tear-blurred eyes, she said, 'At least, because of my brother, we've had shelter. But you can see their condition. Their children died; now, on top of that, they've got our burden to bear.'

Wrapping a dry *gamtcha* round his waist, Chandra came out, puffing away at a hookah pipe. His eyes fell on Chandramani.

'There she goes again. Tell me, Azharbhai, what's the matter with her? I haven't died yet, have I?'

Chandra reprimanded her, 'Go and do the fish. The children have got to be fed.'

Chandramani snapped, 'No, nothing's the matter with me. Look at what's happened to your health, working for us.'

'Run. Beat it! That's enough. What's happened to my health?'

Passing the pipe to Azhar, Chandra showed his biceps. 'Look, Mani, look. Let any son of a gun try punching me down. Go on, go to the kitchen.'

Stroking his moustache, Chandra curled his lips.

Jogin laughed at his uncle's antics.

'You laughing? Come on, then, let's arm-wrestle.'

Three-year-old Jogin was undaunted; he held out his little hand.

Gopal was timid; he observed his brother from a distance.

'Right. Learn to fight like this. Then you can go robbing when you grow up.'

Azhar disengaged his pipe.

'Fine lesson you're giving him.'

Chandra stroked his long moustache.

'I'm going to make robbers of them. Working won't feed them. I'll join a gang as well.'

Chandra has a touch of madness, Azhar thought, but he continued nonetheless.

'So you're going to rob as well, are you?'

'Why not? What good is working to your bone? Religion, God, I don't care for them. There's no sin in thieving if working won't feed you.'

Azhar's eyes climbed his forehead.

'What are you raving about, Chandra?'

'I'm fed up, really. You think there's a God, Allah?'

'God forbid! God forbid!'

Azhar recited Muhammad's praise in his mind.

Jogin was still arm-wrestling with his uncle. Chandra would not shut up. 'We can't feed ourselves by working, they get fed lolling about on their cushions. God's will, they say, fate. Well, I've no use for an unjust God like that. I'll rob and I'll eat! I'll rob and I'll eat!'

Chandra got Jogin to join in: 'I'll rob and I'll eat.'

Chandra's singing stopped as his eyes fell on Azhar.

Azhar Khan was sitting with a sullen face.

Chandra held out his hand to him.

'Are you cross?' he said. 'All right. Now let's get back to the real job.'

'What job?' Azhar asked.

'What I asked you about.'

Of which no trace was left in Azhar's mind. Like a fool, he said, 'What did you ask me about?'

Chandra had a laugh.

'You wouldn't remember that, would you? I'm talking about the fish business.'

Azhar was embarrassed.

'You know my situation,' he mumbled. 'I couldn't raise a loan.'

'And you've been arguing with me. Why don't you open your eyes and look? We can't feed ourselves by working, so we want to do business. But there's not a blind cowrie of capital.'

Chandra fell silent. Chandramani had come back to listen in to their conversation in silence, which she now broke: Jogin's father had also fancied the fish business.

Chandra grunted his agreement.

Jogin's play with his uncle had come to a stop and he was sitting in a sulk. Looking at him, Chandra laughed out loud.

'Our argument holds, eh, son? We won't do business and we won't do farming.'

Azhar thought Chandra was annoyed with him. To wipe away any misunderstanding, he said softly, 'Don't be cross with me, Chunder. Only I know how I've been running the family these last two years.'

Chandra asked Chandramani to get another pipeful of tobacco.

'Why should I be cross with you? All my anger is with – what do you call it? – fate. With fate.'

Azhar was sitting in wet clothes. He could not leave Chandra, as he felt he had let him down.

Chandramani returned with a blazing pipe. After a listless puff or two, Azhar passed it to Chandra.

52

'Khan, let's go look at the paddy in the fields. You'll go home too.'

They walked along the path, Chandra carrying a couple of *topshey* fish with red moustaches. Absent-mindedly, Azhar wasn't looking anywhere. The thought that he could not help Chandra pricked him somewhere in his conscience.

Chandra, without a care in the world, went along at his usual pace. The taint in the horizon had been washed away by the rain. Some egrets were arguing in the shallow water. A kingfisher put out its neck from its nest beside the forest of reeds in the canal and then blended into the blue sky in an instant.

Azhar was following him. As Chandra turned round, he said in a heavy voice, 'Chunder, don't take it hard. It's my fate. I wish we could give the business a try.'

Chandra was surprised.

'Sure I'll take it hard. If you fry this fish and eat it with your children, I won't be cross.'

With a smile, Chandra squeezed the fish into Azhar's hand.

Before Chandra's mind paraded Chandramani, his own family, Gopal, Jogin, and he felt as if a load of sorrow was being lifted; he liked the company of Azhar even more.

'Azharbhai, one day I'll go away to foreign parts with you. Teach me a little masonry job.'

No reply came from Azhar. Looking at his sad face, Chandra kept walking silently. A seagull's sharp note lost itself over the fields in a dreamlike swoon.

Chapter Seven

Azhar had sown a little *aush* paddy on a few *kathas* of land.

A touch of ripeness had coloured the grains. Suddenly he picked up his building tools and went off to distant parts, leaving the affairs of the family in Dariabibi's hands. In the past he used to confer with his wife before going; on this occasion he did not say a word. Dariabibi had seen Azhar getting his tools, but it did not occur to her that he was going away. Amjad, who first got to know about it, told her.

'You're joking, Amu.'

'No, *Ma. Abba* said there's a place called Niamatpur. He's going there looking for work.'

Amjad had been out with his friends surveying the fields when father and son met purely accidentally.

Dariabibi stood stock still for while. Were there such people in the world who would not consider it necessary to tell at least the members of their family before going away indefinitely?

'Ma, looking at *Abba* you'd think he was crazy. Not a word. Pushing on with his head down.'

There was no expression on Dariabibi's face.

'Ma, Abba makes me laugh. Doesn't even know how to wear his *lungi* properly. A tatty shirt on top of that.'

Dariabibi flared up.

'Go away! We've had enough of your lip.'

Amjad turned into a worm.

Dariabibi noticed the evening was drawing in. It was the dark phase of the moon, which would not rise over the highway tonight.

'Didn't he tell you anything else?' Dariabibi asked, touching Amjad's chin, and he cringed, as if she were touching the chin of a fatherless child, her voice weighed down with an excess of emotion.

'He only said, I'm going to Niamatpur looking for work. Where's Niamatpur, *Ma?*'

54

Dariabibi did not reply. She felt angry – an anger born of envy. If only *she* could treat the world in such a cavalier fashion! For her a day dawned with a hundred chores and the reptilian wall of a thousand constraints around her mind.

If Amjad hadn't been there, she would have burst into tears like a little girl. Her eyes on the horizon, she now stood like an idol, leaning slightly on her son.

Naima was attached to her father. She had heard from a boy in the village about her father going away. Her crying would not stop.

'*Abba* didn't take me, Ma,' Naima cried.

'Shut up or I'll thrash you.'

Naima calmed down.

Dariabibi said, 'Amu, go and show her the pictures in your school book.'

She had not realised that the evening lamp had not been lit, so she added, 'Hang on, I'll light the lamp.'

As she took the lamp around, she had a look at the cattle as well. They could be let loose if it did not rain. But Amu was too young to stop them from straying into other people's fields; there was that risk. Those who could afford to pay the fine let their cattle loose even in the harvesting season.

Today the haystack under the *neem* tree looked strange. The homestead felt desolate. Taking the lamp round the house quickly, Dariabibi got back to her children.

A couple of owls flew past and Dariabibi's heart trembled with the fear of things inauspicious. Of late the children had lost a few more of their clothes. The fear of petty thieves disturbed one's sleep. At least there had been a man about the house, and that had provided strength. Once again a sense of loneliness hit her. She had finished her household chores during daylight hours. Now Dariabibi sat beside Amjad and listened to him reading: 'Once on the way to the city of Dehli – '

Naima laughed, 'Dilly billy – '

'Listen quietly, Naima, don't make a noise. Your brother's reading.'

Perched on Dariabibi's lap, Naima swayed back and forth. Dariabibi was alert today. Amjad was reading, making a not inconsiderable noise. She pricked up her ears at the slightest sound by the fence or near the threshold.

A grey future spread out to the horizon. Aridity surrounded her; there was not a trace of green.

A week passed; there was no news from Azhar. Amjad pestered the postman for nothing. Dariabibi got worried; the *aush* paddy would have to be harvested. She was confident Azhar Khan would get back before then.

Two more weeks passed slowly. Dariabibi called Saker and complained bitterly. Saker slipped away with the advice that it was no good worrying about a grown-up male going to foreign parts for a bit.

Dariabibi saw darkness all about her. The household cash was exhausted; would she be able to give the children their daily food? How long could she keep borrowing?

Dariabibi crept about in darkness. If she still had the pair of kids, she could have sold them in these hard times. Allah had forestalled that. With a man around, a way could be found. It was the rainy season – the neighbours just survived somehow. Some had eaten their rice seeds. People hardly employed labourers at this time of the year. With the danger of hunger surrounding them, they were worried about themselves.

The next day Dariabibi went to visit Saker's mother. The old woman's face shone with happiness. At last Allah had fulfilled Hashu's wish. So Dariabibi laughingly broached the idea of being invited to dinner. The old woman not only agreed, she insisted. Dariabibi could not accept the invitation with a simple heart. It stung her. The neighbours would look down upon her if she accepted an invitation when she had no food at home. Nevertheless she accepted it. It would save her a meal. Ashekjan too was invited with them.

Dariabibi, who had had a pitying contempt for Ashekjan, now looked at her differently. Deep inside her she realised that Ashekjan's condition could be weighed on the same scale as her own helplessness. In the past she had never bothered about her; never felt a need to know if and when she ate, slept or starved. Now she felt an urge to bear this burden.

Ashekjan used to go out in the rain. Even a heavy rain would not stop her. She might have had an invitation or she might not – but she always pretended she had.

The stock of rice was nearly exhausted. Ashekjan knew it all. In these matters, Amjad was helpful. When he went to bed, Ashekjan made detailed enquiries.

'There isn't much rice in the rice jar, *Dadi*. Ma was so mad with *Abba*.'

Ashekjan kept quiet for a while and asked, 'Did you have enough to eat today?'

'Yes, *Dadi*, but Ma doesn't eat much.'

Ashekjan fell silent again.

The next day, finding a lot more rice in the rice jar, Dariabibi called Amjad.

'Where did all the rice come from?'

'I don't know, Ma.'

Dariabibi easily guessed what was happening. On any other day, a battle would have ensued. Charity rice could not be allowed to fill the stomachs of her children. Today Dariabibi herself sought to divert the course of the conversation.

'Did you ask the postman if he had any money or a letter?'

'I ask every day, Ma.'

'Ask again tomorrow.'

Amjad could hardly believe his mother's voice could be so smooth.

'Amu, go and see if the paddy's ripe. We'll have to get a labourer to harvest it.'

Amjad nodded agreement.

Ma had come to measure out the rice for dinner. Suddenly she gave him a cuddle. As if unable to say all she wanted to tell him, she had to finish it with tenderness. Amjad was embarrassed by his mother's kiss.

Outside the clump of bamboos murmured.

The following day Amjad was stunned. How could Ma thrash him for such a minor offence? He had asked for his school fees. Perhaps she was not in a good mood, so he shouldn't have asked, but he did not know his mother could wield her hand so ruthlessly.

Thrashed, he sat on the veranda shedding tears for a long time. Naima came over and stood beside him. If only he could find any remorse in her! Instead she started a row on her own, in which arrangements for the fortieth-day feast of Azhar's death and of his fourteen generations were concluded. Amjad slipped away from the veranda.

He went to the fields and found peace. It was in the fields Azhar made his sighs worthwhile. Perhaps in this way Amjad was bound to him by the chain of blood.

He walked about in the fields. There were clouds in the sky, but no rain, nothing to stop him from wandering about.

As the sun set, he felt very hungry. It was the rainy season and there was no other crop except rice in the fields. If it were summer, Amjad would have taken revenge on his mother by eating melons and cucumbers from the fields. As if drawn by an unseen hand, he advanced in the direction of Chandra Kotal's home.

Sitting under a tree near where the river met the canal, Amjad daydreamed. Something kept him from heading straight for Chandra *Kaka*'s house.

With a water pitcher on her hip, Chandramani came to the river. Seeing Amjad, she asked, 'What are you sitting there for?'

Amjad did not reply. His face looked shrunken and there were traces of dried tears under his eyes.

'Did you have a row at home? Let's go, your *kaka*'s at home. What happened?'

Amjad kept his head bowed, refusing to comply with Chandramani's request.

By then Chandra himself had arrived.

'What is it, Chandramani?'

'Look, your friend's son is sitting there without a word.'

Chandra observed Amjad's movements. He was quiet, still, his young and pretty eyes lost in the distance.

Chandra burst out laughing.

'Have you taken to meditating under a tree now, eh? Well, your *abba*'s a pious Muslim. You're his son after all.'

Amjad did not look at either of them. The Kotals kept laughing.

Chandra sang as he whistled: 'My mynah doesn't talk . . .'

Still there was no expression on Amjad's lips. Chandra concluded whistling with a flourish and swept up Amjad and put him on his shoulders. The dumb saint now started sobbing.

> 'My mynah
> doesn't talk,
> Hai, hai-rey . . .'

Chandra started walking along the canal as he sang. Chandramani called out: 'First give the boy a handful of puffed rice to eat.'

Chandra nodded.

'Right. Good job you reminded me, Mani.'

He turned homeward.

Chapter Eight

It was raining ceaselessly. The sky cast its shadow on pools of water in the open spaces of the fields, where birds came to bathe as soon as the rain stopped.

Dariabibi had come out to the bend of the road, something she had never done before; mounted on her head like a cone was a jute sack. A current of rain water flowed under her feet. The jute sack failed to keep the water off her; the upper part of her had got soaked.

Dariabibi stood unconcerned. She was cold, but she was hardly conscious of it. Who was she waiting for?

On one side of the road there was little vegetation so the faraway fields could be seen. On the other side there was a jungle of thickly grown trees and creepers. This lonesome lap of the silent, intimate village under the cover of a cloudy sky was fearful, ghostly – where the slightest sound could startle you.

Dariabibi cast anxious looks at the farthest point of the road, her face as grave as the clouds in the sky.

Suddenly her eyes brightened as a boy's figure became visible at a distance. Amjad was approaching fast with a red *gamtcha* over his head.

His boyish figure, seen through the falling lines of rain, looked enchanting like a dancing puppet.

Dariabibi became cheerful. Before Amjad had come close to her, she said, 'Did you find Shairami?'

His whole body soaked in rain, Amjad was shivering with cold. He could not reply immediately.

He moved close to his mother and panted for a while, then answered with a sad face, 'No, *Ma*, but her sister-in-law said she would come to see us straight from the fields.'

Shairami was a *bagdi* untouchable who lived on one side of the locality beyond the fishermen's quarters. The only living person in

59

Shairami's world was her invalid son; her husband had died long ago. Ganesh had become an invalid following a long illness. He could not stand erect and one of his hands had atrophied. Even in her old age Shairami had to support him. She sold cowpat cakes for fuel, picked greens and ran errands for others. Shairami had learned to bear her suffering through physical labour. She had known Dariabibi for some years. Shairami delivered cowpats at this house; from there a friendly relationship had developed between the two women.

The rain had abated a little. Soft sounds played ceaselessly on trees and leaves. One could hear a bird shaking water off its wings.

'If she doesn't?' Dariabibi broke the silence.

'No, Ma, she'll come. Let's go home. I'm cold.'

As if coming to her senses, Dariabibi rubbed Amjad's head with a dry part of her sari.

'What good is drying it now, Ma? It's raining.'

Dariabibi seemed to have lost touch, unable even to realise that it was raining and so useless to dry his hair out in the rain.

There were several frogs leaping about under a banyan tree. Although he was shivering, Amjad was delighted. A frog had flip-flopped to the middle of the road, quietly eating rain-drawn insects.

Giving it a forceful kick, Amjad said, 'Ma, look, I'm playing football.'

The frog fell at a distance with a thud. Sprawled on its arms and legs panted the son of a frog.

Dariabibi could not suppress her laughter.

'Amu, you'll never grow up.'

Amjad turned grave at his own achievement. Shaking his head, he said, 'You'll have to give me hot rice now. I'm soaked through; don't I get hungry?'

Dariabibi fell silent, the smile on her face immediately put out.

More clouds gathered in the sky. How much longer would the rains continue in Bengal's villages?

Naima hadn't gone anywhere; she was arguing with Ashekjan. They sometimes engaged in mock disputes.

There was some watered rice left. But Amjad became difficult, he wouldn't eat watered rice.

Dariabibi was annoyed, but she kept quiet. Sulking, Amjad did not touch the food.

Dariabibi changed her wet clothes and sat waiting. In the cowshed the cows munched hay. Naima was playing in Ashekjan's room; her voice reached her ears.

There was no break in the rains.

Looking at sleeping Amjad, a hundred waves churned in her breast. She sat in silence, as if enjoying a long-awaited rest, stringing together in her memory the details of her weary days.

There was a little watered rice, but she had forgotten about food. Her eyes became hevy with sleep. Sitting leaning against the wall, Dariabibi dozed.

'*Bhabi*, where are you?'

Dariabibi woke up. Shairami had really come. Her clothes were wet and she carried in her hand a bundle of freshly picked greens.

Putting the bundle on the veranda, Shairami asked, 'Why did you ask for me, *Bhabi*?'

Shairami was dark. Age had wrinkled her skin and the tyranny of wet cold upon her body had shrunk her. She looked very ugly. But the goodness of her heart rang out in her voice. 'You know how busy I've got to be. There's no end of trouble with the boy in the rainy season.'

Shairami really started panting.

Dariabibi had never seen Ganesh. But Shairami's misery was real to her. She did not need any effort of imagination.

'It's fate, *Didi*. To think Allah had to give your breadwinning son such an affliction!'

Shairami placed her two hands on her breast for warmth. She did not want to wait much longer. But Dariabibi hesitated to broach the question; she played for time.

'What's in that bundle, *Didi*?'

'Greens, *Bhabi*,' Shairami said. 'Give me a little oil, I'll have a bath before going home.'

Dariabibi fetched the pot of mustard oil.

Shairami was undoing the knot of the bundle. Unloading some greens on the veranda, she looked up at Dariabibi.

'Any more, *Bhabi*?'

'No, that's enough. What else is there in the bundle?'

'Nothing.'

As Dariabibi curiously touched the greens in the bundle, she found snails under them.

She did not pursue the matter. Dariabibi knew that Shairami

61

wasn't well off. What was there to be secretive about if she had collected some snails for her ducks?

'*Bhabi*, I must go now.'

'Hang on. How much cold can get into those old bones?' Dariabibi said with mock anger.

Shairami pleaded: 'I'll come another day for a natter. Leaving the boy alone at home in the rains, I get no peace of mind, lest something happens.'

Dariabibi did not speak for a while. She was sitting on a *pidi*, looking down; she remained seated. A dark shadow crossed and recrossed her face.

Then with a sudden burst of breath she said, '*Didi*, my gem of a husband left home three weeks back with a dark face. We're in want. There's an old pot – if someone could keep it for five rupees, I'll pay interest every month.'

For Azhar there was unending anger.

'Just look at it. He ran away from home. If I was younger I'd have run away with someone.'

Shairami reprimanded her: 'What inauspicious words you're mouthing at this time of the day! A little wind knocks you over too.'

Dariabibi suddenly fell silent.

'All right, give me the pot,' Shairami said. 'I'll leave it with Adhar Santh's mother and get five rupees for you. The old woman will charge two paisa for interest every month.'

'Give it to her.'

Dariabibi spoke softly, her eyes getting moist.

'My father gave us a dowry. When my first husband died I brought back a little brassware.'

Dariabibi's large eyes misted up. Her face, like a still sky, looked beautiful. Her fatigued fair colour flashed like lightning.

Shairami expressed her sorrow: '*Dada* shouldn't have done this. The wives of good homes don't go out; who'd look after the family?'

'You tell me, *Didi*.'

Dariabibi walked into her room and when she came out after a few minutes she had an old brass pot in her hand.

Shairami repeatedly examined the pot.

'I'll see if she'll give us a rupee or two more. Such good stuff!'

The rain had stopped for a while. Giving Shairami a *paan* to chew, Dariabibi said, '*Didi*, hide it in your clothes. If anybody asks, don't tell them it's ours. By God, *Didi*.'

'After all these years, you think I'm a cobra? Would anybody send away *Lakhshmi* unless she was desperate?'

Shairami stood up. It had started raining again. Dariabibi kept touching the pot. Despite much mental resistance, she had put the brass article in Shairami's hand.

'Don't tell anybody, *Didi*, Swear it on my head.'

Shairami left.

There was a little rice, which could be fried for Amjad. Dariabibi had nothing more to worry about for the night.

The distant thunder travelled down across the fields. The trees tossed about in a flood of green. The silent sky repeatedly cast its shadow on Dariabibi's face.

In these hard times Chandra offered help. He could not offer them even a cowrie with a hole, but is it possible to put a price on the physical labour and sympathy he gave? Two more weeks passed. There was no trace of Azhar. The *aush* paddy would have turned into cowpat in the rain if Chandra himself hadn't got it all sent to Azhar's home. The crop had not been very good, but it would see them through for the next couple of months. Dariabibi sighed and took courage. On Chandra's advice she did not repay the loans. What if Azhar did not return in a couple of months, or did not return at all? Dariabibi felt crushed under the wheel of evil despair.

One day Amjad got back from school and said, 'Ma, moulvi sahib wants my school fees.'

Dariabibi was annoyed: 'All right, *moulvi* sahib needn't insist every day. Don't go to school from tomorrow.'

Amjad's face dried up.

Dariabibi was removing particles of stone from a pile of broken rice. As she looked up at Amjad, the shadow of irritation on her face vanished. Assuming a serious expression, she said, 'Tell *moulvi* sahib you'll pay up when your father gets back.'

Amjad still did not move. Ma had used the same words before to dupe *moulvi* sahib.

Mustering his courage, he protested, 'You say that every day.'

Dariabibi kept sifting the stone particles; she did not even look up at Amjad.

Amjad stealthily watched his mother's movements.

The long silence seemed like a great rock on his chest. He felt ill at ease.

Dariabibi seemed to have forgotten the existence of her son.

'Ma,' Amjad suddenly called out, the sound just emerging through his numb lips.

Raising two grave eyes, Dariabibi simply looked at her son.

'Ma.'

There was a sharp response: 'What?'

'Ma.'

'No. You don't have to go to school from tomorrow. You've had enough of reading and writing.'

Amjad was secretly delighted. He liked the boys, but didn't like the school at all.

'Then what do I do, Ma?'

Dariabibi replied sarcastically: 'What else? Son of a peasant, you'll start with your caste trade, won't you?'

Amjad lowered his head. There was no honour in the hard labour of a peasant.

He said, his smile untarnished, 'Can I push the plough? I'm only eight.'

'Your neck will.'

Amjad was frightened. Ma was really angry.

Just then Chandra Kotal's voice could be heard from the outhouse.

Amjad heaved a sigh of relief.

Chandra had just dropped in to see if there was any news of Azhar. The rice wholesalers often went to Niamatpur, but they had no information about him. In a big market town a nonentity like Azhar was not listed anywhere.

Amjad talked to Chandra. After a while Dariabibi herself spoke to him from behind the outhouse: 'Please do something for us.'

Chandra was surprised that Dariabibi, a woman of purdah, was addressing him directly.

Diffident Chandra's voice lost its usual carefree tone.

'Why, what's the matter, *Bhabi*?'

'What good is counting school fees for a poor man's son?'

Chandra's voice stalled, he kept quiet for a while.

'That's true. But maybe we should give him another year or two. He's only a little boy.'

'If we can't get him far enough, there's no use spending money.'

Chandra raised no further objection.

'Let him stay around with me, learn to fish and row a boat.'

Dariabibi agreed. The child had not yet learned to swim; how was he going to row a boat? But one could depend on Chandra.

After chewing a *paan* and giving Amjad a cuddle, Chandra walked away into the village.

The following morning Amjad was surprised. Ma was really sending him off to Chandra *Kaka* with a small barge-pole. Was a boatman's life really opening up for him?

Looking at Ma's determined face, Amjad raised no objection. Carrying a little puffed rice, he set off towards the river.

Only two years ago Dariabibi could not have imagined such a train of events. She had had so many dreams about the child then!

Don't you dream any more, Dariabibi?

Chapter Nine

Azhar and a few other builders had rented a house in a village on the outskirts of this provincial town.

The last bus had long taken its passengers to the railway station, leaving the marks of its tyres on the highway.

Azhar, perched on the threshold, was still sucking away at his coconut hookah. The sparks flew as he sucked, removing the darkness for a moment to reveal the door.

The room was narrow with a single window on one side. There was a coat of plaster and lime on the mud walls, some of which had come off here and there. On a large mat spread out on the uneven mud floor, Azhar's mates were sleeping. After a whole day's continuous rain, Azhar felt like choking in the room's humid heat. A little while ago he had abandoned his bed for the threshold and a smoke.

A frog croaked in the ditch beside the road. There were too many mosquitoes in these parts so you couldn't take your shirt off. Azhar's tired eyes closed as he smoked. Mosquitoes hummed all around him. Now and then he flicked his *gamtcha* to drive them away.

Darkness thronged in the trees beside the road. Responding to the call of a cool night, fireflies were sleepless.

Azhar's mind had gone inert. Even his tangled thoughts had forgotten to crawl about in the dark. Azhar Khan recalled nothing.

He worked at Niamatpur for only a couple of days. He had a good job, which could easily last for a few weeks. But the place was not to his liking; he didn't like the company of drunken louts. Most of the builders there were bad characters. With a couple of days' earnings tucked away, Azhar had set off again. He was confident he'd get a job somewhere. When he saw the structure of this new building by the road, he approached the owner hopefully. His mates didn't seem to be bad, so though the wages were low, he readily took the job.

The village, called Jahanpur, was a couple of miles from a railway station, which had been opened only two years ago. Within a few days Azhar quietly realised that even now there were opportunities for many businesses and persevered to put away a little capital.

He wasn't feeling very well after a whole day's work; it was hot and stuffy inside the room. Azhar felt uneasy, though without a clear awareness of it. He smoked and yawned a few times, sitting there without a thought. The tobacco was exhausted, but there was no respite to the sound of the hookah. He puffed away vigorously, but the tobacco would not respond. Disappointed, he put down the hookah at one corner of the threshold.

He could do with another smoke. He yawned.

Suddenly he felt the presence of another person beside him — unknown in the dark.

Azhar called out softly: 'Who is it?'

'Me, *Chacha*.'

A boy's voice caused a wave in the dark.

'Khalil, what are you doing here so late?'

'Can't sleep, *Chacha*.'

Azhar's ear caught the hint of a sob.

He shook off his slumber and reached out his hand in the dark and found Khalil, who was sitting with his head buried between his knees.

One of Azhar's mates was called Odu. Khalil was Odu's brother's son. Hardly twelve, he was suffering this exile from home to learn the carpenter's trade with his uncle.

Azhar moved closer to Khalil and, giving him a little shake, said in a soft voice: 'What's wrong, son?'

Khalil would not raise his head, as if by putting his head between his knees he wanted to get away from the world's calumny.

He gave him another shake: 'Come on, raise your head and speak. What happened?'

Their dialogue was conducted softly lest it disturb the sleep of the others. They were all day labourers in the room.

Khalil did not respond. He was sitting without a shirt on. Placing Azhar's hand on to his back, he sobbed again.

As if stung by a scorpion, Azhar quickly removed his hand and called out, 'How did you get those weals on your back?'

Khalil put his hand on Azhar's mouth: 'Don't shout, *Chacha*. If they wake up, I'll get told off again.'

Frightened, Khalil looked around at the sleeping figures. No, Azhar's cry hadn't reached their ears.

Azhar drew Khalil to him and patted him affectionately on the back.

He remembered Amjad, Naima's face, Moheshdanga. And Daria-bibi? No, the image of the industrious, resourceful, firm-bodied Dariabibi did not rise to his mind. Or perhaps it did, in the faded lines of a momentary light.

'Who beat you?' Azhar asked anxiously.

Khalil looked around and whispered in Azhar's ear: 'Odu *Chacha*. With a piece of firewood.'

Swallowing hard, Khalil resumed sobbing.

'What, Odu so cruel?'

Putting his hand affectionately on Khalil's back, Azhar said, 'What did you do that he hit you so hard?'

'I broke Gahar Mistry's spirit-level. It fell on the bricks.'

Gahar was a mason, one of those sleeping in the room.

'Just broke a little spirit-level and he had to beat you like this?'

Khalil broke into a sob.

One could just catch his meaning when he said haltingly: 'I wanted to go home with Odu *Chacha*.'

'Has Odu gone home today?'

'Yes, *Chacha*.'

Azhar wanted to console the boy.

'So what? We're here, you've nothing to fear.'

Khalil had moved away to a corner, his head between his knees. He had no courage to look the frightful world in the face.

After a while he said, 'I don't like it here, *Chacha*.'

'It won't do for a man not to learn a trade. The foreign parts are for men to explore. It's natural to feel a little down now and then.'

Khalil went inert. There was no reply from him.

'Is your father alive, son?' Azhar asked.

Khalil did not raise his head. His tired voice sounded like a scream: 'No!'

'There's nothing to worry about. We're here. Odu'll be back in a day or two.'

Azhar reached out his hand towards Khalil, who now moved close to his side, his tired eyes fixed on the road.

Then looking at Azhar, he said: 'I've been away from home for two months now, *Chacha*. I miss my ma. Odu *Chacha* has been home four times.'

'Learn to stay away from home. To be a good builder you'll have to learn the trade. Then your misery'll end. Look at me, I used to farm at home, didn't bother to come to town. It's a dog's life!'

Khalil found no hope or comfort.

'If I can work for food for six months, I'll get some pocket money. I haven't given Ma a paisa yet. If I'd had pocket money I could have saved something from it.'

Azhar Khan, his heart melting, stared at the child. At this tender age he had learned to tell the colours of the world. Surely Allah would make him prosper and fortune would smile at him.

Azhar spoke again: 'A few more months, son. Then you can save out of your pocket money for your ma. Doesn't she work?'

'She threshes paddy for her food.'

Khalil felt deeply ashamed for having introduced himself as a thresher's son. He'd got carried away.

Azhar sat silently. Who knew where Amjad would be after three or four years?

Amjad's face flashed through his mind. And Chandra's, who had taught him to dream. No other face would hold still in the swirling mist of his mind. There were endless opportunities for business in this expanding village. Would God not look kindly on him for once?

An unknown fear agonised his heart. He recited a verse from the Koran and breathed on himself.

Azhar noticed that Khalil was yawning. He turned to him and said, 'We'll have to go to work tomorrow morning. Go and get some sleep.'

'Won't you go to bed, *Chacha*?'

The sound of the innocent voice was very sweet to Azhar's ear.

'No, son, I'll have another smoke before turning in.'

Khalil went in. Azhar refilled the pipe.

A cool breeze started late at night. Clouds spread out over the village woodland and the face of the sky darkened in an instant.

Azhar Khan stuck to his decision.

After a couple of weeks he rented a small thatched hut near the bus stand not far from his present abode. The veranda was about three feet wide. With the help of a carpenter friend he made a shelf in one corner. A lot of fuss was made about the shop, though there wasn't much merchandise. Azhar had saved twenty-five rupees, of which the carpenter took three, and with the rest he set up a stall with items like needle and thread, trinkets for girls, pencils for school children, lozenges.

Azhar wanted to open a corner for *paan*, but a few *paanwallahs* had already crowded out the business. Yet he had hopes. If his fortune shone, he would brighten his shop with new stuff. Four miles from the railway station, a merchant had set up as a big wholesaler.

Gahar Mistry did not take the matter lightly. Azhar was leaving, so they would have to pay more towards the house-rent. He shot hundreds of verbal weapons to dissuade him. He felt a touch of envy too. Gahar did not know how Azhar had suffered to save twenty-five rupees, neglecting his family like a loafer, on top of the physical hardship. How many people had such fortitude?

Gahar said, 'So you've opened a shop here, eh? See if you can build a mansion.'

Azhar, poor fellow, didn't reply, but those words pierced his heart.

'You've got to make a living somehow. I thought I'd set up a shop.'

Gahar was fair, tall as a palm tree, very thin and wiry. He had clean teeth: he did not chew *paan*.

'No, there's nothing wrong with it,' he said. 'Well, give us a *bidi*.'

Azhar was not easily roused, but even he felt the sting in Gahar's words.

'Haven't got any, all gone.'

Azhar had no hesitation in lying.

Gahar got to his feet.

'Get on with your shop, you might build a mansion. Then I'd probably come and stay with you for a day for having once worked together.'

Azhar was amazed. He said to himself, 'There are people in the world to envy even a poor wretch like me.'

Ants were climbing up the jars of lozenges to which Azhar now turned his attention.

A little later Khalil came. He looked cheerful.

'*Chacha*, your shop looks pretty. Bear me in mind for when you want an assistant.'

Azhar smiled wanly.

'Bless me, son. If Allah wills, it won't take long.'

Khalil hadn't seen so many things in his own village. He looked about in wonder.

'I'm on my own now,' Azhar said. 'I've got to shut the shop even when I go for a dip in the pond. You can relieve me now and then.'

'I will, *Chacha*, as soon as I get back from home. Odu *Chacha* promised he'd take me home next time he goes.'

'Good, good.'

Khalil sat on one side of the veranda.

He looked wistfully at the jars ranged in a row. Unconsciously he picked up a jar of lozenges in his hands.

'What's in it, *Chacha*?'

'Lozenges.'

'How do they taste?'

'Very sweet. Each costs two paisa.'

Khalil promptly put the jar back on the shelf. His hands had gone stiff.

Azhar looked at his face for a while. He was a shopkeeper who had just opened a shop. After a little hesitation, he said, 'Why don't you take one, son?'

'No,' replied Khalil, embarrassed.

Azhar delayed no more. He took out a couple of sweets and gave them to Khalil.

Khalil's diffidence would not pass: 'No, *Chacha*, I don't like sweets. I've got no money.'

'Take it, go on.'

'How's your shop going to survive?'

Such a young boy and yet so aware of the ways of the world! Azhar Khan was amazed.

Khalil chewed the sweets with a smile.

'You wait here for a while. I'll go for the evening prayer.'

Khalil immediately turned into a master. He sat there with a serious face, talking to the customers. He felt amused. If only he could set up a shop like this.

When Azhar returned, Khalil went home.

A little lamp burned in one corner of the shop. Khalil was seen walking along the road, across which fell the shadows of roadside trees.

Such a small child!

Was Amjad, sulking, going back to Moheshdanga?

71

Chapter Ten

After she had sold her greens in the village, Shairami was talking to Dariabibi. Ganesh wasn't well. He had fallen from the veranda a few days ago; his crippled arm was now totally useless.

Dariabibi was listening sympathetically to the widow. These days she often wondered who knew what would become of her own life. Looking at Amjad and Naima, Dariabibi's face dried up. Azhar Khan hadn't sent any news these last few months.

Saker's mother walked in and Dariabibi offered her a *pidi* to sit on.

'You don't step in our direction at all, Dariabou.'

Dariabibi hadn't gone to Saker's for a week. She was abashed.

'So much work, you see. Couldn't make time.'

Saker's mother moaned: 'I have no rest either. My flesh and bones are burning into ashes for this daughter-in-law of mine.'

Shairami joined in: 'What's the matter?'

'Her time's passed, but she won't deliver. I'd like to get the *kaviraj*, but she's got ten excuses.'

Dariabibi expressed her doubt: 'Ten months! No, there must be a mistake in your calculation.'

Saker's mother insisted: 'No, it could be more than ten months, not less.'

Shairami said: 'It takes eleven months for some.'

Dariabibi laughed with the end of her sari pressed to her mouth. 'Why eleven, it takes eighteen months!'

Saker's mother's face darkened: 'Rice won't go down my gullet and you're laughing. My son's getting worse, going who knows where to fight. He'd have cooled down if he'd seen the face of a child.'

'That's the way with men folk,' Dariabibi said. 'There's no news from my husband. One day he'll suddenly drop in. What can you do?'

Shairami offered hope: 'Don't worry, Saker's Ma, God's sure to have good results in store.'

'May gold dust shower on your face, Shairami. I can't sleep I'm so worried.'

Dariabibi talked as she sifted the greens brought by Shairami.

'I'll go and see Hashu.'

'Do,' Saker's mother resumed. 'It's hard to know her mind. Baby, baby, that's all she thinks. These days she won't sleep without me. Maybe that's why my boy's got worse. I say to myself, well, this is her first time, I don't want her to suffer. She doesn't even bathe for fear of catching fever.'

Dariabibi made enquiries about the size of Hashu's inflated belly.

'Like a ten-month-old pregnant woman. Huffing and puffing all the time. She says she's in pain, won't even let me touch. Got the midwife in once, won't allow her to put a finger on it.'

'Good results, you'll see,' Ganesh's mother commented. 'One day you'll say this is what the untouchable woman said.'

But the old woman was not particularly convinced. She requested Dariabibi to go and see Hashu.

'I've got a lot to do today. I'll surely go tomorrow afternoon and diagnose your daughter-in-law's trouble.'

Shairami complained: 'It's these modern times. There's no end to human depravity.'

Dariabibi kept sifting the greens, engrossed in her own thoughts.

'When Sakerbhai gets back, send him round to look for his runaway cousin. I keep saying to myself, I won't stir, I won't worry.'

'Can there be such people in the world? No feeling for the children.' Putting her hand on her shrunken cheek, Shairami stared at Dariabibi.

This pity was not to Dariabibi's taste. She felt her gall rising.

'Please come round for a visit.'

Saker's mother left. Shairami said in a whisper: 'Would you give me half a rotten *betel* nut? I feel a little nausea after meals these days with nothing to put in my mouth.'

Dariabibi brought out not only a *betel* nut, but also the bottle of oil.

'Shairami *Didi*, put a little oil on your scalp.'

Shairami stretched out her wrinkled palm.

As she rubbed in the oil, she said: 'I feel good when I come this way. When I go to the Brahmins in their brick houses, I don't get anything but shoo shoo. This was the destiny I'd brought from God. He's even left my boy crippled.'

73

Dariabibi said: 'It's the same in every community. You've heard, haven't you, how Rahim Bakhsh insulted my husband? Poor Hindus and Muslims get the same treatment, be it from their own community or from another.'

'Well, *Bhabi*, swearing by my head, haven't you had any news from your husband yet, and sitting doing nothing?'

'I don't need any news,' Dariabibi replied in a huff.

Shairami fell silent. Tying up the half of a *betel* nut in the corner of her sari, she got up to go.

'Get me some *pakal* fish if you catch any, Shairami *Didi*. The boy's got an upset tummy.'

Shairami nodded agreement.

'Another thing, don't tell anybody about the jar.'

Shairami laughed.

'You think I'm crazy!'

Dariabibi put her head down in shame. Somehow the jar had hurt her dignity.

'No, but it's better to warn you.'

Dariabibi burst into tears the moment Shairami was out of sight. Her tears would not stop. Then, casting a glance at the courtyard, Dariabibi quickly dried her tears. Ashekjan had gone out visiting. There was no one else to talk to. Dariabibi continued to sift the greens.

She could have spent the whole day with the greens if Amjad's voice hadn't reached her ear.

'Ma, look, *Abba*'s sent this letter and twenty rupees.'

Amjad was so happy he could dance. He had school books under one arm and the money and the money order stub in the other. Amjad had worked as Chandra's assistant for ten days only. Now, by Dariabibi's order, he was to go back to the *maktab*.

Dariabibi's eyes filled with wonder.

'He's really sent money? Who gave you it?'

'The postman. *Abba* sent it to me. The postman got me to put my thumb-impression on it.'

Dariabibi had stood up. Taking the two notes from her son, she handled them.

'Has he given his address?'

'Yes, Ma, it's written here.'

Amjad showed the stub to his mother, as if she was so very literate.

Taking the stub in her hand, Dariabibi focused her eyes on it. For the first time she appreciated as hard truth the value of literacy.

Naima was listening to the two of them. She commented: 'Ma, money, letter.'

Dariabibi picked up Naima in her arms and kissed her.

'Yes, we'll buy you sweets from the sweet shop.'

Amjad commented like an old man: 'Just twenty rupees after all these months. It's more profitable to stay at home and work as a day labourer. Ma, do you know they can take our land away? They won't let us keep the land if *Abba* doesn't come back to work on it.'

Although Amjad was echoing her own fear, Dariabibi didn't like her son's worldly remarks.

'You don't have to play the wise guy. I'll see to that.'

'Two months' fees are due at school,' Amjad replied seriously.

Dariabibi smelled the new banknotes. The afternoon sun brimmed over and the tamarind tree below the homestead seemed enchanted by a leisurely breeze.

Tying the banknotes in her sari, Dariabibi gave Amjad a couple of paisa: 'Go and buy some biscuits for the two of you.'

Naima got off her mother's lap.

Ashekjan got home. There was a *fateha* feast somewhere in the village. That she hadn't returned empty-handed was evident from the little bundle under the end of her sari.

'I got back before cooking time. The children will eat with me. There's enough rice and meat here.'

'No, I'm going to cook now.'

'Would you waste rice for nothing, dear?'

Holding the corner of the old woman's sari, Naima screamed.

'*Dadi, Abba*'s sent money.'

The old woman's eyes were full of happy tears.

'Really, Dariabou, has there been news from our son?'

'Yes, *Khala*. He's sent money too.'

Amjad said reassuringly: 'We've got an address now. I'll go and see him one of these days.'

Delighted, Ashekjan had forgotten that Dariabibi did not like arguing.

'Dariabou, the kids can eat with me,' she said.

'No,' Dariabibi said. 'Amjad, go to the shop. Naima, you go with him.'

Dejected, the old woman advanced towards her hut. Today she's got money, so she despises charity food, she thought, annoyed. But she knew how stubborn Dariabibi could be, so she kept quiet.

Dariabibi repeatedly frowned at Ashekjan as she walked away.

A few months ago when Naima lost a piece of cloth, Dariabibi had thrashed the girl.

Then one evening she went home after losing yet another piece of cloth. Dariabibi did not say a word. On top of a thousand wants, these shocks overwhelmed her.

At Saker's mother's request, Dariabibi went visiting the day after. Saker had been home for the last few days. Perhaps Rohini Choudhury had finished pacifying his tenants.

Dariabibi met him on her way into the locality.

'There you are, *Bhabi*, so suddenly.'

Dariabibi smiled: 'Couldn't make it earlier for pressure of work.'

Saker was notorious for being stubborn and rude, but his behaviour with Dariabibi was all sweetness. He did not even look her in the eye, out of deference, when he talked to her. He quailed in her presence, though politeness was a virtue contrary to Saker's nature.

Pulling the corner of her sari over her head, Dariabibi said, 'Sakerbhai, I think you've got no head-smashing jobs now, so we meet.'

'You too shame me, Dariabhabi. When I wield my stick, true, heads get smashed, but one has got to make a living. Nobody would provide for us if I sat about.'

'Your cousin isn't sitting about either. He's gone exploring. We'll see what wealth he brings home.'

Saker asked with surprised delight, 'Has there been news about him?'

'Yes, he's in a place called Jahanpur.'

'Allah be praised. What a man – it was a deep dive, wasn't it?'

'There's rice and dhal stocked away so who else will play the eel now?'

Saker laughed out loud.

'Everybody feels like laughing at your worthy cousin's activities,' Dariabibi responded, gritting her teeth.

'You're annoyed. You think that's what men are like. But looking for rice and dhal they don't spare themselves, for if there isn't any rice

76

and dhal, faces twist into . . . That's why I go smashing heads. And let others smash mine, who cares? You blame my cousin for nothing.'

Dariabibi said, smiling: 'You were going out, do. I'll go and visit your mother. You don't have to plead for your cousin.'

'As you wish.'

Bowing, as if to royalty, Saker walked backwards for a bit, before turning away.

Dariabibi's laughter rang through the alleyway. A little further away was Saker's courtyard with its gourd *machang*.

Saker's mother was pleased to see Dariabibi. 'You, Dariabou? Laughing like that in the street?'

'I met Sakerbhai. Would anybody feed me, he says, if I don't smash heads? Do I wield the stick for nothing?'

'Don't listen to him, dear. My ears buzz from the same old tune. Come in.'

Hearing the voice of her mother-in-law, Hashu had come out to stand under the gourd *machang*. She looked pale and thin, her eyes puffed-up and pensive like those of a convalescing patient. The mother-in-law flared up at the sight.

'There's the daughter of the unlucky one. Will Allah ever give her a child?'

Hashu did not reply. Her tired eyes were looking for something on the ground.

'Why do you get worked up for nothing, *Chachi*? She's young, a child. If you pester a pregnant woman like that, you'll fall ill.'

'Aren't I ill?'

As Dariabibi approached Hashu, she moved away a little with fear in her eyes.

'Hashu.'

'Yes, *Bubu*.'

'Are you all right?'

'No.' A brief and docile reply.

'You've changed much during the last few days. Did you keep a count of the days?'

Hashu demurely lowered her head.

'Eleven months have passed. Do you have a lot of pain?'

'Yes.'

'Let's have a look.'

'No, thanks.'

Turning to Saker's mother, Dariabibi asked, 'Haven't you put your hand on her stomach to see if the baby moves? There'll be a lot of trouble if she's carrying a dead child.'

'She doesn't let me touch her, dear.'

As Hashubou was walking away, Dariabibi called, 'Where are you going, Hashu?'

'I'm thirsty, *Bubu*.'

'Drink some water and get back soon,' her mother-in-law ordered, while Dariabibi wisely nodded in agreement with her.

'Can't stand so much trouble at my age, dear. I should be sitting on the prayer mat, calling upon Allah to bless them, but no, that won't happen.'

'What can you do, *Chachi*? She's such a simple child, who'll look after the family if you don't?'

Hashu wouldn't come out of her room. The two kept waiting outside, whiling away their time talking about one thing and another.

'You'd better have a look, dear. It'll be trouble if there's a dead baby inside her.'

'Call your daughter-in-law, *Chachi*.'

At her mother-in-law's call, Hashu came out of her room and stood under the *machang*.

She was sobbing away with her head down.

Dariabibi held Hashu's emaciated arm in her own hand and said, 'Why do you cry? I'm a woman too. I understand your sorrow. No woman can be happy if her husband turns into a loafer.'

Saker's mother would have nothing to do with Dariabibi's sympathy.

'She's infertile, dear, she's been married all these years. Saker would have changed his ways if she'd borne him a child.'

Looking at Hashu's anemic fingers, Dariabibi said, 'I've got two children. Did that stop my husband from loafing? Why did you get such a young girl for a grown-up man?'

The mother-in-law did not reply.

'Hashu, let me have a look at your belly. If you're unfortunate and your baby has died inside you, we've got to save you, haven't we?'

Hashu replied, crying louder: 'Let me die, *Bubu*. I'm a bone in everybody's throat. It'd better if I went to my grave.'

Dariabibi put her hand on her chin and said, 'Don't talk rubbish. Let me have a look at your belly.'

'I fall at your feet, *Bubu*, I fall at your feet.'

Hashu's voice was choking in a surge of intense crying. She covered her stomach with her arms like a bird protecting her chicks from the talons of a buzzard.

'It won't hurt. I'll have just one look.'

Hashu kept retreating.

Dariabibi swiftly got hold of her sari at the stomach and gave it a pull. What was this? Wasn't it a mound of fabric crumbling down? Another firm little pull, and a pile of rags came tumbling down from Hashu's inflated abdomen. Naima's lost piece of cloth, a red *gamtcha*, and many other stolen pieces of cloth belonging to the children of the village were in that pile.

In an instant Hashu fainted and fell under the overhanging *machang*. Her abdomen was quite normal – there was no trace of swelling there.

Saker's mother and Dariabibi stood aghast before the pile of rags.

Chapter Eleven

Azhar was careful with money, but he had never learnt to look deeply into circumstantial factors. Mental arithmetic was his mainstay before he set up shop. Now he realised his mistakes at every step. In this situation people without worldly experience looked up to God.

Many railway passengers walked from the station to their villages along the highway. As most of them lived in town, where these articles were cheaper, they didn't care to buy them here. Those who lived in the country, Azhar cruelly realised within a month, had no means. Illusions beckoned from the darkness of the future and pious people like Azhar mistook the mirage as part of faith. Azhar had a small amount of capital, he had sent money home once, what else could he do except survey the future as long as the rest of the capital lasted?

Now and then women on their way back from the local market stopped in front of Azhar's shop. As they had never been to town, they had a strong desire for town articles. But how many paisa could they spend? A cheap celluloid comb, a hair ribbon for two paisa, needle and thread or a pot of red dye to decorate women's feet. These women only visited on market days.

Azhar's dreams, his palace of imagination, had been built around his shop. He hardly ever forgot the central tenet of his dogma that for a man of faith days somehow passed. At times he would not cook, but dine on two paisa worth of puffed rice and *batasha* from the sweet seller. As he had no high hopes for himself, Azhar Khan's profound faith in the creator was never shaken.

On Fridays Azhar put on a prayer cap and a white *lungi* and walked three miles to the mosque to say his Jumma prayers. His shop remained closed only during those few hours. Otherwise one could always see the small wall lamp burning in the shop until the last bus had left for the railway station.

A couple of months passed. As there was no income from the shop, Azhar rejoined the carpenters. Gahar had a great laugh and Azhar stopped talking to him. He could not work out how he could have been mates with such an envious man. The shop opened after the day's work. On market days he did not go to work; on those days he sold a few paisa worth.

One day Gahar came to talk unsolicited: 'Azharbhai, you don't talk to me. Do you think I get angry for nothing? I had my destiny smashed before I got born, nothing will come my way in this life.'

Azhar looked up at him.

Gahar continued: 'If you haven't got the guts, the tricks and the wiles of making money, do you think you can make money by just setting up a shop?'

Gahar's sympathy was unadulterated.

'You won't talk, Khan, so let me. Listen, you've got to cheat your customers, and there are so many ways of doing it. Swear and swear again. Say, I'm selling at the price I paid, sir. If I make any profit, I'm a swine-eater. And when you've eaten seven hundred pigs, you may make some money. Then you can go and become a *haji*. Visit Mecca and Medina, and that's it, you're cleansed.'

Azhar opened his mouth: 'Sure, you can't run a business if you don't want to make a profit.'

'Well, then you'll have to tell lies. If you tell the truth, there won't be much profit, perhaps none at all. You won't support a family on that.'

The words were much after his heart. He felt rather small, yet his mind desperately sought to escape from the maze.

'It's hard to support a family if you're a man of faith,' he agreed.

'Is it just hard?'

Gahar lit a *bidi*.

A few more builders had got back from work. Azhar hadn't opened his shop today. He was enjoying their company.

Gahar called out: 'Odu, are you there?'

Odu, lying in one corner of the room, had his ears open to their conversation.

'What is it?' he replied.

'Do you remember when we worked for the warehouseman at Beleghata? How that swine cheated us!'

81

Odu was tired; he was trying to sleep. Now he sat up.

'Do you know how famous he is now? He's had a couple of mosques built. But he didn't pay for our labour. How much does he owe us, Gahar?'

'Fourteen rupees and six annas.'

Gahar flicked the ashes off his *bidi*. 'He'll burn in hell for fourteen years.'

Azhar replied: 'That's not likely. The angels Keramun and Katebin are writing out our good and bad deeds. On the day of judgement they'll weigh them to find which side is heavier. If you cheat fourteen rupees and then build a mosque, you don't have any sins left, the scales weigh down in favour of good works.'

Gahar taunted: 'Stop preaching, Azharbhai. Can you build a mosque for fourteen rupees? Do you know how many fourteens he's robbed of other people's money?'

Azhar agreed: 'You're right.'

'You won't run a shop if you think like that. Think like that mosque-wallah warehouseman, learn to embezzle and cheat, then you'll thrive.'

'God forbid!'

Gahar giggled.

'You'll do great business! I see your shop stays closed on Fridays, that's when the customers come – will it do keeping your shop closed then?'

Azhar was not easily roused, but today he was impelled to protest. 'What are you saying, Gaharbhai? Is my stomach so much more important than my faith?'

'You'll have to go begging if you're that faithful.'

Gahar laughed derisively. After a while he called out: 'Khalil, son, fill a pipe for us.'

Cooking was going on in one corner of the room. Khalil was stoking the fire under the curry pot. Being the youngest, he ran errands for everybody in the house.

'All right, *Chacha*.'

Gahar was not Khalil's uncle, as Odu's mate he had become one. 'Give us a smoke, I can't bear it any more.'

Khalil brought in a hookah pipe filled with tobacco.

Gahar handed the pipe to Azhar: 'Son of a Khan, you start off.'

'No, you start,' Azhar replied softly.

Gahar was being very polite now; in deference to Azhar he refused.

82

With his eyes shut, Azhar was releasing smoke after he had sucked at the pipe a few times in quick succession when Gahar said, laughing, 'Smoke out the root of your intelligence, son of a Khan. It's a hard world.'

Now languid, Azhar smoked with his eyes shut.

Odu, who also wanted a smoke, was looking at Azhar. Khalil had gone back to his post. In the glow of the burning firewood, one could see his sweating face.

Now with the pipe in his hands, Gahar resumed talking. He had much experience. As a builder, he had seen many people in the business world. The conclusion he arrived at was always the same: There's no place for a man of faith in this world.

Azhar carried a rosary in his pocket. He was pressing an occasional bead in the midst of the raging torrent of words. He was surprised that Gahar had gathered so much experience at his age.

'Odu.'

Odu was lying on his side on the mat. This was Gahar's test to find out if he had fallen asleep.

'What?'

'Odu, listen to this one. I used to live in Howrah at the time. One day a man came to me and said, I've got a job for you. You get paid when you finish. We made a deal. Five rupees for the job. Then, when I asked for the money, he said, There's my house. I've got a ten-rupee note, nothing smaller. You give me a five-rupee note and I'll give you the ten-rupee note as soon as we get home. Come with me. I gave him a five-rupee note. After a ten-minute walk, he said, There's my house. Hang on here, I'll go in and get the money. Clearly, a Muslim house. A jute-sack curtain hung at the door. I waited and I waited. One hour passed, the man did not appear, so I started calling out. A woman came out with a lamp. Who do you want? she said. The master of the house, I said. There's a madam here, she said, but no master. Would you like to come in? I was taken aback. Right inside the red-light district. Beyond the alley, there was a road along which my master had vanished.'

Perhaps in response to the juicy story, Odu sat up and said, smiling, 'Then?'

'Then nothing. I stared at her like a bloody fool.'

'Didn't you wait with the madam?'

'You can't wait empty-handed. But listen, there's more to it. About seven years later I was going through Posta when I saw this big trader, seated. I couldn't believe my eyes, it was the same man who'd cheated me, sitting on a cushion, surrounded by flunkeys.'

Odu clicked his fingers: 'So you got your money back.'

'Money back? I ran away. With my dirty clothes and looks, could I hang on there?'

Though he was pressing the beads, Azhar had his entire attention on Gahar.

'Did you really recognise the man?' he said.

'Sure. My eyes, they're like those of the money-lending Kabulis. I don't make many mistakes, son of a Khan. He'd become a rich man by fraud. Is there a place for piety any more?'

'Is there no way one can live without cheating? No way at all?'

Azhar's question sounded like an agonised cry. He looked so sadly at Gahar that the latter had to turn his eyes away. He too became serious.

'If I knew the way, would I live like this?'

Everybody in the room was quiet. From the pot over the cooking oven came a hissing sound.

Azhar was mechanically pressing the beads of the rosary. His fingers moved fast. Even Gahar had gone speechless. He had no answer.

Khalil had gone out to rinse the boiled rice. They heard a strange cry. Azhar, as if he had had a small electric shock, exclaimed, 'Gahar, what was that outside?'

Odu, Gahar and Azhar ran out quickly.

Khalil was sobbing away. The pot of rice stood on one side.

'What happened?' Everybody had the same query.

'My hand's scalded, oh Ma – '

As Khalil was the youngest, everybody sought their own comfort at his expense. Gahar took it easy much of the time and Odu had become a nawab because the boy was his nephew.

Quickly Azhar said, 'Let's go in. Let's look at it in the light. You should be a little careful, son.'

Odu started shouting at him, 'Such a big lad, yet not one bit of sense. I get into trouble for helping out other people's kids.'

Even Gahar, who usually enjoyed Odu's tyranny over the child, lost his temper.

'Odu, you're saying whatever comes to your head. You think it's easy for a child rinsing three pounds of boiled rice? You yourself don't touch the pot once in six months.'

Odu grumbled to himself. Gahar had a sharp tongue; he didn't dare talk back.

Gahar said in a tone of authority, 'We'll look after the boy. You take the pot in or it'll be dog's feast.'

Odu carried the pot inside, but he was so annoyed he didn't even cast a glance at Khalil.

Soon the tips of Khalil's fingers were covered with blisters. Gahar was remorseful.

'Light the fire if you like, son, but don't ever touch those things again.'

Such sweet words from Gahar! The pain on Khalil's scalded fingers was soothed a little. Had Gahar got drunk?

Azhar said, 'I'll crush a potato and put it on the burn. It'll stop the pain.'

He began to crush a potato, as Gahar cooled the blisters with a palm-leaf fan. The curry had not been cooked yet. Odu got busy with a pot. He was not concerned otherwise.

Azhar covered the fingers with the crushed potato and tied a rag round them. The pain abated gradually.

Once again Khalil looked gratefully at Azhar's face.

He said as if to himslf, '*Chacha*, when your shop gets bigger, will you let me run it?'

Azhar looked at him and smiled, but did not reply.

Taking it to be a novel mode of agreement, Khalil became cheerful. 'I don't like this job.'

Odu cast a glance at Khalil and got back to cooking. Whatever was in his eyes was not visible.

Gahar had not yet dropped the fan. An occasional ah-uh escaped from Khalil's lips. Though the burning sensation had passed, his hand throbbed up to his wrist with a dull pain.

'Azhar *Chacha*, if only Allah'd made your shop get bigger.'

'May gold shower on your face, son.'

Gahar did not make any remark; he put down the fan and got up. He needed to wash his hands and face. Azhar started fanning instead.

Khalil feared Odu like Yama, the angel of death. Uncle and nephew hardly ever talked openly.

Yet after a little hesitation, Khalil said, 'Odu *Chacha*, please don't tell Ma, she'll cry.'

Odu did not respond first. After a while he said, 'I'll take you home within a day or two. It's no good your eating up rations for nothing.'

For a brief moment Khalil glowed with happiness, but his uncle's last few words seemed to pour ink over his whole body.

'No, *Chacha*, I'll not go home until I've learnt my trade.'

'Right, so be it, and much good that'll do.'

Odu pressed his lips together and took the lid off the curry pot. The pot was steaming with a hissing sound. Khalil turned his tired eyes to it.

Gahar got back and picked up the fan. The evening conversation had irked him; no mocking word or smile came from him.

After the cooking was over, Gahar mixed the curry and dhal with the rice on Khalil's plate. Azhar raised the food to the boy's mouth in silence. The blisters on Khalil's fingers had gone red by then.

It was Friday. Azhar had gone to a neighbouring village to say his Jumma prayer. The shop didn't have to be shut. Khalil was unable to go to work for the mishap, so he looked after the shop in Azhar's absence. His uncle didn't like his eating without working for it, so he had asked Azhar for two annas for his labour. He told him that he had to make such a shameless request because he was poor. Khalil had gone home for lunch with his wages; he would return in good time for Azhar's late afternoon prayer. Azhar was sitting quietly. There weren't many customers today. Whatever he had sold he had done so in the morning. A wind was blowing. Because of the dust from the road it was hard to keep things clean. Azhar dusted the shop furniture and got back to rest.

The wind whined in the shaggy branches of the *shirish* trees behind the shop. The clouds were charcoal black; perhaps there would be a storm. A flock of birds kept company with the aimless clouds, but Azhar wasn't aware of it.

When he sat idle, all sorts of thoughts thronged his mind and he had no peace.

The wind suddenly dropped. A cuckoo called out sharply and flew into the clump of bamboos across the road. After a while one could hear someone whistling round the bend of the highway.

Were new birds arriving in the area? The sound of whistling got closer. Azhar was surprised as he looked down the road.

Before he eyed Chandra from head to foot, the later had concluded whistling with a flourish and perched on the bamboo bench in front of his shop.

'You, Chunder?'

Chandra's eyes danced. He resumed whistling.

> 'Now you've returned to Mathura,
> About Brindaban you forget.
> I know you now, Shyama,
> I haven't lost my eyes yet.'

Azhar was eager to make queries, but Chandra's song wouldn't stop.

'Chandra, will you stop for a bit?' Azhar called out firmly.

'Give me a *bidi* first.' Chandra dangled his legs.

'I'll give you *bidi* – *paan* – tobacco, everything. How are the children at home?'

Stroking his moustache Chandra did not reply; his head bent, he smiled like a cat.

Azhar was getting impatient: 'Is everybody well?'

After another prolonged stroking of moustache, he shook his head. 'How should I know that?'

Stretching out the palm of his hand, Chandra smiled mischievously.

'Are the children all right?'

It was nearly time for the late afternoon prayer. Khalil arrived and stood quietly in front of the shop. He was taken aback by the stranger.

Chandra's eyes fell on Khalil.

'Whose son, Azharbhai? Ah, you've really settled down here then? Have you married someone with children?'

Khalil was dying with shame. Embarrassed, Azhar said, 'Stop it, Chandra. Khalil looks after the shop now and then. The nephew of one of my mates.'

'Good. Everybody's all right at home. First give us a *bidi*, then I'll give you the details.'

Azhar said, 'Chandra, let me get some sweets for you, then you can smoke.'

'No need of that.'

So Azhar gave him a *bidi* and matches.

Puffing away and relaxed, Chandra said, 'Everybody is all right. After all, God's time does not stop for anybody. But then sometimes it walks on two feet, sometimes it crawls on hands and knees, and at other times it has to be pushed.'

Levity was not Azhar's forte, but today with an imaginative flight he cruelly understood everything. Shrewdly, he looked for distractions to conceal the pain. 'You've come a long way,' he said. 'Have a rest and then have some sweets. Have you got any other work here?'

'Work?' Chandra frowned. 'Lots of work. We'll have to pack up your shop and set off for Moheshdanga immediately.'

Azhar said, sceptically, 'Chunder, you're impossible.'

'That may very well be. But now hurry up.'

Everything seemed to be getting mixed up for Azhar.

'What's the hurry? I'll try and run the shop for a while.'

Chandra now turned truly serious.

'You've had enough of it,' he said, bitterly. 'You don't have to be a millionaire. Come and see for yourself what's happened to your home in these few months. Rahim Bakhsh has taken back your land. How long is he going to leave it fallow? Your family is intact thanks to Dariabibi; anybody else would have raised a stink.'

Azhar lowered his head in shame, his eyes becoming tearful.

'We don't want to wash dirty linen in public. Let's tie up those few things in your *chador* and get out.'

Khalil was watching the movements of the crazy stranger like a dumb, innocent child.

'You've had enough of these foreign parts. Now let's go back to Moheshdanga. You may have to eat leaves, but at least you'll see the family in front of you.'

Like a snake, charmed by the tree-roots, Azhar did not raise his head.

Chandra was stubborn. Azhar gently raised a few objections, but nothing worked. Within an hour, the articles of the shop were packed in Azhar's wrapper. Chandra himself sold off the wooden shelves to a *paanwallah* on the highway without loss. He was no Azhar Khan.

To Khalil, Chandra seemed rather like a barbarian. Rounded in height and width, this moustachioed giant had suddenly appeared in Jahanpur to leave the place in ruins. His only consolation was a little puffed rice and some lozenges Azhar gave him.

The builders hadn't got back yet. Not that Azhar needed to see any of them. He went there to collect his tools. Khalil's pensive mood saddened him.

'Come to our village when you can,' he said. 'Moheshdanga, by the Grand Trunk Road.'

'All right, *Chacha*.'

Khalil came with them a long way. He was losing a sympathetic soul in this butcher's pit.

Chandra carried the merchandise on his back.

'Don't worry, Khan,' he said as he walked. 'All these things will be sold off at *pir*'s fair on the day of the next full moon.'

Azhar, who was walking with a small bundle, did not reply.

It was the end of the day. Shadows of trees grew longer, wiping out the brightness of the road.

Chandra started singing as they left the houses behind:

> 'Leaving Mathura, Chandra crosses over in Yama's boat,
> In the fields the cowgirls in their tears float.'

Azhar broke into laughter. He said, 'Chunder, get the dance-troupe together again. You can still make songs.'

Chandra shook his head and the bundle of merchandise shook as well.

'If people were better off, would Chandra carry loads?'

The bundle was hanging from his left shoulder; he switched it to the right and gave it a shake.

> 'Oyo, oyo, oyo, Shyama, how you make me suffer . . .
> Like the glowing fire of husks and the forlorn wind.'

The snaky road would merge into distant Niamatpur. Mohesh-danga was ten miles further away from there. The twelfth moon had already taken over in the sky. There was a resonant sadness in the woods around.

Chandra kept whistling:

> Oyo, oyo, oyo . . .

Chapter Twelve

It was an early morning in the month of Aghran. Dariabibi had got up a long time ago, sacrificing the night's rest to boil the paddy.

It was a little cold. The dull stars still sparkled over the mist-covered trees.

Covering her chest with the end of her coarse sari, Dariabibi was putting away the parboiled rice on one side of the courtyard. It felt cold filling the pot with paddy from the vat. But then she found warmth near the oven for a while.

Dariabibi hadn't slept well; she was yawning. Azhar and Naima were still asleep. And so was Amjad in Ashekjan's room. Behind the bamboo wall a cockerel was crowing from time to time; it sounded rather shrill.

Dariabibi was tired keeping the fire burning. It pained her to think that she would have the laurel of being the mother of a new baby after about four months. Despite her swollen abdomen, she had no time for rest. Why did they have to come crowding the homes of the poor? Naima's eyes were not getting better. What if she went blind? Perhaps nobody would marry the poor girl. The charity hospital was five miles away. How could a little girl walk that far? Amjad would finish *maktab* this year; how was he going to continue his education? Chandra Kotal had got Azhar's land transferred to his own name, protecting their means of livelihood from farming – otherwise that too would have gone.

Suddenly Dariabibi felt a dull pain in her stomach. In the light of the oven, her pale, rock-still face darkened. Loosening her sari at the waist she warmed her stomach in the heat of the oven, but the pain got worse. She had two more pots of paddy to boil. Not a sound escaped from her lips. Hot steam was rising from the heap of parboiled paddy stacked away in the courtyard. Pressing her stomach on the hot pile, Dariabibi lay down on top of it, fearing that she might faint any moment now.

A little while ago she had been shivering with cold. Now she started sweating all over. Beads of perspiration glistened on her forehead.

Dariabibi looked about her. The trees below the compound were drinking in the morning light in silence. Above the blue banana trees the morning star looked brigher than on other days. Yet the sky remained grey.

Dariabibi was lying embracing the pile of paddy. Her legs trembled in unbearable pain. Making an 'ah' sound and then gritting her teeth, the image of the naked mother Eve lay still.

When the pain abated in the warmth of the parboiled rice, Dariabibi got back to the oven. She pressed a grain between her fingers and found it was time to remove the pot. She got busy.

Why was Dariabibi so work-mad? Was the family meant to be borne on *her* shoulders only? Didn't she have a husband, wasn't Azhar alive?

After removing the pot, she stoked the fire and was soon engrossed in her thoughts.

Her eyes were closing in sleep, but there was no way she could loosen the boa constrictor of duty. She fed the fire slowly. Sitting on her haunches, her backbone ached, so she fetched a *pidi* from the veranda.

The tide of morning light had just been released at the horizon. The night birds sought rest in the solitude of the woods. To the enchanting rhythm of the morning, birds and beasts, trees and creepers, as well as the inhabitants of the farming community, woke up. The muezzin's 'Allahu-akbar' from a distant village left a sound-trace on the trees and waters of Moheshdanga.

Around the homes of the Khans, perhaps nobody except the young wives wanting a bath had got up. Dariabibi often sacrificed her rest to her duty without resentment. She hadn't noticed that tears had gathered in the corners of her eyes. She became alert as a hot tear rolled down her cheek. Wiping her eyes, she looked about her. Suddenly the shadow of a human being startled her.

Thieves did not come in the morning; Dariabibi was not easily scared; she got to her feet. But as she advanced, the shadow moved away. Dariabibi opened the gate and looked around. No, there was no trace of either human being or animal.

A little mystified, she returned to the oven.

Next time there was no reason to doubt her eyes: that shadow was once again on the gate. But as she advanced, it vanished again.

Puzzled, Dariabibi wondered if it was not a djinn or ghost. She was a little frightened. But as she opened the gate the third time she saw a ten- or twelve-year-old boy standing under a jackfruit tree. The sun wasn't there, so the boy's face was in the dark.

'Ey, boy.' Dariabibi called out. The boy hesitantly advanced a few steps into the morning shadows.

'Wait!' sounded the voice of a determined woman.

The boy stopped; suddenly he covered his face with his hands and started sobbing.

Pulling him into her arms, Dariabibi said, 'Whose child are you? Has your father beaten you? Have you run away?'

The boy did not reply. He was sobbing; now he stopped, though an occasional sob stirred the morning air.

'Whose child are you?' Dariabibi held him close to her warm breast in unconscious affection.

A smile played on her lips.

'What a child! Won't you talk?'

Darkness still lingered here; idle wind whispered in the leaves.

The boy started sobbing again.

Dariabibi said, 'I'm not letting you go. Let's go in.'

With Dariabibi's arm round him, the boy walked as if enchanted.

'What's your name, my child?'

The boy turned his wide eyes on Dariabibi, who now noticed a black birthmark on his eye-brow. And the darkness of forgetfulness was wiped away in an instant.

'Monadir, my Muni.'

Before she had half-uttered the words in a tear-soaked voice, Dariabibi held the boy deeply in her arms and sat down.

Putting his head in his mother's lap, Monadir cried loudly.

'Wait a bit, my son.'

The boiling paddy was overheated; there was a burning smell. Leaving Monadir, Dariabibi quickly removed the pot from the fire.

The parboiled paddy was poured out immediately. Monadir sobbed from time to time. His eyes were not drowned in curiosity at this strange environment. He just kept staring at his mother.

When the work was over, Dariabibi raised the boy's young face and looked into his large eyes.

'You remembered your poor slave of a mother at last?'

After she had said the words in a tear-choked voice, Dariabibi repeatedly kissed the boy on his young face and lips . . .

'Were you well, son?'

Muni replied shyly: 'Yes, Ma.'

Dariabibi placed him on her lap and made detailed enquiries.

Azhar came a little later, back from his morning prayer in the outhouse. He was surprised to see an unknown boy in Dariabibi's arms.

'Whose child is that?'

Quickly pulling the end of her sari on her head, Dariabibi said, softly, 'My son has come.'

'What a handsome boy!' Azhar said. 'Such pretty eyes!'

Dariabibi blushed.

'Muni, son, greet your father.'

After touching Azhar's feet like a mechanical doll, he was getting back to his mother.

Azhar said, 'I won't let you go.'

Touching the boy's chin, he gazed into his eyes.

'From today you're my father and I'm your son.'

Azhar laughed at his own joke, a real exception to his nature.

'Tell me your name.'

Monadir shyly lowered his head. It was Dariabibi who answered, 'Monadir Hussain Khan. I used to call him Muni.'

'Good, good. My Muni *babaji*.'

Azhar started calling out loudly, 'Amu, Naima, Amu . . .'

Within moments the children had left their beds to get there.

'Amu, Naima, come and meet your elder brother.'

They looked at one another in childlike bewilderment.

Dariabibi was pleased at Azhar's excitement. While Monadir was seated on his lap, Amjad and Naima kept their distance.

'Come, come closer, he's your big brother.'

Monadir did not say anything; he took Amjad's hand in his hands. Although his affectionate eyes fell on Naima as well, he felt a little put off by her pus-filled eyes.

Dariabibi forgot all her frustrations and fatigue.

'Get the children to know one another,' she said. 'Yesterday I saw a touch of colour on some bananas. They may be ready today. The children will have a good breakfast.'

Dariabibi walked away quickly, Monadir staring at the path she took.

Azhar said, 'You play, I'll go and light the hookah. Amjad, you don't have to go to the *maktab* today.'

Happily, Amjad started running all over the courtyard.

Chapter Thirteen

It was as though a fresh enthusiasm for work had been restored to Dariabibi. Azhar was surprised. There was a mutual bond between husband and wife in running the family, yet so far everything had seemed rather empty. Now an intimacy was blossoming around the peasant couple. Azhar had care and affection bestowed on him beyond his imagination.

Within a few days Monadir broke down fences between strangers. Azhar seemed more affectionate to Monadir than to Amjad. Monadir was not required to run errands. Azhar got him admitted to a junior school a mile from the village. When Amjad finished with the *maktab* in two months, the two brothers would go to school together. Yet two months! Dariabibi was worried because Monadir had to go to school on his own. The day he failed to get home until after evening, playing with other children by the river, midnight passed before they finished their evening meal.

Monadir could not bear the sight of Ashekjan and trumpeted her dirty habits to his mother. There were only two rooms. Monadir was reluctant to sleep in the same room as Ashekjan. The old woman's hair was so full of lice that Dariabibi had to put him up in her room. But there the boy felt ill at ease and, as she realised, couldn't easily fall asleep. Dariabibi wanted a shed built for him. Extending the roof of the house, Azhar made an extra room with walls of plaited bamboo. Chandra offered not only his labour, but also ten bales of hay. Monadir and Amjad did their homework there, kept their books. There was this abandoned area with trees beside the extension. On moonlit nights, Monadir and Amjad talked to their hearts' content until they fell asleep. Ashekjan moaned that Amjad had moved away from her. On some nights, she crept into their room. If the boys happened to be talking, they would fall silent. Neither did the old woman fancy Monadir. 'Would an old bird be tamed, Dariabou?' she said. 'Feeding him is all you'll do.' Reprimanded by Dariabibi, she never repeated those words but nursed a hidden bitterness in her heart and avenged herself by telling tales to Amjad when she found him alone. Amjad too avoided Ashekjan. 'Your son, Dariabou, has grown up. Why should he sleep in my room?' she said with resentment.

Yet Monadir was not aware of one particular aspect of the family. Dariabibi did not want him to notice their poverty. The husband and wife whispered their money matters. If there was a shortage of rice, Dariabibi did not raise her voice about it as before, lest Monadir should hear. He might leave if he knew. Though an orphan, surely Monadir hadn't lived in such poverty. Azhar Khan's *lungi* was torn in places; it was doubtful if his prayers were acceptable to Allah the way his knees got exposed when he sat down to touch his forehead to the ground. Rather than buying a *lungi* for himself, Azhar bought shorts and a shirt for Monadir.

Monadir was very friendly with Hashu, who had taken this son of Dariabibi close to her heart. On school holidays, Monadir spent the whole day at Saker's house. Amjad and Monadir read stories from books to her; she tasted the fullness of life again. Monadir was close to Saker as well. Amjad used to avoid Saker; of late he had followed his brother to be friendly to Saker *Chacha*. Saker taught Monadir how to wield the *latthi*. Dariabibi did not like it as she was afraid that it might turn her handsome boy into a ruffian.

The woods and fields of Moheshdanga spoke a new language to Amjad, who did not like running errands any more; he just loved roaming about with Monadir. Azhar had been working harder because of the addition of another person to the family. He needed Amjad even more now; but he wouldn't go within hailing distance.

Together with Chandra, Azhar had grown sweet potatoes. The little island in the river was covered with young plants. But Monadir and Amjad loved pulling out the plants to taste the sweetness of the roots.

One day Chandra Kotal caught the two red-handed.

'Eating all the tubers, eh?'

Chandra, drunk with toddy, was lying behind the *babla* bushes. His eyes had fallen on this sight of vandalism when he woke up to the sound of boyish voices. Opening his eyes wider and puckering his moustached lips, he called out gravely, 'Eating tubers, eh? *Chowkidar! Chowkidar!*'

He cried so loudly one would think robbers had attacked the whole village.

Amjad was scared. Monadir had seen the man before, but not in this state.

'No, Chandra *Kaka*, we were looking to see if the potatoes were growing.'

'If potatoes were growing, eh? Let the *chowkidar* come. Don't you run away!'

Amjad advanced, pleading, 'He's my elder brother.'

'You're a thief too. The watchman will arrest you both.'

Monadir shrank in fright, his eyes tearful.

Chandra looked about him and yawned.

'The watchman's not coming, so I'll have to arrest you. Two thieves, come with me – '

Amjad was stunned. His feet would not move.

'I'm not letting you go.'

Chandra stroked his moustache.

'Oh, I know. You won't walk.'

Chandra sat down on his haunches and said, 'Right, two thieves, get on my shoulders.'

What could Monadir do? Like nice boys the two climbed on to Chandra Kotal's shoulders. Afraid of falling off, they hung on to Kotal's long hair.

'Oh, Pathan cubs, horse-riders – '

Chandra started walking. The riders were scared out of their wits. Tears rolled from Amjad's eyes. Monadir was silent.

The riders found no pleasure in the bumpy ride on Chandra's shoulders.

Suddenly Chandra laughed out loud.

'Ey, let's go to your *Kaki*'s prison. Who knows if she's at home?'

Over his head the two boys looked at each other, as lines of laughter formed on their faces.

Then Chandra Kotal started singing and their eyes nearly popped out.

> If you had to take my life,
> O thief, with your own hand
> Why did you leave the cuckoo
> In this godforsaken land . . .

The *baul* tune filled the heart of the open fields.

Monadir said, 'Chandra *Kaka*, put us down.'

'No, that won't do. You'll have to go to your *Kaki*'s police station. There's sweet potato there, you'll have to eat it all night.'

The sun was setting. A gentle wind rustled in the pampas grass. Chandra was entirely absorbed in the song, his heart troubled by the estranged cuckoo, whose agony was resonant in his voice.

Elokeshi was picking lice from Chandramani's hair.

Chandramani said, 'Oh, *Dada*, put them down on the ground. They're somebody else's children; if they fall . . .'

Chandra cried, 'They'd become wise men if they fell.'

Perched on Chandra's shoulder, Monadir now started giggling.

'Oh, look at the thieves laughing now they're at the police station. On to your *Kaki*'s police station! She'll feed you with sweet potatoes.'

Amjad too started laughing.

Chandramani said, 'Don't climb on to the courtyard with them on your shoulders; you'll break your neck.'

'Just like that?'

Laughing sceptically, Chandra rushed on to the raised yard in one bound.

Climbing down from Chandra's shoulder, Monadir felt shy. He had never been here before.

Looking down, Chandra resumed singing. With mock anger, Elokeshi said, 'Sister-in-law, there's a world of lice on your head. In your brother's brains and on his sister's head.'

Chandra stopped singing.

'In my brain? Come and pick them then.'

Elokeshi laughed. 'How could I find the brain under such long hair?'

A pummel was lying around in the courtyard. Pointing at it, Chandra replied in mock-anger, 'Give it a blow with that. Smash the brains out.'

Chandramani got very annoyed.

'You say whatever comes to your head. It'll bring bad luck.'

'There she goes again,' Chandra said. 'If there are sweet potatoes, give some to the children.'

He had bought sweet potatoes from the local market town. Elokeshi served puffed rice and boiled sweet potatoes in bamboo bowls to Amjad and Monadir.

Chandra's eyes danced.

'Eat sweet potatoes as much as you can, but don't go anywhere near those plants. I'll take you to the cattle pen if I catch you again.'

Gopal protested, 'They don't take people to the cattle pen, do they?'

'They do, they do.' Turning to Amjad, he said, 'I'll take your father to the cattle pen for running away from home.'

Amjad made a face as he munched puffed rice. Monadir only smiled.

Sounds and colours and bird-calls signalled the beginning of evening. Monadir didn't know that this was how the faded faraway villages looked from a house compound. The picturesque rows of still palm trees, a white country path, perhaps a traveller or two, a tired white calf, clouds and flocks of birds made a strange signal to his boyish mind.

Chandra had joined in with others in their game. Only Monadir remained listless.

Amjad startled him, 'Munibhai, it's getting dark. Let's go home.'

'Hang on. It's a moonlit night, perhaps Chandra *Kaka* will take us home.'

Chandra demurred. 'No, I've got a lot to do. The cattle haven't been brought in. Then I've got to put the fish-nets in the river. There isn't much time before the tide comes in.'

Amjad said, 'Do you get any fish in the dead river?'

'No, son, just enough for the pot.'

The two boys happily set off on their way to the village. Monadir had gone dumb. He had never been in the vast expanse of the field.

Suddenly he opened his mouth: 'Chandra *Kaka* is crazy, isn't he?'

'*Abba* says so too.'

There is a certainty about pre-adolescent conclusions which beats the elderly. It was as if in the glory of this the two brothers started laughing.

Amjad said, 'Munibhai, can't you sing?'

'I can, but I feel shy.'

'Sing a song, Munibhai.

Even when he lived with his uncle, Monadir did not fear anybody. When everybody went to bed, he could go and spend a whole night with a local market folk opera group and get shouted at the following morning.

Monadir began singing in the *baul* style of Ramprasad. He did not understand the meaning of the song, but the sweetness of his voice

99

would have brought rapture to the hearts of love-lorn village girls. Amjad had not known that Monadir's voice was so sweet.

His respect for Munibhai grew.

When Monadir finished, Amjad said, 'Munibhai, why don't you take lessons from Chandra *Kaka*?'

'Does he sing?'

'*Does* he sing! He used to lead a folk group! You heard him sing, didn't you?'

'I liked it.'

'*Abba* doesn't like singing. Says, those who learn to sing go bad.'

'Get lost. I'm going to learn to sing.'

On the following day they got together in Hashu's room, gossiping.

In Monadir's view there was a mad man in the village called Chandra Kotal. He was telling his story in detail.

They stopped when Saker's mother walked into the room.

Looking at Monadir she said, 'Nice boy. Stay with your ma, child. A stranger can't become kin.'

Monadir was not prepared for this, but Saker's mother went on, 'Do you know, Hashu? This is what's called the pull of blood. His uncle who reared him with gold couldn't bear it when he broke a writing slate. What does your uncle do, son?'

Monadir was silent.

'Stay, stay with your mother. A mother doesn't become a stranger just because you've lived away from her for five or six years.'

Monadir was sorely vexed. In his mind he called her a witch. He would have felt better if he could call her a firewood-picking hag.

As she got no response, Saker's mother left, grumbling.

The interrupted gossip resumed.

There wasn't much furniture in Saker's room. In one corner there was a large bed, on one side of which Hashu sat with her back to the wall. Monadir had a book in his hand. Across the bed with a pillow under him lay Amjad, listening.

Monadir was reading the story of Ali Baba and the Forty Thieves when Saker entered the room.

'Reading stories, eh?'

'Yes.'

Hashu pulled the corner of her sari over her head, her eyes alert, fixed on the person who had entered.

Monadir asked: 'Where are you going, *Chacha*?'

'There's talk of a fight. I've come to get my *latthi*.'

All eyes turned to the oiled staff in the corner.

Standing erect, Hashubou said, 'You don't have to go anywhere.'

'No, I've taken an advance.' Saker's voice was grave.

Monadir took Hashu's side.

'No, *Chacha*, you'll give us a lesson this evening. Don't go away.'

Staff in hand, Saker stood there for a while. He had indeed noticed Hashu's quiet and serious face. Perhaps for the first time in his life the insistence of the boys made him give up.

'All right. You carry on.'

Saker walked out.

They did not go back to the story. Hashu started talking. How she wanted to drown Monadir in affection!

'Good boy,' she said, and suddenly taking Monadir in her arms as he lay in bed, kissed him again and again. Her motherly affection had found an object.

Monadir could not breathe. The young woman's lips on his large beautiful eyes, fair young lips, left a sort of unpleasant taste.

On their way home, he asked Amjad, 'Ey, does Hashu *Chachi* kiss or bite?'

'Why?' Amjad asked innocently.

'Here, look at these teeth-marks on my face.'

Chapter Fourteen

Monadir loved this village. Abandoned homes, little woods, occasional footpaths through them – all these attracted him. In his own village there weren't spots like these to play hide and seek, and the difference enchanted him.

The two brothers roamed up and down the village like vagabonds. Amjad, who had become daring, no longer ran errands as before. At times Dariabibi got very annoyed with him. But she was always cautious about Monadir for fear of losing him if she should neglect him. Monadir was a daredevil by nature; now, with nobody to restrain him, he became even more reckless.

There was a large number of date trees to the west of the overgrown graveyard. It would be a couple of months before the blue bunches of dates would ripen. The boys lacked that much patience. With Amjad's help, Monadir brought home a whole bunch of green dates. You had to be a daredevil to do that. Poisonous snakes were not uncommon in the dense cane-bushes. Besides, wild plants made one so itchy all over that many would not dare go anywhere near the place even when the dates were ready.

Monadir played the guide. He held the wild creepers apart to make way and bore the unpleasant touch of wild plants. But Amjad's body itched severely; once out of the bush, he burst into tears. Like an elder brother, Monadir consoled him, but at home Dariabibi was stunned with fright and anger.

'One of these days the two of you'll drive me round the bend. I've told you again and again, don't go anywhere near that graveyard – but my sons just turn a deaf ear.'

The brothers did not reply. Dariabibi wiped their bodies with a wet *gamtcha*.

'Munibhai said the green dates were lovely to eat . . .' Amjad was telling his mother.

Monadir protested, 'Did I say lovely? I said bitter.'

Casting a sidelong glance of disapproval at Monadir, Dariabibi kept wiping Amjad's body.

Monadir was quiet. Dariabibi noticed his silence and turned to him, 'Come here, Muni, let me give you a rub down.'

Monadir sounded sulky. 'Leave it. My body doesn't itch.'

Dariabibi did not heed his protest.

'Look, you've got black weals on your body. Don't ever go into such thick bush. There are big snakes there.'

'What sort of snakes, Ma?' Amjad asked.

'Very poisonous snakes. Cobras.'

Monadir laughed.

'Snakes my foot. We didn't even see the tail of one.'

Amjad joined in the laughter.

'They drop their tails when they bite, don't they, Ma?'

'Yes.'

Monadir did not believe this.

'Huh, drop their tails when they bite! My *chacha*'s got a little dog; he's bitten so many people he shouldn't have any tail at all then.'

Dariabibi had been grave so far; now she couldn't help bursting into laughter.

'Oh my dumb mynah, who says dogs lose their tails?'

Scratching himself, Monadir said, 'Well, Amu said – '

'Are you still itchy?' Dariabibi asked.

'No, Ma.'

'Still don't want to tell me?'

Putting his arm affectionately round his mother's waist, Monadir pointed at Amjad, 'It was him who took me.'

Dariabibi eyed him with mock anger.

'I swear I'll never go anywhere with you again, Munibhai,' Amjad said, sulking.

The next day Amjad broke his promise. After school the two roamed down country roads. Other boys played football in the school grounds, but Monadir didn't like their company. He felt very small amongst his fellow scholars. Their clothes were different; there was a shine about them. Monadir preferred Amjad's pleasant company.

After school they drifted away towards the fields. Chandra Kotal was not at home – he had taken the harvest to the market town – so there was not much to keep them there. Amjad picked up a few kite feathers from one side of the silted canal and presented them to Monadir. They would make good quill pens.

Before dusk Monadir lost Amjad while playing hide and seek. They lost their way in the excitement of the game.

Monadir had no great difficulty finding his way back. He was glad when he turned a bend and found a familiar path. The narrow track, like a white ribbon, had turned and twisted towards the other end of the village, with many kinds of trees on both sides. Ahead of him he saw a sturdy fence beside a moss-covered pond. There was a sudden stirring in the water. Monadir looked down curiously at the sunset-tinged scarlet pond. A brass pitcher stood on the coloured steps of the ghat; a village wife was bathing. One could see her fair face. It was getting dark. Monadir hurried along. By a moss-covered pond some home-seeking egrets were chattering in a clump of bamboos. Monadir was cheered by the *cawk-cawk* call of their chicks. On one side of the pond stood a few old *betel-nut* trees; beside it a cowshed, where a calf was lowing. Beyond a palm-leaf fence, the householders had begun their evening chores. Thick smoke rose through the trees. Monadir walked past the silhouette of a dry banana leaf, swaying in the wind over the fence. Suddenly there was a scraping noise by the road. He was scared, but stopped out of curiosity. Was it a snake? He heard the sound again. Monadir had lifted his leg to run when he heard the warning voice of a girl: 'Ey, boy.'

Monadir had thought an elderly woman was watching his movements; he stopped and looked hard at the fence.

'Ey boy.' No elderly woman, but a very young face, making an opening in the young banana leaves, was moving her lips. Sitting on the root of a dead jackfruit tree, she had put out only her face. Monadir had no ready answer. The girl came to his rescue.

'Which side of the village are you from?'

Monadir replied hesitantly: 'From there.' He did not forget to point his finger.

'From there?' The girl giggled. 'Isn't there a name to it? Have *you* got a name?'

Cheeky girl! Monadir was angry.

'I haven't got a name. Have you?' he said, choosing the form of the pronoun used for inferiors.

'I have a name and so have you,' the girl said.

'Sure, I have,' he said, putting out his tongue as far as he could.

'What a cheeky boy! Whose child are you?'

Then rising from the roots of the tree, she came out through the fence. Monadir saw a plump girl, nine or ten years old, her hair swinging over her back. She had a round face, fair and lively; her big eyes under sparrow-like eyebrows were restless.

'Whose child, eh?' The girl made a face.

Monadir was really mad now. As he could find nothing to throw at her, he was exploding with rage.

'I'll grab your leg and trip you up,' he said.

Quickly withdrawing her legs, the girl made a face. 'You want to touch my feet to salaam me?'

Monadir rubbed his fist in the palm of his other hand.

'I'll trip you up.'

'Just you wait, you cheeky thing.'

The girl vanished behind the fence. Monadir could hear her footsteps. He was scared. He broke into a run towards the road.

He could hear the girl calling: 'Ey, boy, listen, I won't say anything . . .'

Monadir did not respond to her appeal. He was frightened. At a distance, standing in the dark shadow of a tree, he looked behind. A vague silhouette, her hair dishevelled, the young girl he had met by chance was standing there. Yes, it was her, no mistake.

Somewhat depressed, Monadir returned home.

Chapter Fifteen

The next day, after the midday meal, Monadir walked to the village path, the dimly seen world of last evening's journey. As he looked absent-mindedly around in the midday light, everything seemed new to him. He set our to rediscover the lost route.

It did not take long to recognise the stump of the dead jackfruit tree between two stretches of a palm-leaf fence. He looked about him in surprise. It was a miniature world of insects. A group of ants was advancing over a wooden bridge with food in their mouths. The line of small red ants seemed to be trembling like the hanging thread of a severed kite. Their zigzag movement disappeared under a palm leaf.

Monadir turned his eyes. There was a peasant's compound beyond a couple of betel-nut trees. A small bird went *dig-dig* looking for insects under a tamarind tree.

'Ey, whose stupid child is that?' a girl's voice called out. Startled, Monadir was going to turn round when he was stopped by a soft hand. It was the same girl he had seen last evening. Monadir was not prepared for this. Holding him by the hand, the girl pulled him along towards the farmer's house, as if he were an insect trapped in a cobweb.

There was no time to protest, it had all happened like magic. He found himself standing like a criminal in someone else's courtyard.

'Ma, come out and see a stranger.'

The girl was giggling.

'What is it, Ambia?' a woman replied from the veranda of a thatched cottage in front of them. She was plastering the walls with clay.

Ambia laughed her head off. 'He's out early today to steal something, Ma.'

The woman was busy. Turning in that direction, she stopped work.

'Ambia, whose pretty boy is that?'

The girl's laughter continued unabated.

'He was standing near the *betel-nut* trees, I went and got him.'

Holding a rag soaked in red clay, the woman came down from the veranda.

'Where do you live, son?' asked Ambia's mother, Amiran.

That a smart boy like Monadir could be so puzzled was hard to believe. Words caught in his throat.

'I – I live at the Khans'.'

Amiran cleaned her hands with water from a container.

'Whose son are you?'

Monadir was very embarrassed. Whatever he was, Azhar was not his father.

'Dariabibi is my mother,' he said.

Amiran was older than Dariabibi. The mark of advancing years was visible on her face and she was rather sickly.

'Daria's son, Daria's son,' said Amiran as she walked towards him. Ambia was still laughing.

Turning towards her in mock anger, Amiran said, 'O unlucky one, who do you think you dragged in like that? Go and say sorry.'

Ambia hadn't imagined they were related.

'We'd heard you'd come, son. We're poor people, we've got to work all day. Up to here with work. Haven't been to the Khans for some time.'

Ambia was curiously watching the movements of her mother and the stranger. Now she started digging the ground with her toes.

Amiran called out, 'Go and get a cane stool. Come on, son.'

Ambia quietly obeyed her mother. Mechanically, Monadir sat down on a cane stool. Sitting beside him, Amiran spun a web of family stories. Ignoring his protests, she gave him some puffed rice in a cane bowl.

'Your *chachi* is poor. Have I got anything to give you, dear? Your *chacha* died two years ago and I'm suffering with that unlucky one. She won't listen to me, just roams about under the trees.'

Mother and daughter exchanged looks; Ambia became serious.

'When did you come?'

'Many days now,' Monadir replied as he munched puffed rice.

'I get no rest. So much to do since morning. There's a cow, chickens, goats and what with that crazy one – I haven't got time to breathe. I haven't seen the face of the Khans for months.'

Monadir felt that his new aunt was not inept at continuous chatter. Nodding, Amiran agreed with herself, 'Very pretty boy. Very pretty boy. And what about Dariabubu? Not for nothing her son looks like a prince.'

Monadir blushed.

'We just survive, son. Our destiny is nothing but work. Your *chacha* was a good man. Like your present father, he didn't open his mouth even if he was slapped ten times in the face. We suffer the result now. We had an acre of land, but now that's gone into other people's bellies.'

Then, whispering, Amiran pointed at some thatched roofs across the courtyard.

'Ambia's second *chacha*. A real devil. Grabbed two *bighas* of our land. Wouldn't give us a share of the harvest; now he's gone and got it registered as his own property. Let him have it, Allah will deliver justice. He buys so many things, but doesn't let the orphan girl touch anything.'

Monadir obediently listened to the story. Ambia was an orphan like himself. Yet he was eager to leave.

'During the rains last year there wasn't even a handful of rice at home. I went to borrow some from him, but he wouldn't give any. Mother and daughter, we nearly died of starvation. He took our land, but we didn't have a grain in our stomachs.'

Tears gathered in the corners of Amiran's eyes, which she dried with the end of her sari.

Monadir said, 'So long, *Chachi*', and got up. Let someone else listen to her sad stories. He was feeling miserable.

Chapter Sixteen

One day Amjad brought news that Shairami's son had died. She would find some peace now that the life of her crippled son was over. Together with her son, Dariabibi recalled many stories of their own. Poor Shairami.

Dariabibi said, 'Could you go and ask Shairami to come and see me?'

The next day Monadir and Amjad went to the untouchables' quarter. Shairami was bedridden, being looked after by a widowed distant relative.

Every day Amjad brought news of her. One afternoon he said, 'Ma, Shairami *Pishi* won't live much longer.'

With a distressed look on her face, Dariabibi stared at her son.

'No, Ma, she's grown so thin, it's hard to recognise her.'

Dariabibi recalled memories of a long friendship with this untouchable woman. The pawned pot had not yet been reclaimed. Family expenses were going up every month. Where was the money coming from? Chandra Kotal was planning a new business, as if one could do business without capital. For a few months all they had done was talking. Dariabibi wanted some cash to release the pot. She couldn't let an old object go like that.

Dariabibi said, 'Isn't she going to get better?'

'No, Ma,' Amjad shook his head. Monadir had gone with him; he agreed.

Let the pot go to hell, can't I even see Shairami? The thought bothered Dariabibi. The untouchables' area was not far away; it was fifteen minutes' walk. She could go in the dark and see Shairami without violating the purdah. But would Azhar agree? In these matters, Dariabibi feared Azhar. Purdah was not strictly observed in a peasant home. Dariabibi could easily visit her neighbours. But if her visit to a different area, particularly that of the untouchables, got known in the Muslim area, they would have no honour left.

But the more the evidence of Shairami's simple heart came rolling down the road of indelible memories, the more she became restless. Once Amjad had malaria; there was no hope for him. Shairami used to visit him every day. One day she put some sweets in Dariabibi's hands.

'What for, Sharidi?'

'Give one to the boy.'

'What's it for?'

Shairami did not lie. She had made an offering at the Shiva's temple for Amjad. The sweets were from the offering.

There were religious prohibitions against it for a Muslim. Daria-bibi had her misgivings. But sitting by the head of a son who could die, she did not want to hurt anybody in case a curse fell on the boy. She had given the sweet to Amjad in Shairami's presence. Didn't Allah, who saw everything, see into people's hearts?

The shame which humiliated one in hard times could vanish without a trace if one had a companion like Shairami, who had appeared in Dariabibi's life rather accidentally.

'Can she talk, Amjad?'

'Her voice is very faint, Ma.'

'I'd like to go and see her.'

Like an elder, Amjad said, 'Will you go to the untouchables' area?'

'What's wrong with it? Aren't they human?'

Monadir said, 'You can't go that far in your condition.'

Dariabibi was embarrassed as she looked at herself. Her son too had noticed her swollen belly. That was another problem. If Azhar came to know that she, a pregnant woman, had gone to the untouchables' quarter like a night-walker, he would kill her. In these matters, her husband was more dangerous than a cobra. Yet he was so meek. Dariabibi wondered why he got so mad if he noticed her slip up in the observance of religious rituals.

So it was decided that after Azhar had fallen asleep, Amjad, Monadir and Dariabibi would go and visit Shairami. It was unseemly visiting a sick friend empty-handed; they needed at least two annas. Amjad took the responsibility of cadging the money from Ashekjan.

The opportunity offered itself when Azhar, after a whole day's labour, fell asleep. The three of them set off along the country road.

110

Dariabibi whispered, 'Amjad, do you know the way?'

'Sure. I've been ploughing it up, haven't I?'

Thick vegetation bordered the narrow path. There was a gentle wind. Dariabibi felt intoxicated, like a caged bird let loose into the sky. She hadn't had much opportunity to see the world beyond her home and its immediate neighbourhood.

It was past midnight. Lamps still burned in a peasant house; perhaps the inmates were playing cards. Dariabibi walked confidently. The whiteness of the narrow path shone even in the dark.

She shuddered as she entered Shairami's shack. It was filled with pots and pans. Shairami lay on a dirty mat, her head resting on an even dirtier pillow. To protect the ramshackle huts from the ravages of a storm, poor peasants had resigned themselves to having no windows. The stench in the room nearly choked Dariabibi, but the call of love wiped away her signs of unease. Shairami opened her eyes and stared on.

Dariabibi called, 'Friend.'

Shairami didn't reply; she motioned her to sit down. A female relation of Shairami's was sitting by the patient's head, fanning her.

Dariabibi said, 'How are you now?'

'Not so well,' the relative replied sadly.

Phlegm had accumulated in Shairami's throat, making a rattling noise. She made an effort to reply.

A faint female voice was heard, 'Very well, thanks.'

Shairami started panting. The relative complained: 'We're poor. If at least you're in good health! Now she's got this disease on top of her bereavement. Hasn't God got even a punctured eye?'

Shairami was looking unblinkingly with her tired and feeble eyes at Dariabibi. She coughed a few times to clear her throat.

'When I get better, I'll come and see you,' she said.

Dariabibi took the patient's lined, dirty hand in her own.

'Your pot,' Shairami whispered. 'Jaya!'

She had great difficulty speaking; she pointed at the clutter of pots and pans.

Her lips moved a little. 'I – I got it released. You can give me the money.'

Tears rolled from Shairami's eyes. Jaya put a brass pot in front of Dariabibi.

From the expression on her face, it seemed she would like to speak.

111

But she kept quiet. The noise in her trachea came faster. Dariabibi sat like a rock.

The *chowkidar* called out the hours of the night. The boys sat like stupefied onlookers, their eyes heavy with sleep. Dariabibi did not wait any longer. Squeezing the two-anna coin into Jaya's hand, she took leave. The woman came out to see them off.

'It's fate. At least she's had a visitor from another part of the village. Nobody here gives a damn. She won't last the night. The cough's got back, you see.'

Jaya hurried back.

The brass pot was under Monadir's arm. Clouds had gathered in the sky; the moon was lost in their darkness. The wind was screaming in the thick clumps of bamboo. Suddenly they heard a cry from the direction of Shairami's hut.

'Wait, Amu.'

Dariabibi pricked up her ears and listened to Jaya's heart-rending scream.

Amu said, '*Pishi*'s died, Ma.'

Dariabibi stood still like a lifeless object. Then she turned towards Shairami's compound.

Amjad said, 'Where are you going, Ma? A Hindu dead in a Hindu home. What are you going to do there?'

With a surging cry, Dariabibi pressed her hands to her chest and sat down.

The news of Shairami's death spread in the morning. Dariabibi had developed an affection for this untouchable *bagdi* woman; she found no relief even in the midst of her daily grind.

On Monadir's insistence, they went to visit Amiran that afternoon.

Amiran was busy with the ducks and hens. Dariabibi's arrival after a long absence delighted her. Ambia smiled mischievously at Monadir.

While the two village women moaned, Amjad and Monadir walked off to the main road with Ambia in tow.

She watched as the brothers played marbles.

While aiming his marble at the hole, Monadir asked, 'You go to *maktab*, Ambia?'

'Why not? I'm old enough, aren't I? Shouldn't I learn to read and write?'

'Oh my grandmother!' Monadir stopped playing. 'Let's go and see what you read.'

Holding him by the hand, Ambia dragged him home. She fetched a rhyme book instead of the reader. The children's book in pretty colours was full of verse and pictures. Monadir hadn't seen one like it before; he was amused.

'Can you read it?'

Ambia curled her lips: 'Why not?'

She read a rhyme in her fine voice.

'Not bad,' Monadir said. 'Where did you find the book?'

Rahim Bakhsh's daughter went to the same *maktab* as Ambia. Some relation of the girl's had sent her it as a present.

'You're a smart old woman. A wizened old woman.'

'Who are you to call me old?' Ambia made a face. 'I'm only seven.'

Amjad laughed. He paled before Monadir and felt a little envious of this stranger. He had joined the rhyme-reading session as a mere spectator.

Amiran called out, 'Why are you making such a fuss over a book? How much longer can I send you to the *maktab*?'

Dariabibi protested, 'You scold the girl for no reason. She's a very good girl. Clever. Keen on learning.'

'Clever? That girl will be a rock on my chest in five years' time.'

Monadir was now reading out a rhyme. When he finished, Ambia said effusively, 'Munibhai, please read another one. You read so well.'

Monadir read another rhyme while the mothers talked about their misery. Amiran's relatives were not kind to her; they would love to see her evicted from her home, letting them lord it over these few trees and the pond.

Dariabibi rehearsed the tale of her own old relatives.

She noticed how neatly Amiran tended her little patch. The courtyard, the path to the pond, the veranda, everything was spick and span. *Lakhshmi* reigned over the *machang*, the plants and the vegetable patch.

Dariabibi's heart weighed heavy as she walked home, though she was all right so far. She felt as if right in front of her, Shairami, carrying a bundle of greens on her head, was trudging along, on a weary evening.

Chapter Seventeen

They had made a loss on sweet potato. Still with a smile Chandra said, 'Our fate is weighed down under a rock.'

Azhar was unresponsive. The number of dependants in the family was rising. He was so worried he couldn't sleep well at night. The machine of his brain was not very active anyway.

Chandra Kotal was not sitting idle. He found ways of making money. Azhar was surprised to see that Chandra had built a shed beside his hut. There he stored a battered harmonium, an old violin, wigs and *baiji* costumes. Chandra was in the shed, talking to a young man.

'What's all this, Chandra?'

'Come and sit on this mat first. I'll tell you. I'm organising a comic folk theatre group.'

Sitting on the mat, Azhar kept smoking.

'Do you have to do this in your old age?'

Chandra laughed as he rubbed his stomach.

'Old age, yes, but this place doesn't know how to get old.'

'The rehearsal's going on, is it?' Azhar said.

'In full swing. We're doing Krishna Stealing the Gopis' Clothes.'

'You used to do that one well. Where did you find the money?'

Chandra slapped the young man on the back and replied, 'Here's our Rajendra. He's been in town for a long time. He's brought us town manners but not its money.'

Rajendra was born a child of this peasant village. Now he had a *dhoti* and a short-sleeved shirt on and he flaunted a modish haircut.

Embarrassed, Rajendra said, 'Leave it, Chandrada. I don't think this will bring any money. But we'll have a good time.'

'Now that we've found Rajendra, we'll do well, you'll see. He's equally good with both voice and instrument. There's nobody to match him playing the fiddle. The other *jatra* groups will collapse, you'll see.'

Azhar Khan didn't feel comfortable in this atmosphere. A few saris were hanging from a bamboo rack. He asked, 'Are they costumes for dancers?'

'Yes,' Chandra said. 'Rajendra has brought them from town.'

Rajendra was notorious in this area. Seven years ago he had eloped with a married woman from the fishermen's village. Many stories of his exiled life in town had reached the village. That the runaway woman had now found refuge in the red-light area of the town and that Rajendra lived on her income. That a theatre singer had fallen in love with Rajendra and pursued him until she was reduced to begging. That Rajendra Das, son of Abhoy Das, was now a man of substance; thanks to him, the sons of Hatem Bakhsh were flying their peacocks in town. There was no end of rumours.

Rajendra was hard to recognise. He was fair; he had become brighter in the shadows of the town. His conversation was without the fault of the peasant tongue; he sounded as if he had studied long in school.

Did Chandra have to set up business with such a man? Chandra drank, so he would soon go to the dogs. But Azhar didn't dare speak his mind.

Chandra had no end of enthusiasm. He frequently stroked his long moustache.

'You'll see, Azharbhai. If there's a good harvest, there'll be no end of commissions.'

'Harvests are a matter for Allah's kindness,' Azhar replied in a weak voice.

Rajendra pulled up the harmonium and played some notes. Chandra drummed on the mat. Azhar sat without saying a word.

'Azharbhai.' Chandra kept smiling.

Azhar understood little. A new way had opened up and Chandra's face was flooded with the dream of a mirage. He called to the idle Azhar, but his voice had a touch of sarcasm, which Azhar did not catch.

'I've other things to tell you, Azharbhai.' Chandra looked Rajendra in the eye, asking him to wait.

'Khan sahib, come and join our group.'

Azhar cast a sad look at Chandra. He was even more surprised when he sat down on Chandra's veranda. There was a touch of prosperity about the cottage. He had substituted a wooden pillar for a ramshackle bamboo one. Chandra might have cheated him in sweet potato. Chandramani had recovered from her illness; she had a clean white sari on. She must have had a *paan*; red lips suited her. You wouldn't think she was the mother of two children. Azhar couldn't indulge any mean thoughts about Chandra. Chandra was no cheat. Perhaps Rajendra was spending money on their new group. All these rumours about him might not be baseless after all.

There was no fault in Chandra's welcome of Azhar.

'Truly, Azharbhai, I don't fancy swaying the hips in my old age. That Rajendra lad insisted, so I said, let's give it a try, see what fate's got in store for us.'

Chandra used to work with a dancing group in the past and had been called to play at the market townships ten to twenty miles away. During his exile he had found Elokeshi for a companion. Elokeshi was not his married wife. Azhar didn't have the nerve to complain to Chandra about Rajendra's activities.

Azhar's voice was lifeless when he said: 'Give it a try. And do another farming job with me.'

'Sure, sure. I'll never give up my caste trade. This is an extra job; who knows if we'll get any commission at all.'

'I'm up to here with life,' Azhar said despondently.

'Same here.'

Chandramani was like a sprightly butterfly; she looked prettier, with the shine of her health. The two children were dancing about in the yard. Wouldn't such an air of wellbeing touch his own family?

Azhar finished his tobacco and got to his feet.

'Think about it, Chandra.'

'Right. Right.'

There was a burst of happiness in Chandra's voice. Azhar felt envious for a moment.

On the lonely path through the fields, a sadness weighed on his chest like a rock. The sound of the harmonium came floating by. Rajendra and Chandra had started on a duet.

Chapter Eighteen

Dariabibi had never had to spend this long in the lying-in room. A healthy woman, she usually got back to setting her house in order after the fifth day of delivery. Ashekjan used to help her during this period. Now that she couldn't see well, the old woman was of no use with housework. Azhar sought Amiran's help. She was a busy widow, but she promptly agreed and soon painted a picture of an orderly home. For a few days the two cows would not be set free – let them have their fodder in the cowshed. Ambia was put in charge of the hens and ducks.

Dariabibi was overwhelmed with gratitude. Ashekjan's room was now the lying-in room. Daylight did not penetrate here; cobwebs hung in the corners; an unhealthy smell nearly suffocated you. Dariabibi lay there with the newborn girl, who looked like a lotus on a partially cleaned quilt. The mother's features were evident in the baby's face.

She had a little temperature. A *kaviraj* had been called, but no good came of his potions. So medicines were now being brought from the District Board Dispensary. But the dispensary was three miles away; Amjad's and Monadir's faces dried up in the sun. Azhar was busy working on Hatem Khan's land and planning to raise a loan. The household was in a mess. Children were not fed on time. So much pus accumulated in Naima's eyes she could not open them until midday. Sitting beside Ashekjan, she snivelled. When Dariabibi scolded her from her bed, she stopped for a while – and then started again.

One could not blame Amiran. She could not be bettered in housework but, unused to someone else's home, she took her time.

Monadir had gone quiet. He didn't like sitting beside his mother. Even if he responded to her, he did so without enthusiasm, as if he found the atmosphere unbearable. He felt a certain shame as he looked at the newborn baby; the conscious realisation of any reason

117

for this feeling was, however, beyond him. So he spent more time sitting under trees with Ambia and Amjad when they should have been at home running errands for their mother.

All Dariabibi could see of the outside world was through the open window. Her active, restless mind found no peace in the dark room. She kept watch from bed: had Muni eaten? Where was Amu? How bad were Naima's eyes? and a thousand little queries like these. The District Board Dispensary doctor had ordered complete bed rest. How much of the instruction could she observe? She used to get up to go to the toilet, to the embarrassment of Amiran, who had insisted on removing the patient's excreta and urine.

'Get well and then you can repay,' Amiran said.

'Repay?' Dariabibi made a face. As the newborn baby moved her hands and legs and cried out, she gathered her to her breast. Continuing, she said, 'Repay? Not in this life. Let Monadir grow up.'

Dariabibi fell silent; she had a headache.

'Let me give your head a little massage,' Amiran said.

'No, you'd better finish cooking.'

'Yes. I'll do that. Then I'll have to run home for a bit. I told Ambia to fill the trough with water. Who knows if she's raised water from the well. The cows could die of thirst.'

'Nobody can repay, not in this world, what you've given, *Bubu*.'

'Don't worry. Allah will see you through.'

'Allah, Allah!' Dariabibi said with sarcasm. 'If Allah does everything, what does he get out of our misery? I'm losing faith, *Bubu*.'

'You shouldn't say such things.'

'Leave Allah alone. If you're ill, you take medicine to get well. It's people who have to find ways to get well. Allah didn't put that in their brains. Then why talk about Allah? We'll have to fight our sufferings and disease ourselves. It Allah exists, let him; if he doesn't, who cares?'

Amiran was stunned.

'What are you saying in your fever? I don't understand all this.'

Dariabibi closed her eyes in pain. A dark shadow had fallen over her world. Then she opened her eyes to look at Amiran with gratitude.

'Don't be angry, *Bubu*. I know you say your prayers; I've stopped doing it. I can't put my mind to it. It's no good doing something you don't care for.'

118

Placing her hand on Dariabibi's head, Amiran said, 'Now keep quiet, dear. You aren't well in the head.'

'Hm.'

Dariabibi felt an unbearable pain in the joints of her legs, which she tried to stretch out.

'Now go to sleep. I'll be back after I've finished work.'

'Could you call the boys, *Bubu*?'

Amiran went in the direction of the kitchen.

The boys were not anywhere around. Hashu sometimes came to make enquiries and nursed the patient in her spare time. She wasn't allowed to stay out for long. Her mother-in-law wanted to keep a watch on this simple, sickly girl, who was being sent to perdition by djinns and ghosts. Without any offspring, her son would not look towards his home. Though she was peevish with Hashu, Saker's mother was in fact quite kind to her. Hashu had offered to keep the boys for a few days, but Dariabibi did not agree. They were not very well-off either. She feared that the trials of kinship might destroy the natural harmony of their relationship. When Monadir found no affection among the trees, he went to see Hashu, but, following his mother's strict orders, refused to take any food there.

This refusal scene was being rehearsed at Hashu's that afternoon. Hashu had a few *sandesh* in her hand. On the bed sat Amjad, Ambia and Monadir.

Hashu said, 'Come on, eat it up like a good boy. Yum-yum.'

'No. Ma'll tell me off.'

'Is she coming here to catch you out?'

'They'll tell her.'

'They're going to eat too.'

Freed from fear, Monadir put out his hand to take a *sandesh*. That set off the chorus of yum-yum and Hashu rolled over in laughter.

Saker's mother walked into the room and had a laugh too.

'Hashubou!' she said, suddenly changing her tune. 'Go to the kitchen! Daughter of an ill-fated one, it's not in your fate to have a home and children.'

Hashu was petrified. Amjad and others, having bitten into their *sandesh*, now sat without moving their jaws.

The old woman jabbered on: 'These ill-fated ones! They can't even fulfil one's wish for a child. Who knows where Saker's gone with his *latthi*. Allah knows what fate has in store for him.'

The old woman walked out. Not so much an old woman as a nuisance! Laughter broke out again.

Monadir started reading from a story book and everybody listened. Hashu, who found Monadir's gestures and style of reading charming, sat close to him.

Time passed. Monadir finished the story and looked out. The sun was declining to the west. It was time to go. He was hungry.

He called out to Ambia: 'Let's go. Don't you want to go home?'

'Let's go, Munibhai,' Ambia said.

Casting an irate look at her, Hashu said, 'Ambi, go if you want to. Why are you dragging him?'

'I'll go with him,' Ambia said, embarrassed.

'No, I'll go.' Monadir got to his feet.

Her petulance having proved fruitless, Hashu said, with entreaty in her voice, 'Monadir, I'll go and see Dariabibi.'

'Let's go then.'

Monadir was not exactly delighted, but he had acquired a natural courtesy.

'I won't let you walk,' Hashu said. 'Come, let me carry you.'

Monadir protested: 'What, am I lame or have I put henna on my feet?'

Hashu brushed off any opposition and hoisted him on to her hip.

'Big boy on hip!' Amjad taunted.

'What's that to you?' Hashu snapped. 'If one's a big boy at ten or eleven, what are you?'

Perched on Hashu's hip, Monadir had no peace in his heart. Of course, people would laugh at him.

As she stepped forward to go, Hashu said, 'Darling, put your arm round my neck or you may slip and fall.'

Home had little attraction for Monadir. Hashu was giving Dariabibi a head massage. Monadir talked to his mother for a minute or two and got up to go; Amiran was serving food for everybody. Azhar's food was left covered in the kitchen. Nobody knew what, apart from his work on the field, he was doing with Chandra Kotal, or where he was doing it.

After the midday meal, Monadir peeked into his mother's room and then disappeared in the village. Ambia had gone home; there would be a better opportunity to play there.

Hashu called out for him but there was no response.

'Don't know what's happened to him since I've been bedridden,' Dariabibi said with a sad expression on her face.

'He could have stayed with me these few days,' Hashu said, 'but you don't agree.'

'No, Hashu, it won't do. He's come to me after a lot of trouble. I'd like to keep him before my eyes.'

'A lot he is before your eyes!'

Hashu left after a while.

Late that evening neither of the boys had returned. These days Ashekjan did not sleep here if she had an opportunity to spend the night elsewhere. Not that she was much help anyway. And all Naima could do was to doze sitting on the veranda; she couldn't see well after dusk. A hospital doctor had examined her eyes and made out a list of things she should eat, but there was no money in the family to buy food for preventing disease. Amiran had gone home for a while to put away her ducks and chickens for the night.

Dariabibi was calling out in a feeble voice: 'Fetch me a glass of water!' When there was no response for a long time, she cried out with all her strength: 'Have you all died?'

Naima had responded, not that she could be of any help. At that moment Azhar got home. The plough was still on his shoulder; hearing Dariabibi's scream, he didn't go to the cowshed to put away the plough.

'What is it, Dariabou?'

'A little water.'

Putting down the plough on the ground, Azhar poured water from the pitcher. Dariabibi had just handed the glass back to her husband after drinking the water when Amjad, a bamboo cane in hand, was seen coming across the courtyard, Monadir following.

Putting down the glass on the ground, Azhar rushed forward with the speed of an arrow. 'Where have you been, you *haramzadah*?' he said, and holding Amjad by the ear, he slapped him across the face and hurled him down on the ground. Then the same severe punishment was meted out to Monadir. Azhar thrashed both the boys hard with a bamboo cane.

'Sons of beggarly *haramis*, all you do is eat and loaf about. Sons of swine, haven't you died yet?'

Naima was crying loudly. Though she couldn't see what was

121

happening around her, she nonetheless had a cruel realisation of it, which made her cry and scream.

Azhar Khan rushed up to her and gave her a clout.

That the meek Azhar Khan could suddenly turn into such a brute was beyond anybody's imagination.

Dariabibi came out, leaving her bed, and started screaming: 'Just you wait! Damn your manhood! You dare to strike my children!'

She rushed out onto the courtyard. How she got there from the veranda only that moment could tell.

Azhar Khan broke off the battle and, plough on shoulder, retreated in the direction of the outhouse.

Biting the dust, Amjad and Monadir lay on the ground. Blood flowed from several wounds on their bodies.

Before she could reach them, Dariabibi collapsed in a faint on the ground.

A little later, carrying a hurricane lamp, came Saker, Hashu and her mother-in-law.

Chapter Nineteen

Thanks to Amiran's great nursing skill, Dariabibi got well. Without treatment or diet in this poor home, she recovered through sheer willpower. During these three weeks she had found new friends and companions in Amiran and Ambia. When she was confined to her sickbed, Shairami's miserable death scene had flashed across her mind and she feared she might die a similar death. Amiran had helped in the gradual recovery of her mental health. Dariabibi felt indignant as she looked at her newborn daughter: the gold of her loveliness would turn to copper in this poor home. She had realised this looking at Amjad and Monadir.

Dariabibi would have recovered sooner if Monadir hadn't hurt her so badly. There was no trace of him. Beaten up, he lay burying his face in bedclothes and vanished without a trace the following morning. Saker made enquiries at Dariabibi's first husband's home, but Monadir hadn't gone there.

Dariabibi shed many tears and stopped talking to Azhar. She devoted herself to the daily grind, doing the duties of a wife, but remained speechless. Looking at her unmerciful face, Azhar did not dare speak to her. Unable to understand each other and with no need for communication, these two lived together like dumb creatures.

Chandra Kotal was deeply absorbed in his work with the comic theatre. Elokeshi and Chandramani had visited Dariabibi during her confinement. Chandra knew that Monadir, reprimanded by Azhar, had left home, but he did not know that a mountain of silence had reared up between husband and wife as a consequence.

One day Azhar told Chandra the whole incident and lowered his head in shame.

'So there's anger in you too?'

Chandra kept laughing. If timid cats could sometimes swallow the

head of a large fish like *ruhi* then it was hardly surprising that Azhar
could get angry.

'I shouldn't have beaten him like that.'

'Have you fallen at Dariabhabi's feet?'

'God forbid! You go and tell her things can't go on like this.'

'Why not? You've talked for ten years; can't you do without talking
now?'

'Get off, crazy!'

They had had a good harvest this year, so Azhar was not very
worried about supporting the family. He too loved imagining.

Later that day Chandra teased Dariabibi with jokes and laughter.

'*Bhabi*, I can't invite you to the theatre, you've got such religious
restrictions.'

'I'll come and see you perform at your home one day,' Dariabibi
said from behind the door.

'You're talking to me. Why aren't you talking to Azhar Khan?'

Dariabibi fell silent. The reply came a little later: 'If someone
throws my son out of the house – '

'That was criminal. What if I brought the boy back?'

'First bring him back.'

'Of course, I will.'

'I didn't mind when he beat up Amjad. But an unfortunate child
had taken refuge here, he lifted his hand to him, didn't care to think of
me.'

'He's done great injustice there.'

'My Muni is such a wretched child, and he raised his hand – '

Chandra realised she had burst into tears.

Returning to the outhouse, he reprimanded Azhar: 'Really,
Khanbhai, don't you understand a mother's love for her child?'

Azhar was smoking the hookah. Closing his dispirited bovine eyes,
he replied, 'Hm.'

Chandra Kotal had lost out today; he kept quiet.

'Look for the boy, Chunder.'

'I'm going to get someone to do it.'

Chandra got up to go.

Azhar kept smoking. He was losing interest in everything.

He had raised a good crop on a couple of *bighas* of land; this might
see them through three months. As soon as he got some money,
Azhar went and bought a handloom-woven sari for Dariabibi. As

124

there was no communication between the couple, Azhar put the sari on the bed and said a word or two, indirectly addressing Dariabibi.

For a few days more, the harvest was brought home. One day Azhar noticed that old Ashekjan was wearing the sari he had bought for Dariabibi. He stared for a while; a hundred questions churned in the heart of the meek man.

Later that afternoon, Azhar Khan set off with his building tools in the direction of a different village. The following day when Amjad raised the question of his father, Dariabibi stopped him with a reprimand.

Chapter Twenty

Yakoob had gone to the market township to buy onions and potatoes
wholesale. As there weren't many traders on that day, not much was
bought. Travelling five miles to get home only to return to the market
the following day was troublesome. Azhar's home was close by; there
was also an opportunity to cement an old relationship. With this
intention, Yakoob set foot in the courtyard of his poor maternal
cousin after many years.

Dariabibi could not immediately recognise Yakoob, who had
changed much over the last few years.

'Can't you recognise me? I'm that brother-in-law of yours who
used to tease you so.'

'Come in. Come on in.'

'It was useless coming to the market, *Bhabi*. I haven't bought much
stuff.'

'That explains why at a poor man's hut an elephant . . .'

Yakoob caught the proverb in midair: 'Not an elephant. A tiny bat
may be more appropriate.'

Yakoob had changed since he last came to this house many years
ago. He had a long *dhoti* on and his curly hair was parted in the
middle. He flaunted black leather pumps and a loose *kurta*. His teeth
were stained at the base with betel juice and his smile hinted at a
crooked mind.

Yakoob had a hundred *bighas* of land. He traded with the paddy
grown on the land as well as seasonal crops like potatoes, *potol*, onions
and jute. Dariabibi knew that he had made money over the last few
years. Further evidence of his prosperity was that he now had two
wives. He had recently made arrangements for another wedding but,
tormented by his neighbours and his second wife's kin, he was forced
to abandon his fond wish.

'Where is Azharbhai?' Yakoob asked, sitting on a mat.

126

Dariabibi had given him a glass of water and was now preparing *paan* for him. She continued to do so and did not respond.

'Where's my cousin?' Yakoob asked again.

'How should I know? Been gone for fifteen days and hasn't even sent word.'

'Funny man! He only dreams of business. But business is not for a good sort like him.'

'Who's going to tell him?' Dariabibi said, putting *paan* in Yakoob's hand. 'He has these urges now and then.'

'Azharbhai's like that. He set up so many shops at so many places, but never stuck it out. That's his great fault.'

With a wave of laughter, Yakoob took out a ten-rupee note from his pocket.

'*Bhabi*, don't mind my saying so, but I'd like to eat *khichuri*. Get someone to buy some ghee and quality rice. Can you find a chicken in the village?'

'You'll find one here.'

'Very well.'

Dariabibi refused to accept the note. She wished such guests never came. The humiliation pierced her heart. Yakoob insisted. Amjad and Naima stood by him, watching his antics. Yakoob squeezed five-rupee notes into their tiny fists.

'You buy sweets for yourselves,' he told them.

Dariabibi protested, but Yakoob turned a deaf ear.

'If you do this sort of thing, then don't come to our house. We're poor.'

Sulking, Yakoob said, 'My nephews and nieces – aren't they mine? You can say what you like. Let Azharbhai come.'

He burst into an open-hearted laugh as if he had made a great joke.

So Dariabibi had to get up. Hospitality was no small matter.

Amjad carefully folded his note and gave it to his mother to keep. He had jobs to do. He would have to go to the dairy farmer for ghee. Paid at this rate he was not prepared to neglect his work. He set off with a jar.

A chicken was slaughtered immediately. They had a large rooster, but it hadn't returned home yet and there was no way of telling when it would. Killing a hen stopped a source of income; people bought eggs and chicks for convalescing patients.

Dariabibi was busy in the kitchen when the little girl started bawling. Yakoob reassured her: 'Get on with the cooking, *Bhabi*. I'll take the baby.'

The baby stopped crying and Yakoob walked into the kitchen swinging her in his hands. Dariabibi had little time to arrange her sari decently.

Yakoob, embarrassed, walked out, saying, 'Your baby's lovely.'

'Yes, she's quite pretty.'

Dangling the baby, Yakoob entered the kitchen again.

'Naturally,' he said smiling. 'Look at her mother.'

Dariabibi blushed red. She was putting spices into the meat pan. She needed to fry coriander, so she put a hot plate on the fire. Yakoob's presence was a little embarrassing.

Dariabibi called, 'Yakoob-bhai.'

'Yes?'

'Why don't you go out? You're not going to learn to cook, are you?'

'Who'll teach me, *Bhabi*?'

'With two slave girls to do it for you, you don't have to learn.'

'Of course one has to.'

'Take the baby out in the fresh air. It's stuffy in here.'

Dariabibi got back to her cooking.

As if there was no end to what Yakoob had to say, he went in with the baby again.

'*Bhabi*, Azharbhai has gone fifteen days now and he hasn't sent word? Only you could live with him.'

'We're nothing to him, are we?'

Dariabibi was blowing into the fire through a bamboo hose, filling the whole kitchen with smoke.

'Even the love of such a pretty baby can't tie him down,' said Yakoob.

Dariabibi was getting a little irritated.

'I'll try to find him,' he said.

'There's no need for so much kindness. Who cares if he doesn't want to come back?'

Yakoob looked at Dariabibi's eyes. They were filled with tears, perhaps caused by the smoke or by life's whiplashes; Yakoob tried to work out which.

Dariabibi did not want any sympathy and would have been pleased if she were left alone. Watching him from the corner of her eye, making the smoke-filled kitchen even smokier, she said, 'Take the baby out of the kitchen, will you? Smoke harms their eyes.'

Yakoob left unwillingly.

Household chores, special cooking for the guest, it got quite late. There were only two rooms; finding a bed for Yakoob was another problem. Amjad had to sleep out on the veranda.

After he had finished his job at the market township, Yakoob stayed on for another three days. He was apparently making enquiries about Azhar. Melting with gratitude, Dariabibi was particularly watchful that there was no slip-up in her hospitality. Yakoob was spending with both hands. The children of this house only tasted *sandesh* on special occasions; Yakoob brought home varieties of sweets and made arrangements for ghee, *parata* and other delicacies.

The house put on a festive air. Yakoob didn't even allow Ashekjan to eat elsewhere. She too was a guest in this house.

Diffidence kept Dariabibi from protesting, but she could not quite approve of this show of charity.

Yakoob left after two more days. Amjad went a long way with him to see him off.

Chapter Twenty-one

At midday Hashu came to fetch Amjad. They did not go to her place, but went and sat down under a tree on the other side of the village.

'What is it?' Amjad asked.

'Why don't you sit down, there's a good lad. I'll buy you *sandesh*.'

'No, tell me.'

Hashu hesitated.

'Muni, isn't he coming back?'

'How should I know? Ma cries for him, doesn't talk to *Abba*.'

Hashu said: 'Now your father's left home. Muni's a bad boy.'

Amjad didn't agree. He was losing his shyness as he was getting older.

'But you're very good,' Hashu said.

Moving away a little, Amjad taunted, 'You don't have to cuddle me. Just because Munibhai isn't here.'

Hashu was surprised; he was only a little boy, but jealousy had touched his mind.

She moved closer to him and fondled his hair. 'No, you're really nice. I'll be nicer to you if you can do something for me.'

'What?'

'Make enquiries about Muni.'

'How am I going to do that?'

'Why don't you go to their village?'

Amjad said he couldn't.

'It's not very far. I'll pay for the bullock cart.'

'*Ma*'s going to tell me off.'

'Tell her you're going to school.'

Hashu untied a knot in a corner of her sari and took out a half-rupee coin.

'Here, keep it. It won't take you very long.'

'If *Ma* gets to know?' There was fear in Amjad's eyes.

'Nobody will tell her.'

A flock of wild birds suddenly called out from somewhere unseen.

'You'll go, won't you?'

'Yes,' Amjad nodded.

'Good. Good boy.'

Looking into the eyes of the innocent boy, Hashu held him in her arms, and the silence of the woodland gently shuddered.

'You're a very good boy.'

'Let go of me.'

'No.'

'Don't you bite my cheek like you did Munibhai's, Hashu *Chachi*.'

Stunned, Hashu loosened her embrace and moved away.

Amjad laughed, 'Hashu *Chachi*, Munibhai's crazy. Once he caught a butterfly and said he'd dye his shirt with its colours.'

Hashu did not respond.

'Well, can you dye shirts with the colours of a butterfly?'

'Yes, you can. I'll dye your shirt for you. First get some information about Muni. Don't you see how your mother cries for him?'

Amjad felt sorry for his mother. He said firmly, 'Of course, I'll go. Four annas for the bullock cart; with the other quarter I'll buy puffed rice.'

'Good.'

Hashu put out her hand towards Amjad, who had by then dashed out of sight.

Chapter Twenty-two

Dariabibi named the little girl Sharifan; her pet name was Shari. Shairami had of course come to her mind, specially the closing moments of her miserable life. Let Shairami's memory live in the child's pet name. It was, as it were, the feeble effort of a peasant mother in one corner of this land confronting religion and caste as they raised their reptile hoods against humanity.

But in the village, Hindu–Muslim communal riots were about to break out.

A fifty-*bigha* fenland had been a bone of contention between Rohini Choudhury and Hatem Khan over the last few years. Until recently the fenland was in Choudhury's control. Despite Hatem Khan's rights to the property in title, he had not been able to get anywhere near it. A few Muslim fishermen, called *atraaf*, the poor, by respectable Muslims, had taken over the lease of the fenland. The income from the fen was not inconsiderable. Hatem Khan had persuaded some *atraaf* Muslims to stop paying rent. Rohini Choudhury, who knew exactly what was going on, now got together some low-caste Hindu peasants and provoked them to start a communal riot in the village.

Of late Hatem Bakhsh had become a fanatical Muslim. His sons drank at home and he did not say a word; he himself never cared about prayers or fasting; but he was seen in the mosque for prayers on Fridays. His black and white beard now looked whiter for the white dye he put on. Wearing a knee-length *pirhan* shirt and carrying a stick, he walked about in the darkness of the village with a bodyguard, organising sittings, intrigues, disputes. He urged people to say their prayers even before prayer times, for to delay a prayer was sinful. The village *maktab* was falling apart and he had never spent a paisa on it; now he called the Muslims to a feast of pilau and korma and found ways and means to spread the word that the infidel Hindu *zamindars* would finish off the Muslims.

Excitement had returned to the dreary life of Moheshdanga. In the Hindu area of the village, Rohini was not being very miserly either, nor was he lacking in propaganda power.

Until now Hatem Bakhsh didn't much care for Saker, whose skill with the *latthi* was well known. Hatem Bakhsh now bought him up by feting him and bribing him with money. Saker turned into a fierce Muslim. One who said his prayers only twice a year, on Eid and Bakr Eid, with the set formula 'My wishes are whatever the Imam wishes', was now learning to say his prayers. He had gone and bought a Bangla Teach Yourself Namaz from the market township. Hashu got severely told off when she laughed at his incorrect Arabic pronunciation. 'A new crow is an avid shit-eater,' the timid wife was supposed to have remarked.

Chandra Kotal had become the king of the pack. Last month he had an argument with a Muslim of Sheikhpara over land borders. Rohini Choudhury's flunkeys made use of the incident. Chandra was now going round saying, 'If Muslims utter a word, blow them away.'

One day two groups of tenant farmers had a scuffle beside the fen. A few were wounded and criminal cases were filed at the court. The wounded ones didn't have money, but as long as Rohini Choudhury and Hatem Bakhsh did, they would not lack any.

The village was sombre with fear.

One early afternoon Azhar Khan returned carrying over his shoulder a bag containing an assortment of articles like tops, a bottle of red dye and glass bangles for girls.

Naima and Amjad were delighted. Everybody had a present. Amjad got a writing book, a pencil and a rubber; he acquired a top and string too. Naima got earrings and a few glass bangles.

Dariabibi broke her silence, but the bridge between husband and wife remained unrepaired. Azhar Khan brought home thirty rupees; he hadn't been sitting idle these last four months. He also ran a shop for a month, but it had not worked.

Dariabibi too had money. Yakoob spent generously whenever he came, and he often came on market days. She wouldn't have been in want even if Azhar hadn't returned. Not only had Yakoob promised to pay Amjad's monthly school fees, he paid them for three months in advance.

Azhar was surprised by what he heard about the village. Amjad gave him a brief history. Saker was believed to have said that the season had arrived for making money and that he was grabbing it from both the *zamindars*. He was said to have assured Rohini Choudhury that he wouldn't touch his *latthi* on the day; 'We'll see how many *latthi* fighters Hatem Bakhsh can fetch!' And to Hatem Bakhsh, he had pledged: 'As the son of a Pathan, I'll play my *latthi* for the last time.'

Without further delay, Azhar Khan went to the field. It was important to see the condition of his field first. The family looked well because he had raised a good harvest that year. Peasants were planting seasonal crops. Some were building fences around their fields to protect them from the damage by the cattle. They were going to grow *potol* this year. Watermelons didn't do well last year, so gourds and horse-radishes were being planted instead.

He was a little late, so he'd have a late harvest, but Azhar wasn't particularly penitent. He needed to see Chandra. Chunder, he laughed to himself. But Chandra, who was sitting on the veranda, didn't greet Azhar, didn't ask him to sit down.

'Chandra.'

Chandra did not respond.

Elokeshi brought out a *pidi* for Azhar to sit on and Chandramani followed her.

'Chandra!' Azhar called.

As Chandra did not reply, Azhar turned to Elokeshi, 'Is he drunk?'

Elokeshi raised her voice. 'What's going on? Sitting like a clown! Why can't you talk? There's Hindu–Muslim trouble in the village, so what have you got against a brother? *Zamindars* are quarrelling. The rich against the rich, so what does it matter to you? Will they give you their *zamindaris*? There he sits; Rohini Choudhury'll give him the fen, so he's going round the Hindu areas day and night.'

The one at whom these verbal arrows were aimed remained seated like a lifeless idol. Blinking his foolish eyes, he looked at Azhar and turned away.

Chandramani brought a pipe of tobacco for Azhar. Smoking quietly, Azhar called out between puffs: 'Chunder.'

Dejected, Azhar sounded hurt: 'Chunder. I've been away so long. I thought Chandra would be there when I wasn't. The rich have their arguments; why should we, poor people, get into it?'

Elokeshi hurled another shower of verbal arrows at Chandra, who now smoked a hookah, reclining on a mat on the veranda like

Bhishma on his bed of arrows. Elokeshi's assaults might not have been entirely futile, but Chandra was not humbled; there was no sign of it when he yawned.

Evening had set in. The courtyard was quiet; calves were lowing in the distance.

Before he got up to go, Azhar said, 'Jogin's Ma, I'll come back tomorrow. He's not in a good mood today.'

Azhar walked down to the field, now brushed with the colour of dusk, and as empty as his own mind. He listened to the sound of the wind.

Azhar once pricked up his ears; Chandra was being abusive: 'No, I haven't got eyes, I can't see. Look at the Muslims; they haven't got their eyes either.'

Elokeshi's voice mingled with that of Chandra: 'How can you see? You're up to your eyes with toddy.'

Azhar turned round to look at Chandra's homestead and an inexpressible pain filled his eyes with tears.

The following day Azhar was preparing the field for the seasonal crop. He hadn't grown any horseradishes for some time; he would put some in this year, as well as sweet potato along the edges of the field. Amjad had come with him. He avoided his father these days, but much feared his quiet gravitas. He didn't like working in the field. He went to school, so why should he go to the field at his age?

He was quietly obeying his father's instructions. Azhar had cut a few bamboos; Amjad was peeling the palings for a fence round the field. Because of the cattle, there wouldn't be much of a crop without a fence.

Other peasants were busy in the distance. Only recently the windswept paddy had kept the fields embellished in colour and line. Now they were empty. Haystacks had risen in the farmyards instead.

Azhar didn't look round him as he worked. Amjad, who was also working quietly, started at the sound of whistling. It must be Chandra *Kaka*; his field was beyond a few *bighas* of land. Chandra's figure gradually came into view over the bank.

Amjad's mind was no longer on his work. Soon Chandra *Kaka* would be coming over and he wouldn't have to work any more. But Chandra did not come to the field. He remained behind some banana trees before revealing himself; his spontaneous whistling had stopped.

Amjad was the first to greet him: 'Oh, Chunder *Kaka*!' Their eyes met; suppressing a smile Chandra looked away.

135

'Oh *Kaka!*'

The uncle didn't respond.

Azhar was tidying the ground with a spade; he raised his eyes and then looked down.

With a smile on his face, Amjad was going to move in the direction of Chandra, but Azhar reprimanded him, 'Get on with your work!'

Chandra was standing at a distance, his eyes turned away. Azhar quietly worked with his head down as if they did not know each other. Amjad kept looking at their faces. The village was on the brink of a Hindu–Muslim riot; was this the consequence?

Chandra walked away slowly across the field and vanished beyond the trees as evening approached.

Amjad asked, 'Why didn't Chandra *Kaka* talk to us?'

'No.'

What with the nature of his father's response, Amjad was not encouraged to make any further queries.

The whistling came floating down: Chandra *Kaka* obviously. Saddened, Amjad kept looking up across the fields.

Chapter Twenty-three

Azhar had a chance meeting with Chandramani, who sometimes came visiting in the village. Chandra alone had left the village; his relations still lived in their ancestral homes.

Azhar was walking absent-mindedly; surprised by the call, he did not look at the caller's face. Chandramani was not easy to recognise. She had a clean sari on and her lips were tinged red with *paan* juice, as if she wasn't a widow. Taking her to be someone else's wife, Azhar looked embarrassed.

'Oh, *Dada*, I'm Chandramani.'

Azhar was surprised. Chandra's income must have gone up. He had done well setting up the comic theatre group with Rajendra.

'Oh, Mani, it's you. I thought it was someone else.'

Chandramani laughed like a young girl. Only a year ago she had been reduced to such a miserable state by malaria.

'Why don't you go to our place any more, *Dada*?'

Azhar lowered his eyes in shame.

'How can I go? Chandra doesn't even talk to me.'

'That's why Elokeshi-boudi quarrels with him.'

'I saw him the other day. He didn't look very well.'

Cowherds were bringing in the cattle. Azhar and Chandramani moved to one side of the road to continue.

'He drinks too much,' Chandramani said. 'Something's happened to him.'

'What's happened?'

'He can't stand me. Scolds me all the time.'

'Just like that?'

'Yes.'

Azhar expressed no sorrow at Chandra's downfall. Another lot of cows were coming along. Turning his eyes in that direction, Azhar said, 'Chandra is a really good man. Why has he changed so?'

'Who knows?'

'Has he fallen into Rajendra's clutches?'

Chandramani did not reply; she fell silent.

Azhar continued on the subject: 'That Rajendra lad is not very good. Perhaps he drinks too much *toddy* with him.'

'No, *Dada*. Rajendra – '

On the evidence of her voice, Chandramani was ill at ease.

'The rich folk's quarrel has put him off,' she said.

'The other day I didn't talk to him either. I lost my temper too.'

Chandramani laughed, 'Both my brothers are crazy.' The joke didn't touch Azhar.

Continuing, he said, 'How's he doing these days?'

'Very well, with Mother Lakhshmi's blessings. He's making a few paisa from the theatre.'

Azhar suddenly felt a pang of envy; Chandra Kotal was doing fine.

'So long, *Dada*. Come and see us one day.'

Chandramani did not wait any longer.

Chapter Twenty-four

The two *zamindars* were locked in litigation. There was no further trouble in the village. The temporary excitement had died down. Chandra Kotal avoided Azhar. Elokeshi often clashed with Chandra over his relationship with Azhar, who went close to Chandra's house but lacked the courage to meet him. Saker had become friendly with Rohini Choudhury. The peasants were busy with seasonal crops and had no enthusiasm for the *zamindars'* quarrels.

One day Elokeshi came to see them on her own initiative. Azhar was not at home; he had gone to another village to buy seeds.

Dariabibi was sitting in the sun, eating watered rice.

'I've come at the right time,' Elokeshi said, laughing.

'Come on in, *Didi*.'

Dariabibi busily offered her a *pidi* to sit on.

Elokeshi showed even greater urgency: 'Have your meal, go on, I'll soon be on my way.'

'Why? Have you got a quarrel with me?'

Elokeshi started laughing.

'What's going on, *Didi*? Arguments everywhere. In the village, at home.'

'With Chandra Kotal?'

'Yes.'

Dariabibi quickly finished her meal. Elokeshi took out a ten-rupee note: 'Keep it for me.'

'Why me?'

'Keep it.'

Then she whispered into her ear: 'There's no way I can keep anything at home, is there?'

'Is money coming in from the opera?'

'Yes. That Rajendra lad is quite a man of parts. Now he wants to set up a *jatra* theatre group.'

Suddenly a stranger's shadow fell in the courtyard. Elokeshi had not seen the man before; she quickly pulled the corner of her sari over her head.

Dariabibi looked up and laughed.

'Come on in,' she said with a humorous smile.

The stranger was Yakoob. Dariabibi whispered into Elokeshi's ear: 'My husband's cousin.'

Yakoob sat down on a mat on the veranda. He had a package in his hand; he gave it to Dariabibi for safe-keeping.

'Is everything all right?' Dariabibi asked. Elokeshi was sitting like a new bride. In a tone of reprimand, Dariabibi said, 'Remove your *ghomta*. He's only our cousin.'

Elokeshi removed her *ghomta* and had a good look at Yakoob.

'I'm not very well, Dariabhabi. I've had fever these last four days. Now I've come to your place.'

'So you left home with fever?'

'Yes.'

Elokeshi took her leave.

'Was there nobody else to see to the business?'

So far Yakoob had not betrayed any restlessness; now he said, 'Make up a bed for me, Dariabhabi. I've got to lie down.'

'I'll do that. But what sort of women are my sisters-in-law that they let you come with fever?'

Yakoob kept quiet. The sun felt good, so he stretched his head out from the veranda. Dariabibi made a bed in the children's room and got back.

'It's too bad. You had fever and yet they let you come. Maybe nobody knew.'

'Of course, they did,' Yakoob said. 'Touch my head and see.'

Dariabibi felt the temperature on his forehead.

'It's hot. You don't look ill though. Go and lie down. What sort of people are they,' Dariabibi repeated, 'to let you come with a temperature?'

'I'm coming from the market,' Yakoob said.

In fact there weren't many liars like Yakoob in the world. His family life had brought him no happiness. The two wives quarrelled openly. Besides, the activities of a professional lecher like him must have reached his wives' ears. He had left home following an argument with his wives, not an iota of which Dariabibi got to know.

Yakoob had been visiting this house over the last few months. His generosity attracted respect, so Dariabibi allowed no fault in her nursing. To bring his fever down she washed his head with cool water. She spread a thick quilt on the bed – which, however, was bought with Yakoob's money – and covered him with a clean hand-woven sheet.

Ashekjan, who hardly went out of her room, collected information from Amjad. She had an old shawl in her chest, some dead person's property, given away by relatives. Dariabibi replaced the sheet with the shawl. Yakoob enjoyed the homely pleasures.

Amjad gave Yakoob a head massage and Naima looked on curiously with her fetid eyes.

Even today Yakoob had observed impeccable kinship manners and had brought sweets and other delicacies for the children, things which to them were as good as caskets of jewellery. He hadn't forgotten the little girl, for whom he had brought a fine dress.

Dariabibi brought him his sick man's meal and Yakoob looked around him with great satisfaction.

Dariabibi said, 'Let's call a doctor.'

'No,' Yakoob protested fiercely, 'I'll get well without one. I hate swallowing medicines.'

Finishing his sago, he took out a ten-rupee note. Dariabibi did not protest; that would be futile. Yakoob was stubborn.

At midday he was moaning with fever. There was no one in the room. He woke up at a little sound of the door. Dariabibi was standing before him.

'Are you all right?'

'No, Dariabhabi.'

He started moaning again. His head was splitting, he said, and he would feel better for a head massage.

Dariabibi called out for Amjad. There was no reply. Yakoob motioned her to sit on the bed.

'All right. I'll give you a massage.'

Dariabibi started massaging Yakoob's forehead.

'Dariabhabi, I owe you too much.'

'On the contrary, it's me . . .'

Yakoob lifted his hand to cover her mouth. Moving her head out of his reach, Dariabibi said, 'It's we who owe you much.'

Yakoob took out another ten-rupee note: 'Then owe me a little more or I'll die. This could be my last illness.'

What a man! He must be talking in delirium. Dariabibi handled

141

the note and then put it back in Yakoob's bag. Yakoob observed her without a word.

'Let's call a doctor, what do you say?'

'If you call the doctor, I'll go home with fever.'

Yakoob soon fell asleep and Dariabibi stopped the massage. When she heard Amjad's voice, she left Yakoob's bedside and came out. A thousand household chores awaited her.

Azhar returned before sunset with a sack on his head. He hadn't found *potol* seeds; seedlings were expensive and dried up. The news that Yakoob was lying with fever reached his ear but he did not show much interest in meeting him. He washed his hands and face and, after having something to eat, sat on the veranda, smoking.

Dariabibi said, 'Go and see him. Haven't you got any decency? What's he going to think?'

Azhar was pleased at the reprimand. Dariabibi was discussing family matters with him again; this was the sort of co-operation he expected from her.

Azhar had a long talk with Yakoob about the family, his farming, the children's education, Naima's eye trouble and so on. He told him about the *potol* seedlings as well.

Yakoob took out twenty rupees from his pocket, put it in Azhar's hand, and said, 'Azharbai, you've tried hard on your own. Now work in partnership with me. Nothing will stand in your way.'

Holding the note in his hand, Azhar finally accepted the gift with hesitation.

'What do you say?'

'It's been so hard. Doing business in partnership with you is a very good idea.'

Azhar kept talking late into the night, calling it a day at Dariabibi's reprimand.

When serving supper, Dariabibi laughed and said, 'You weren't going to see him; now you seem to have got glued together.'

Chapter Twenty-five

One stormy night of *Vaisakh* old Ashekjan died and nobody even knew what time she died. Recently Amjad had been sleeping in the other room. Late in the morning when Ashekjan failed to get up, Dariabibi went to her room to look. The cold body of the old woman was lying there.

Dariabibi cried for a while as Amjad, Naima and Azhar dumbly watched her. The old woman had no relatives, so Azhar concluded the burial with the help of a few neighbours.

A case belonging to Ashekjan was opened and ten or twelve rupees in change and a few clothes were found. Dariabibi didn't make much profit. The shroud cost ten rupees.

Dariabibi thought of the helpless old woman and wondered how her own life would end. Perhaps she too was destined to die an ignoble death.

Ashekjan was forgotten in a week's time. For the *chahram*, the fourth-day commemoration of her death, Dariabibi gave food to two beggars.

For a few days following Ashekjan's death Amjad could not sleep alone. Monadir was not around. He was too frightened to sleep in his own little cubicle.

'What are you scared of?' Dariabibi remonstrated. 'Your *dadi*'s gone to heaven.'

Yet Amjad could not get rid of his fear. He had heard of ghosts from his school. The impression was not to be wiped out so easily.

He asked his mother, 'Ma, do people turn into ghosts when they die?'

'Only bad people do.'

'What about *Dadi*?'

'She was a good woman, she's gone to heaven.'

'Do good people eat at other people's houses?'

'She was poor, wasn't she? Poor – '

Dariabibi suspected that her reply didn't satisfy her son.

'I'm scared. *Dadi* sleeps next to me.'

Dariabibi spat to protect Amjad from the evil consequences of his inauspicious remark.

'You only feel that way because you've grown up sleeping beside her,' she said.

'I'm scared, Ma.'

'You're a big boy. Haven't you got the pluck – '

'So!'

Amjad continued to sleep close to his mother. When a gust of wind hit the jackfruit tree outside, he clung to his mother. Ashekjan *Dadi* was going somewhere, stick in hand, to eat at the fortieth-day feast of someone's death.

When the matter reached Azhar's ear, he took Amjad to the *moulvi* of the *maktab* who said a Koranic verse and blew on Amjad and then on a glass of water. Two holy blows cost Azhar one full rupee. The *moulvi* asked Amjad to come back on Friday. To put away another rupee, Azhar said to himself.

Unable to get rid of his fear, Amjad couldn't even stay on the veranda on his own. But he suppressed this with his mother. He overcame his fear for another reason.

Apart from the money Azhar had received from Yakoob, he had a bit more now. Unknown to Dariabibi, Ashekjan had put a small box in Azhar's safekeeping. In it there were about twenty rupees of which Dariabibi had no knowledge.

Altogether Azhar had about fifty rupees now which he could invest in fish or in some other business. But he didn't like Yakoob, whose parted hair, colourful *lungis* or loose *dhotis* irked him. He couldn't possibly do business with him. Yakoob was younger and Azhar did not consider it right to do his bidding. As the capital would come from Yakoob, he would have no choice but to dance to his tune.

If only Chandra was around. But Chandra hadn't stepped in this direction since the Hindu–Muslim trouble. Elokeshi had come the other day. What a sensible woman she was! 'We're only straws in the battle of kings,' she said. 'Why should we go and have our heads smashed?' Elokeshi was right. With Chandra it was a different matter. Azhar Khan had lost hope in him.

In this village lived Muslims of two persuasions – Hanafis and La Majhabis, of which the La Majhabis were the majority. Hatem

144

Bakhsh Khan was a Hanafi and it was through his enthusiasm that a big religious gathering was organised in the village with the approval of both sects. Three or four *moulanas* were invited for the occasion.

Religious spirit was flagging among the Muslims. Water tax had helped to raise the spirit a little, but Hatem Bakhsh was not satisfied. Muslims were becoming faithless; some Muslims were still on the Hindu Rohini Choudhury's side. It was important to rouse the religious spirit. To Hatem Bakhsh Khan's great despair, Muslims were not getting together. Hundreds of cracks appeared in his heart at the sight of the decline of Islam.

The meeting had been arranged in the village *Eid-gah*. A great marquee had been set up as well as a raised platform for the *moulanas*. Mats and cotton rugs were spread out on the ground. Many Muslims had come from neighbouring villages.

The sermon began as one of the *moulanas* embarked on his speech. 'Brothers!'

Brothers pricked up their ears. Recalling the poor state of Islam, the *moulana* burst into tears. Swallowing, he said through a tear-choked voice, 'Islam is in danger. That it still survives is because pious souls like Hatem Bakhsh Khan are alive. When he goes to his grave, who knows if Islam may not do the same. Muslims are becoming faithless, and even *ferishtas* are weeping in despair. Yet Muslims don't care. These disobedient creatures of Allah are like so many spears piercing Allah's heart. Ya Allah!'

He cried once more. Hatem Bakhsh, who sat on a rug in front of him, frequently dabbed at his eyes with a handkerchief.

The hearts of the listeners, if not their eyes, were soaked too.

'Dear brothers, my Allah, the great invisible omniscient, says in the Koran, Get together and hold on to one rope. Hold tight, firmly – '

The *moulana* made a tight fist.

'Hold it firmly, just as Hatem Bakhsh Khan holds it firmly.'

As Hatem Bakhsh's name was uttered repeatedly, some respectable Muslims felt ill at ease, their main motive being envy.

'Dear brothers,' the sermon resumed. 'If you don't obey Allah's injunctions, you'll burn in hell and you'll not have the benefit of the Prophet's defence in your behalf on the judgement day. Certainly not – '

'Certainly not, certainly not – '

All the heads in the gathering nodded together. Taking a deep breath, the *moulana* said, 'Now recite the words in praise of our Prophet.' The recitation of the praise in Arabic was heard for a long time.

'The fire of hell never goes out. Tough punishments for toughened sinners. So much fire – such burning heat – '

The *moulana* was exhausted describing hell. His throat had gone dry, perhaps from the heat of hell fire; he swallowed a glass of water. Then, burping, he resumed recreating the fire of hell. It was a hot day. The meeting got even hotter.

Meanwhile someone sprinkled the listeners with rose water. With the fragrance in the air, the meeting got going in earnest. Then another *moulana* rose to his feet. He was invited by the La Majhabis.

For a while he described the sad state of Islam. The names of other leading Muslims were now heard. They were the only true Muslims. Hatem Khan's name was not included in this list. So he now nursed envy in his heart.

The *moulana* then started on Islamic legends. Muslims like Hazrat Ali are not born any more. Ali, said the *moulana*, was a tall man with gravitas, his beard reaching down to his navel.

'No!' another *moulana* protested. 'Hazrat Ali was not that tall and his beard was not that long either.'

'Silence!'

'Why should I be silent?'

'Don't be irreverent about the Hazrats.'

'Who's irreverent? Was Abu Hanifa wrong?'

'Who's Abu Hanifa?'

'The Imam.'

'Then the Imam is not right.'

At which the Majhabis were very pleased. A hum of pleasure swept through their ranks. But the Hanafis, the followers of Imam Abu Hanifa, got annoyed with the *moulana*.

'Shut up!' cried the first *moulana*. But his adversary was not to be silenced.

'In which documents have you found such absurdities? According to the Holy Tirmiz, Hazrat Ali's beard was *not* navel-length.'

'Your Tirmizi is false.'

The Hanafi supporters of this *moulana* would not remain quiet any more. Angry whispering started in the meeting.

'Shut up!' shouted the Majhabi *moulana*.

'No, I'll not shut up!' the Hanafi *moulana* shouted back.

146

'You're impudent.'

The adversary's patience gave way. He shouted, 'You are a son of an impudent one.'

'Is that it, *haramzadah*?'

He suddenly got up and slapped *moulana* Shah Fakhruddin in the face. Then they held each other by their beards and had a hairy scuffle. The meeting broke up as two groups of supporters rushed to join in. The dispute between the *moulanas* opened the way to a fight among their followers.

'Beat up the Majhabi *salas* – lay out the Hanafi *salas* – '

In the holy gathering the pious Muslim brothers suddenly started swearing obscenities at one another.

Hatem Bakhsh, now stimulated, started shouting in support of his *moulana*. When he realised that the scuffle was not going to stop, he slunk away in the dark and saved his honour like a clever fellow.

Azhar Khan too had come to the meeting. Usually a placid man, he was a pukka Muslim in matters like these. He could turn into such a barbarian. The lights had gone out. He had a go with both hands to his heart's content. He split his throat shouting: 'Finish off the Hanafi bastards!' Who could now say Azhar was a helpless man, he – such a proper Muslim, that he could not bear any insult to his religion!

The dispute started over beards. Many did not get home with their beards intact and some were injured. Not only that; the two villages turned into contending forts.

The following day the Majhabis found an opportunity to beat up some Hanafis, who then proceeded to avenge themselves. The *moulanas* conducted this village feud as generals. But these field marshals were not to be found in the fields. Staying put in their headquarters, they tasted pullet liver accompanied with pilau and *parata*.

This troubled situation lasted for a week. Who knows how much longer it would have continued if Saker had not done everybody a favour? He too had got carried away in the beginning. When he realised what the *moulanas* were up to, that they were at the centre of the trouble, he got very angry. Armed with his *latthi*, he first went to the Hanafi village. Even before he entered, he started shouting: 'I haven't come to fight, though I've got a stick in my hand.'

Villagers gathered around to see the fun. Nobody would take on this stubborn man in a fight with staffs.

Saker dragged a *moulana* from a veranda and administered two slaps on the face and a knock with his *latthi*.

'Clear out of here,' he said. 'You're here to start a row, aren't you, *sala*? Can't control his own anger, just like a dog, and he's come to make disciples!'

The disciples were stunned; nobody rushed forward in the face of the *moulana*'s discomfiture.

Saker himself was a Wahabi. He chased off the *moulana* of his own village after a good thrashing.

The village sighed in relief. Some were annoyed with Saker in the beginning, but soon they raised their hands in thanksgiving. Many women sought Allah's blessings for Saker. Mothers, who were worried that their children might get hurt, now felt relieved.

In a couple of days normality returned to Moheshdanga. Azhar became quiet again. These last few days even Dariabibi had feared the look on his face. He seemed to have turned into a beast in the name of religion, though he never showed such a temper in any other matters.

Dariabibi once took an opportunity to ask him with a touch of sarcasm: 'When someone oppresses you through no fault of your own, where does this temper go?'

'What temper?'

'You wouldn't remember, would you, when the *zamindar* took away your harvest for no fault of yours and you sat back like a wet cat?'

'Hm.'

'Hm!' Dariabibi taunted. Then as she proceeded to praise Saker, Azhar quietly walked away to the field.

Amjad had already gone to the field. He had a school holiday. He was ashamed to work in the field but, thinking of the sorry state of the family, he quite liked helping his father, though his respect for him was steadily diminishing.

A bed was being prepared to sow chilli plants. Ploughing was over, tidying up was all it needed. A strong fence would have to be put up as chilli plants attracted cows and goats.

Amjad liked doing this sort of work. With a small spade he was heaping up soil in a straight line. Just then came a shower of rain, making it unnecessary to carry water to the bed.

Azhar's sudden appearance did not please Amjad.

'I see you've got some work done.'

'Yes, *Abba*.'

'Good.'

'This time we'll not take our chillies to the market. We keep buying them all the year,' said Azhar.

'Will you remember that when we're in want?'

'No, we'll not sell them this year, if Allah wishes – '

Azhar hesitated. He had some money now, but he was not without misgivings. How long would it take for Allah's pity to run out?

The light of the day dimmed and the look of the field changed. Father and son did a little work on the seasonal crop. Suddenly they could hear someone singing in the distance. Father and son were all ears. The singer sang, repeating the lines. 'Bhagwan, take this broom on your head . . .'

The voice was familiar. Azhar got back to work.

'Chandra *Kaka*, isn't it, *Abba*?'

Azhar did not respond. Amjad looked across the field. The singer was still out of sight.

Amjad was negligent with his work, Azhar noticed. He did not like careless work.

'Get on with your job, Amu.'

'It's Chandra *Kaka*, isn't it?'

'Yes, so what do you want to do about it?'

The singing continued:

> 'Bhagwan, whoever looks at you
> gets chilli in his eyes . . .'

Amjad laughed: '*Abba*, Chandra *Kaka*'s crazy. *Bhagwan* means Allah, doesn't it?'

'Get on with your work.'

Chandra emerged on the footpath from behind some banana trees. His voice was getting closer. Amjad felt happy, but his happiness was short-lived. Chandra *Kaka* would not come their way. Hindus and Muslims were quarrelling. Damn your quarrel!

Azhar again told Amjad to put his mind to work.

The singer was coming this way. Amjad noticed that Chandra *Kaka* had not stopped outside the fence. He was steadily advancing towards them. Coming closer, Chandra Kotal now stood beside them.

Azhar was quietly working away as if to ignore Chandra's presence. Amjad did not look up at him either, so as not to offend his father.

All three were quiet. They had never been in a more embarrassing situation. Finally Chandra laughed out foolsihly. Casting a sidelong glance, Amjad got back to digging.

'Azharbhai, oh Khansahib,' Chandra called out and hesitated. The other side was still quiet.

'Son, has your father gone deaf now?' Chandra addressed Amjad. 'Deaf *abba*, eh?'

Azhar did not budge, though he had stopped working. Giggling, Chandra suddenly sat down in front of Azhar and looked into his eyes. Their eyes met. Chandra's laughter was infectious. Azhar could not restrain a smile.

Chandra clicked his fingers and leaped up, hoisting Amjad on to his shoulders. Amjad had grown up now; he felt shy about getting on people's shoulders. But did he have a chance to protest? He was already in the air.

Dancing about, Chandra said, 'I don't care for religion. Saker has done the right thing.'

No sooner had he finished than the sound of his laughter filled the late afternoon field.

Suddenly putting Amjad down on the ground, he said, 'Give us some tobacco.'

The others had no opportunity to talk. Chandra said, 'When our priest comes, I'll tear off his beard.'

Azhar at last opened his mouth: 'Crazy Chunder!'

Shaking his long curly hair, Chandra accepted the title. Then looking at Amjad, he said, 'I'll tear off your father's beard as well, son.'

Now they all started laughing.

'What happened to you, Chandra?' Azhar asked.

'I was possessed.'

'Must have been a raving ghost.'

'Yes, Khanbhai, my eyes were opened yesterday.'

Chandra fell silent. His face trembled and eyes became tear-filled.

'What's the matter, Chandra?'

Azhar put out his sympathetic hands.

'Shibu, Ismail, they died in the district hospital.'

'Died?' Azhar was speechless. Shibu and Ismail were badly wounded in the riots over water tax. These two close friends had been in the district hospital since.

The three of them sat in silence for a long time. Evening brushed its ink wash across the horizon.

'Shibu's wife and children will maybe die of hunger. It doesn't matter to Rohini and Hatem, the bastards.'

Their faces were not visible in the dark. Breaking his silence, Azhar said, 'Come, Chandra, let's go home.'

Chandra stood up. He did not utter a word. He was already on the footwalk.

Speechless, father and son walked homeward. Amjad felt uneasy. He had met Chandra *Kaka* after a long time, but the evening was wasted in the field. After a while he heard Chandra singing.

Azhar said, 'Really mad is Chunder. Must have drunk *toddy*.'

'No, *Abba*, his breath didn't smell at all.'

The folk tune, in the embrace of the evening breeze, came floating down across the dusky fields.

Suddenly Amjad asked, '*Abba, Bhagwan* means Allah, doesn't it?'

'Yes,' Azhar replied coldly.

Chapter Twenty-six

Hashu often came to visit Dariabibi and wouldn't budge unless sent for urgently by her mother-in-law.

Amjad went looking for Monadir. Dariabibi did not know that Monadir hadn't gone back to his old home. Hashu had dissuaded Amjad from telling her lest she get even more worried. Amjad lied: 'He's there, Ma.'

Hashu was saying, 'Sister, your new baby's so lovely. Give her to me. I haven't got a child.'

'You're crazy.'

'I so want a baby, even if it's a blind or a lame one.'

Dariabibi sympathised with the infertile woman.

'You'll have one if Allah wishes. You're not past it.'

Hashu released a sigh and remained silent.

At this point Amiran walked in with Ambia.

'Come on in, *Bubu*.' Dariabibi was delighted to see them.

'I've found some time at last,' Amiran offered as explanation. 'I'm rushed off my feet with work.'

'Actually you don't care for us.' Dariabibi looked at her with a shrewd smile.

'You'll say that, *Bubu*, but there are a hundred problems. Rice doesn't go down my gullet.'

'Why not?'

Amiran told them about her brother-in-law who was desperately seeking to grab her property, which would come in handy after a few years to get Ambia married. Perhaps she could find a bridegroom to stay on the property, as it would be be impossible to live on her own after that slip of a girl had gone.

'Don't worry about Ambia,' Dariabibi said. 'Entrust Allah's property to Allah. But your brother-in-law is a mean sort.'

'Looking out like a vulture.'

Ambia was not beside her mother; she was busy talking to Amjad under the jackfruit tree.

'So Muni won't come back?'

'Ma still cries for him,' said Amjad in a doleful voice.

'He's good.'

'Isn't he?'

'Yeah. Why don't you bring him back?'

'I went looking for him.'

The truth was nearly out before he remembered Hashu's command.

'I've seen him,' said Amjad, twisting around. 'He'll come when he wants.'

Ambia was not satisfied with the reply.

'That's a lie. Why shouldn't he come if you saw him?'

'He doesn't want to come.'

'He reads so well.'

Monadir was the central topic of their dialogue, as if there was nothing else in the world to talk about.

Amiran, Hashu and Dariabibi talked about household matters. Words had power to salve suffering. One's tale of suffering could put out the fire of another's, forging a link of sympathy.

'The unlucky one,' said Amiran to Hashu, 'you want children. Look at us, how we're burning.'

'I don't even have anywhere to burn.'

Of late Dariabibi had been in a better mood, as a little wind of well being had penetrated the world of this indigent family. Time passed in talk. Once here, Ambia was reluctant to go home.

It was nearly evening, time to go home, but her mother's call hardly registered in Ambia's ear.

'You go, Ma.'

'You stay here as Daria's daughter-in-law then.'

Dariabibi too had built this imaginary castle. Monadir would soon be sixteen. Then –

'All right. Leave her here,' Dariabibi laughed.

'That'll give me some rest. First you'll have to feed and clothe her to make a woman of her.'

Hashu took the words seriously: 'Give her to me. I'll feed and clothe her.'

'Right. Take her away.'

'Come, Ambia,' Hashu called out. 'Come on, darling.'

Just at that moment Saker's mother's loud voice was heard from a distance, Hashu left.

Amjad saw his aunties off. He wouldn't listen to his mother; he wasn't afraid of ghosts any more. Waves of Chandra *Kaka*'s songs had driven his fear away.

Mother and daughter walked carefully along the footpath through the woodland. After a while Amjad stood stock still.

A dusky evening wind murmured through the canebush. One evening he had been here with Munibhai. Suddenly tears filled his eyes; he really loved him.

Chapter Twenty-seven

Chandra Kotal was busy.

A good harvest that year created a demand for comic folk theatre and Chandra had many commissions. Rajendra provided costumes to give the group a little glamour; now they were called to perform in many villages.

Azhar could not find a partner. Chandra told him to wait for a few days, but Azhar was disappointed; he might not have any money by then. He thought he must find something on his own.

Yakoob, who came on market days, raised the subject. He did not just drop in; along with him came merchandise: chicken, ghee, even fine rice. Azhar didn't approve; it hurt his self-esteem; he didn't like the idea of being Yakoob's partner.

But Dariabibi had grown to accept Yakoob's ways; her self-respect did not turn defensive so easily. Yakoob was kin; it wouldn't do to be so sensitive about the gifts he brought.

Azhar kept quiet. Dariabibi seemed to be an enthusiastic hostess. After a long time there was the fragrance of pilau rice in the house. Yakoob had asked for *luchi*, but Dariabibi said he could have *luchi* for breakfast. The name Yakoob *Chacha* delighted the children. Little Naima even salivated at it.

Yakoob had regularly been paying Amjad's school fees.

A couple of years ago, Dariabibi used to scold Ashekjan for accepting little charities; that spirit had vanished now. Dariabibi knew what her husband thought but that did not soothe her grievance against him. It wouldn't do to apply such strict rules to dealings with one's relatives.

Azhar concluded his evening meal with dhal and curried potato. Yakoob had brought catfish, but he didn't touch it.

Dariabibi asked, 'Won't you have some meat?'

'No. I've got an upset stomach.'

155

Azhar suppressed the real reason. The money he had taken from Yakoob was like a thorn in his flesh. There was no way he could return it, for that would bring his dream world crumbling down. Had he not been so constrained he would have told Yakoob to his face to stop the charity.

Dariabibi knew very well where it hurt most.

'It's hard enough paying Amu's school fees month after month. God knows what'll happen if we don't get a good harvest next year.'

Azhar did not respond.

'You talk of business. Haven't you wasted enough money?'

'It doesn't take long if Allah wishes.'

'You've spent ten years talking about Allah's wishes,' Dariabibi said, annoyed. 'It's your wishes we're waiting for.'

Azhar was going to reply, but thought better of it.

'Why don't you start a business with Yakoob-bhai? Let's see which way Allah's wishes turn.'

'It won't work.'

'No, why should it!'

Dariabibi, who had hotted up, now offered a hundred analyses of Azhar's foolishness. But her opponent remained silent; he had fallen asleep.

Over a sumptuous breakfast the following morning Yakoob gave Dariabibi an account of his profits. He had made three thousand from jute, two thousand from warehouse business, and so on.

Azhar was not around at the time; he had gone to the field.

Yakoob said, 'Our brother's a bit funny. If he had worked with me, Allah would have looked kindly on him.'

'He's crazy. Who'll ever be able to change him?'

'I'd have earned a hundred thousand if I had your wisdom.'

Dariabibi was pleased with the compliment. She was preparing *paan* for her brother-in-law. There weren't any *betel* nuts left so she rose to go over to the *shika* for them and, looking back on her way, found Yakoob staring at her backside. Though it was not quite obvious, his look did not seem to be decent.

Dariabibi returned to the *paan* bowl, a little diffident. She did not look Yakoob in the eye. It was probably an optical illusion, or perhaps that was how he usually looked at people.

When alone, her mind was a little agitated. Perhaps the man wasn't bad, just indecent. Having no knowledge of these lecherous businessmen, Dariabibi tried to work out a solution through such

156

conflicting thoughts. Azhar, who had a better knowledge of the man, kept his distance.

Yakoob left that morning. When tidying up his bed, Dariabibi found a ten-rupee note under the pillow and stood stock still for a while, absent-mindedly crumpling the note in her hand. When she became aware of what she was doing, she tied up the note in the corner of her sari.

After working for a while, Azhar had gone to see Chandra, who was busy dressing up in theatre costume; they had a commission.

Chandra offered Azhar a seat and started preparing a pipe. Shibu's wife had come earlier. A four-year-old boy sat clinging to his mother's body, sucking his thumb, and a little girl was sitting on her lap.

As Azhar's eyes fell on her, Shibu's wife pulled down the *ghomta*.

'How are you?' Azhar asked.

'God's killed him; how would you expect me to be, *Chacha*?'

She followed Shibu in calling him *Chacha*.

Chandra, holding a hookah pipe, came and sat down beside Azhar.

'Can you see, Khan, what our religions do?'

'I can see.'

'You can see? You see nothing. Religion! If Hatem Bakhsh is a Muslim and Rohini Choudhury a Hindu, then who's the untouchable? They're religious for the sake of money. And two poor fellows had to lose their lives.'

Addressing Shibu's wife, he said, 'Did you go and see Rohini Choudhury?'

'I did. He gave me five rupees,' Shibu's wife said in a dejected voice.

'Listen to that, Khan! Five rupees! Piss on it. The price of a man's life is five rupees. Azharbhai, as long as we live, I'll not listen to a word of religion. I too fell into Rohini's trap. *Sala* Rohini!'

'Don't be rude for nothing.'

'Don't be rude? Would you support Shibu's wife? Even if you were prepared to do that, could you give her her husband back? You say I shouldn't be rude.'

Red-eyed, Chandra puffed away.

'Don't be rude, he says! Ismail's wife has gone back to her parents with her children. They're poor too. Shibu's wife has nobody to go back to. She hasn't even got two bales of hay for a roof over her head. I keep telling her, come and live here, I'll build another hut. The boys of the village, Bashid, Paru, Ganesh, they said they'd work for nothing.'

Azhar said, 'Call me whenever you need me.'

'Of course, I'll call you. Hatem Bakhsh is a Muslim, his whole clan drinks, and you do what he tells you to do, don't you?'

'You yourself danced to Rohini's tune.'

'True,' Chandra replied, shamefaced. 'But no more. Bugger their religion. And Azharbhai, I don't like your timid ways. You must raise your voice and beat your breast when you talk to them.'

'They're rich. The police and the rest – '

Chandra interrupted, 'Aren't there any laws? We're not just a couple of ordinary folk. There are thousands of poor in the village. If the police don't go by the law, if they think they can do what they please, we've got our *latthis*, haven't we?

Chandra's large eyeballs swivelled round. Suddenly stopping, he said, 'It's getting late. I've got a lot of preparations to make. Come and see us later, Azharbhai.'

On his way home Azhar thought about Shibu's wife. Like her, he didn't know where his next meal was coming from. Only the open road held out any hope. He would set out again. He had suffered so much humiliation for money: it wouldn't do to stay put. Wouldn't his fate ever take a good turn?

How long would it take if it was God's wish?

Chapter Twenty-eight

Dariabibi had finished early with her household chores and was now sitting with little Shari on her lap.

It was soon after dusk. Dariabibi was yawning. Amjad was reading loudly in his room. Azhar sat on the veranda, absorbed with his hookah, emitting a steady *gurook-gurook* sound of smoke passing through the water in the coconut shell.

'Muni's Ma,' Azhar called. He had changed Dariabibi's name since Monadir came to this house. Only once in a while did he call her 'Amu's Ma'.

'What is it?'

'I went to the other village.'

'Why?'

'To buy paddy seeds.'

'Is there any need to tell me that?'

'No. Just – '

Azhar fell silent, but it was obvious from his voice that he hadn't finished.

'Muni isn't there in that village,' he said.

Dariabibi pricked up her ears.

'Not there?'

Dariabibi was sitting at the edge of the veranda; she moved close to her husband.

'Who isn't there?'

She thought she had misheard.

'Who isn't there?' she repeated.

'Muni.'

'Muni isn't there in that village?'

'No.'

'Since when?'

'He never went there.'

Amjad was summoned. He came over, leaving his books.

'Amu, didn't you say your Munibhai was at his uncles'?'

'I didn't go to their house. I just heard – '

'You heard?' Furious, Dariabibi glowered at her son.

Amjad nearly burst into tears. Azhar was no less penitent; he reproached himself repeatedly.

'My vile temper flared that day. Let leprosy smite this hand of mine.'

Dariabibi did not utter another word. It was doubtful if anything that was said registered with her. Suddenly the veranda went completely silent.

Amjad slunk away to his own room. His reading had stopped; his voice could not be heard. Azhar sat with his head between his knees; he didn't even notice when Dariabibi left with Shari. He fell asleep in that position. When he woke up the whole place looked unfamiliar. There was no lamp on the veranda. Darkness had amassed in the courtyard. A great number of cicadas were screeching breathlessly; their screeching echoed in Azhar's brain. Carefully he knocked on the door. No, everything was quiet. Amjad's room wasn't open either. They had gone to bed without their evening meal. Rolling out a mat on the veranda, Azhar lay down.

Very early in the morning he went away to the field.

At Dariabibi's request, Amiran promisd that she would make enquiries about Muni. She returned dejected in the afternoon. It was true Muni had not returned to his uncles' house. Dariabibi cried inconsolably. Hashu came to see her; her own tears wouldn't stop either.

'If he hadn't come to me, I wouldn't have cared. But he came and I drove him away.'

Dariabibi sobbed away.

Amiran said, 'I'll go to the astrologer. He'll tell us where he's gone and when he's going to get back. My sister's brother-in-law – '

Amiran told them the tale of how the lost man had returned.

Dariabibi was not reassured, but still she said, 'I'll pay five paisa.'

'He takes five paisa and a betel nut,' Amiran told her.

'Here, take it now.'

Amiran couldn't wait much longer. Ambia was at home. It was quite dark; she would have to walk through the wood. Amiran and Hashu took leave.

Azhar had returned from the field, but only Amjad knew this. He had taken one look at his father and gone to his room to read quietly in the light of the oil lamp; but his mind was not on his work.

When the visitors had left, Dariabibi went to Amjad's room.

'Amu.'

'Ma.'

'Can you go to the village tomorrow? Then to the market town.'

'All right, Ma. I too feel bad about Munibhai.' Amjad's eyes filled with tears.

'Hasn't your *abba* come back from the field?'

'He has. I saw him.'

Lamp in hand, Dariabibi entered the room. Azhar's *lungi* and *pirhan* weren't there on the bamboo rack. His builder's tools were kept in a niche in the wall. The hole was empty.

Dariabibi looked around sharply and immediately realised everything.

Chapter Twenty-nine

'Your father's gone to catch big fish again. You think tiddlers will do for the Khans?'

When Chandra said it, laughing, he hadn't realised that Dariabibi was standing behind the outhouse. When he did, the smile on his face instantly disappeared.

Dariabibi had called him in. Amjad knew that when in trouble, it was Chandra *Kaka* she first remembered.

'That's right,' Dariabibi said.

Suppressing a smile, Chandra said, 'That's right. I haven't seen another man like him. These whims that seize him from time to time. Two weeks have passed. A man should at least send word, but not him.'

Dariabibi's sigh reached Chandra. A master of making light of heavy scenes, he himself turned pensive.

Amjad said, 'You know, *Kaka, Abba* can't stand the sight of us. That's why he keeps running away.'

Chandra protested: 'No, it's not that, son. He's a whimsical sort. When the world hurts him, he runs for it, thinks misery will go away. But misery doesn't go away that easily, does it? It's the British Raj. Let the British go, let Rohini–Hatem Bakhsh bastards go, then our misery will go.'

Amjad did not understand all this, but he was not prepared to agree with Chandra. He had a grievance against his father.

'But the thing is,' Chandra said, 'your father's a – '

'A quiet devil,' Dariabibi completed Chandra's sentence.

Chandra laughed as if he was himself again.

'Right you are, Dariabhabi. If I feel something, I blurt it out. But Khanbhai, ooh, he won't say one extra word. If someone needed a quiet devil for a thousand rupees, I'd sell your father, Amu.'

Chandra laughed and Amjad joined in.

Dariabibi called out to Amjad in a tone of reprimand: 'Amu, ask your *Kaka* about the land.'

That put a stop to their laughter. It was not Amjad, but Chandra, who answered.

'Don't worry about it. I'll harvest the paddy myself. Hay's selling at a good price this year, people are thatching their houses. I think we can hold on to some of it and sell the rest.'

'Keep at least a *kahan* of it,' Dariabibi suggested.

Chandra said, 'Apart from harvesting paddy, I'll put in some melons and gourds in a *bigha* of land. I've got these commissions for the theatre, but there's Amjad; we'll see what we can do.'

Addressing Amjad, Dariabibi said, 'Amu, give your *Kaka* some *paan* and tobacco.'

Chandra protested, 'No, not today. I must be on my way, Dariabhabi. A lot needs doing in the field.'

Chandra got to his feet and Amjad followed him. If only he could walk about with Chandra *Kaka* in the woods and waters of Mohesh-danga, he wouldn't care for anything else. What an abundance of comic songs, jokes and heartfelt affection he would receive from him!

Chandra's reassurance gave Dariabibi strength, but her anxiety did not pass. It had happened so many times before, but the wretch had always returned. What would happen if he didn't? Until now Dariabibi had depended on her physical strength. Her health was still intact, but her mind seemed weak and lonely.

Absorbed in her thoughts, Dariabibi was feeding the goats with the leaves of a jackfruit tree. Shari was quietly asleep on the veranda. She was a good girl who cried only when she was hungry and slept when she was full. That put Dariabibi's mind at rest and she could go about doing her household chores unhindered. The goats were very dear to her; they gave birth to kids every year. People bought goats for Eid and other festivals. It was good to sell them then, for they fetched a good price and brought relief in hard times.

Dariabibi was busily feeding the animals and hadn't noticed when Amiran had come into the courtyard. Feeding was an everyday job; she wasn't looking at the goats, just pushing the leaves and twigs forward, her mind absorbed.

Amiran looked at Dariabibi's solemn face and called her softly.

With a welcoming smile, Dariabibi said, 'When did you come?'

'You didn't see me. That's how listless the minds of housewives are when they're estranged from their husbands, eh?' Amiran said and laughed.

Driving away the goats, Dariabibi held Amiran by the waist and said, 'Let's go in, *Bubu*. What a husband! *Do* I worry about him?'

Amiran responded with sympathy, 'What a man!'

'Let's go and have *paan*. Let's talk.

> 'Live by the river
> Sorrows for ever!'

The two women talked shop for a while, about the village, neighbours, about where Saker had gone to fight, how Hashu suffered at the hands of her mother-in-law, and so on.

Amiran was a busy woman, a queen in her kingdom of cows, calves, ducks and hens. She did not have much time for gossip. She had come to pass on a piece of information and was looking for an opportunity to do that. Suddenly she said, 'Dariabubu, I've got news.'

Alert, Dariabibi looked with intense eagerness at Amiran.

'I've got news about Muni.'

Without showing much enthusiasm, as if she would have been happier if she had received any other news, Dariabibi said, 'What news?'

'Muni goes to school ten miles away from his old home. He has no contact with his uncles.'

Amiran offered the information fast.

'Let him keep well wherever he lives,' said Dariabibi. 'He's not my son, is he, what right have I got over him?'

'Who says he's not your son?' Amiran protested. 'You'll see he'll come back to you.'

'Doesn't make any difference. Let him live wherever he is. How did you get to know?'

'A maternal cousin of mine lives in the village next to the one where Muni lives now. I'd told him to look for the boy.'

'You're kind.'

Amiran got up in response to the call of duty. Ambia was at home alone; her brother-in-law was hatching plots to deprive her of her property; she could not stay any longer. But Amiran was surprised that Dariabibi did not raise the matter of her son today. On other days the topic figured large for hours on end.

Dariabibi walked with Amiran up to the outhouse and asked her to come again. But as she turned back, it seemed as if her feet would not move any further. Slowly she walked up to little Shari on the veranda and stared at the child's sleeping face. Only Dariabibi knew what she was thinking about at that moment.

Chapter Thirty

On his way to the market Yakoob had dropped in to look them up. He didn't come empty-handed. Apart from sweets for the children, he brought enough things to keep any family happy for three or four days. In the beginning Dariabibi used to raise objections. These days she opened the packages with her own hands, though without showing much enthusiasm.

On this occasion Yakoob brought lobsters and large *koi* fish. Azhar sometimes when fishing. Only on these occasions quality fish got into the pot.

'Dariabhabi, I couldn't find peas. I love lobster with peas.'

The children kept Yakoob surrounded. Naima – who often asked, 'When's *Chacha* coming, Ma?' – would not be separated from him. Amjad sat close to him. Being shy, he talked less, but would not leave Yakoob alone for hours.

Formalities were swept aside. Though a guest, Yakoob would dictate his menu, having himself bought the ingredients.

Dariabibi was frying *luchi* in the afternoon. The children weren't around. Naima had come in with a childlike craving, but her mother shouted her out of the kitchen. Amjad too was told off: 'Such a big boy, you go to school, why are you so greedy? Haven't you seen *luchi* before?' Even a glutton would have run away in shame.

Azhar was not mentioned by the children. Yakoob hadn't asked after him the whole day. He hadn't observed a relative's normal courtesy in this matter.

There was the sizzling sound of *luchis* being dropped in hot oil. Dariabibi was working, absorbed in thought. Her fair round face was sweating in the heat of the oven.

'Dariabhabi, how far along is your cooking?' Yakoob called out as he entered the kitchen.

'I've done the aubergines. I'm frying *luchi* now,' Dariabibi said without looking at Yakoob, as she pushed a piece of firewood into the fire.

'Come on, let's have hot *luchi.*'

'Right. But where are you going to sit?'

'I'll show you where,' said Yakoob and sat down on his haunches.

'Your clothes will get dirty,' Dariabibi said. Yakoob had on a silk *lungi* and a white shirt. She wasn't joking.

'I'm no child, you know,' Yakoob said, laughing loudly, as if he had cracked a great joke.

'All right, sit down. I'll get the plates down.'

Dariabibi got some crockery from the *machang* and started serving *luchi* and aubergines.

'Call the children,' Yakoob said.

'They've had theirs.' A prompt and brief reply. Yakoob saw her rolling out the *luchis* while keeping a watch on the pan, in which oil was boiling.

'Have they really eaten?'

'Yes.' Her voice sounded a little sharp. She drained the hot *luchis* and put them on his plate. Yakoob started eating slowly.

'A little water, Dariabhabi.'

Dariabibi promptly obeyed the order. Conversation didn't seem to make much progress. Yakoob actually feared Dariabibi, couldn't easily look into her eyes. Her solemn expression was the image of a reprimand. Yakoob felt ill at ease. But then he had two wives; he had a hidden self-confidence. Yet things went cold in her presence. So calm was Dariabibi and yet Yakoob felt so ill at ease.

'When I come to your place,' he said, as if to himself, 'I find a peace I cannot find anywhere else.'

'Why?' A brief query.

'Why? Who takes such good care of me?'

'Good care?' Dariabibi laughed out loud. Yakoob pricked up his ears; was she being sarcastic? He couldn't quite make it out. Without giving him any further opportunity, Dariabibi said, 'Where do you find "good care"? You bring the stuff and I cook it like a hotel cook would.'

Her tone of voice had the quality of a shopkeeper about it, which annoyed Yakoob, but to close the gap between them, he said, 'No, Dariabhabi. All this is a matter of fate. I don't find such peace anywhere.'

'You've got two wives, by the grace of God.'

'Wives!' Yakoob guffawed, spraying crisp particles of *luchi* in all directions.

'Wives? Where do you see wives, Dariabhabi?'

'What are those two, then?'

'Mounds of flesh!'

Laughing, Dariabibi looked at Yakoob and lowering her eyes said, 'I haven't seen your wives, but if being fat makes one a mound of flesh, I must be a hill of flesh.'

'No, Dariabhabi, you're a *Lakhshmi* of the family.'

The compliment pleased Dariabibi, who laughed and said, 'That's new, Yakoob-bhai'.

It was this gift of intimacy which Yakoob so desired. Laughing, he said, 'Give me two more *luchis* and call the children.'

'They'll eat later. You eat now,' Dariabibi said simply.

After his meal, Yakoob said, 'Dariabhabi, I'm going for a walk. Your village is a bit jungly. It won't be a good thing to carry money on me. Keep my wallet for me.'

'How much is there?'

'Five hundred.'

'That's a lot of money. If it gets stolen – '

'Thieves won't come to steal money from you,' Yakoob said, throwing her a smile.

'Then for what will they come?'

'Haven't they got any fear?' Yakoob said, changing tack. 'You have courage. If my mounds of flesh were to live in a place like this, I would have to employ ten guards for them.'

Dariabibi put out her hand and Yakoob promptly put the wallet in it and walked out in the dusk. Tying up the wallet in the corner of her sari, Dariabibi got back to her work.

The next day Yakoob was to catch the boat to the market township.

'Give me the wallet, Dariabhabi,' Yakoob said, when leaving.

While returning it, Dariabibi said, 'I have a favour to ask of you.'

Yakoob looked very eager; he thought she would ask for a loan.

'Give me your orders.'

'Keep a look-out.'

'Of course, I'll do that. Do you think I'm not one of your own?'

Yakoob looked at Dariabibi, but she was looking down, as if searching for something there.

'I wasn't talking about us,' Dariabibi said softly.

168

'Who then?' Yakoob asked, disappointed.

'Your cousin.'

'Oh, Azharbhai? He's a whimsical sort. He'll come back one of these days,' Yakoob replied nonchalantly. 'Why are you so worried about him?'

'Are you asking me why I should worry about my husband?' Dariabibi looked straight at Yakoob.

'No, no, not that. He's an unworldly sort; what good is worrying over him?' Yakoob lowered his eyes and replied in a guilty tone of voice.

'Yet you can't help worrying. I'm asking you because your men go to the townships to buy things.'

'Of course, I'll do that. You can count on me.'

'Please. Allah will do good to you,' Dariabibi said without irony.

'Time to go. Rest assured I'll keep you informed.'

Yakoob did not wait any longer.

Chapter Thirty-one

With the exception of one or two homes, Dariabibi hardly went visiting. Besides her own diffidence, she feared Azhar. He was a quiet sort, but he wouldn't stand for any violation of the Sharia. Now, to run her household in her husband's absence, she had to go far.

Amiran's house was at one end of the village, the path to it overgrown with bushes, usually lonely. Even Dariabibi feared the path and usually took Amjad with her. Naima, who wouldn't stay at home without her mother, also accompanied them. Amjad, however, liked the path and often said, 'Let's go to Amiran *Chachi*'s.'

There were other attractions there. Amiran always kept puffed rice balls and coconut balls, both with molasses, for the children. And Ambia was a lively girl with whom he could play while the women gossiped.

That day Amjad badgered Dariabibi to go to Amiran's. She had already cooked both meals and would only heat up the food for the evening, so she had no objection. Going to Amiran's lightened the burden of her heart.

Amiran, who had just finished giving fodder to the cows and was now washing her hands, suddenly saw Dariabibi and her children and smilingly welcomed them. 'Come, *Bubu*, come. Amjad and Naima are here too. Oh Ambia, come and see.'

The girl was there before her mother had finished. Ambia had grown a little but she was as lively as ever. Holding both Amjad's hands, she said, 'Amjadbhai, let's go look at a dove's nest in the *karanja* bush by the palm tree.'

'Let's go.'

As Amjad ran off following Ambia, Amiran called out from behind, 'Don't go far into the jungle. Snakes are becoming a menace.'

But who would listen to her? Amiran prepared *paan*. Dariabibi did not usually chew them, but she did not reject Amiran's offer.

'My brother-in-law,' Amiran began.

Dariabibi interrupted her, 'Has he started being nasty again?'

'Old habits die hard. The other day he cut two bamboos from my clump. Well, let him.' Then a burst of fire came from Amiran's throat: 'They'll come in handy to bury his son.'

Dariabibi also expressed her indignation.

'Far from helping a widow, to go and steal from her! It won't go unpunished.'

'It comes easy to them. They get rich at other people's expense. But his cover is fine. These days he works as the muezzin of the mosque.'

Naima's eyes were watering. She didn't like running about. Her *chachi* had given her a couple of puffed rice balls; she was busy munching them. Perhaps they had stuck in her throat; she asked her *chachi* for a glass of water.

Dariabibi looked around the yard. Visiting Amiran gave her strength of mind. Though a widow, she was running her household well. The yard was always neat and tidy. There were beds of vegetables around the yard. Last year she had planted a lemon tree, which had now grown and was fully blooming with leaves. Her family wasn't big, so she could cope, Dariabibi thought.

Amiran handed Naima a glass of water.

'You've given her a glass; she'll break it now,' Dariabibi warned.

'I'm holding it,' Amiran objected. 'What have we got anyway? This glass – he was alive then – he bought from the fair at Harishpur.'

'They've broken everything at our place. There are only one or two glass things left; I've put them away. You need them when someone comes.'

Amiran had little time on her hands. Looking after the cow and calves took up much of the afternoon. The vegetable patches needed watering. Amiran was talking fast. She did not raise the question of Monadir or Azhar lest it hurt Dariabibi – lest a snake emerged while she was looking for an earthworm.

But a snake nonetheless raised its hood.

Amiran was saying, 'Do you think I'd have cared if I were alone? My mother didn't produce such a timorous sort. But that bone in my throat!'

Unable to understand, Dariabibi looked enquiringly at Amiran.

Amiran laughed. 'Haven't you seen the bone in my throat? You'd have seen it if you were a doctor. Wait a minute. I'll show you the bone. Ambia!' Amiran called out. 'Oh Ambia!'

They were somewhere near; Amjad and Ambia showed up.

'That's the bone in my throat,' Amiran said, pointing to Ambia.

'What is it, *Ma*? Ambia asked. They had broken off from their play; they were not willing to wait much longer.

'Go and play.'

As the children ran away, Dariabibi said, laughing, 'You made a fool of me.'

'Isn't she a bone in my throat? If I were alone, I'd have been free, I'd have done what I pleased. Now I worry so much I can't sleep at night.'

A shadow played across Amiran's face.

Dariabibi sighed, 'Look at mine. They're my leg irons.'

'Yet a home doesn't look right without them. Look at Hashu. She's a piece of grit in her husband's eye, a bone in her mother-in-law's throat, because she hasn't got a child.'

'She's all right. Those who've got no children have one worry; those who've got them have a hundred.'

'True, *Bubu*.'

'If my Muni was here, I wouldn't have feared anything.'

Amiran wanted to avoid this issue, but Dariabibi wouldn't let go.

'If Muni was here, I'd have taken Ambia off your hands. Or he could have lived with you. You haven't got anyone else; you'd have had a boy in your family.'

As if absorbed in a lunar dream, Amiran said, 'Will that ever happen to me? Even if you agreed, what about your husband? You're an old Khan family.'

'What can he say? He's not his father.'

Amiran was pleased, but she knew that it was only a fantasy.

'But he's run away.'

Dariabibi turned very sad. Amiran called the children and gave them coconut balls. The noise of the children brought the atmosphere back to normal. It wasn't long before sunset. Dariabibi knew how important work was. She let Amiran off.

How vast was this world! How much of it could you see through the lattice of a *palki*? Like Amjad, Dariabibi too savoured a strange taste as she walked along the footpath through the bushy vegetation.

It was past twilight. In the woods, fireflies had started snatching the light from one another.

Chapter Thirty-two

Chandra was going home drunk on a lot of *toddy*. As he approached his home, he was seen carrying on his shoulder a half-burnt piece of firewood which he had obviously picked up from the cremation ground.

At midday there wasn't anybody in the field and Chandra was singing to himself, but as he got nearer home the song stopped and the singer turned into a warrior. As he swung the firewood round, making it hum, he yelled at everyone to get out of the way: '*Hat jao, hat jao!*'

Chandramani, her children and Chandra's wife came out of their hut at this sudden cry in Hindi. First surprised, they now watched the fun. Chandramani's children laughed their heads off at their uncle's antics. But Chandra's wife was very angry. *Toddy* was as good as water to Chandra. Her objection was not to that; but that he should appear at this odd hour with cremation wood on his shoulder was so inauspicious that she couldn't bear it.

'You come here and I'll show you your "*Hat jao*",' she cried.

'The older he gets the nastier he behaves,' Chandramani said with her eyes on her brother's wife.

'Just you get on to the yard with that wood!' Chandra's wife challenged.

Chandra suddenly stopped swinging the firewood and asked, in Hindi, what had happened: '*Kia hua?*'

'*Kia hua!* Just you get in and I'll show you "*kia hua*".'

Chandra swung the wood round again but stopped as he approached some *karanja* plants on the edge of the yard. Little Jogin addressed his uncle, 'Mama, don't come up. Mami will beat you.'

'Shut up, son. I'm a *zamindar*. Who dares to stop me?'

Like Bhima with club on his shoulder, Chandra stood erect, straight as a bolt, his long hair dishevelled in the wind, his drunken eyes large and round. Frightened, Jogin's elder brother sought shelter under the end of his mother's sari.

Tying the end of her sari round her waist, Chandra's wife roared, 'Throw away that wood and go and bathe in the river before you come in or else – '

Chandra considered his wife's clenched fist.

'*Hat jao!* I'm the *zamindar!*' he cried, gesturing at the fields behind him with a semi-circular sweep of his finger. 'All those lands are mine. You stop me? Are you joking?'

'Just you get into the yard!' Chandra's wife said, making a face.

Without answering her, Chandra started bashing away at the plants, shouting, 'There are my tenants – do you hear me?'

'Lunatic!' his wife cried.

'Lunatic?' The warrior raised his club and stopped. First with a sarcastic laugh, then with a challenging pose, he roared, 'Lunatic! How can a *zamindar* son of a bitch be a lunatic?'

'Lunatic, lunatic,' the children shouted, laughing.

'I'll kill 'em all,' said the club expert and proceeded to pacify the imaginary tenants again. His drunkenness was at its height.

Finding the contenders falling about laughing, Chandra took a step towards the yard. His wife immediately picked up a piece of firewood.

'Lunatic!' Chandra shouted. 'If you're not a loony would you bash people?'

The play of the pummel started again. Who knows how long this would have continued if Amjad had not arrived with orders from Dariabibi? He was taken aback at Chandra *Kaka*'s new antics. He was quite frightened by the warrior figure and was wondering whether he should return with his mother's orders undelivered. Suddenly the warrior's eyes strayed in that direction. The tenants got off without further punishment as the great hero, holding up his club, slowly advanced towards Amjad, whose face turned pale in terror. Mustering all his courage, Amjad suddenly blurted out, '*Kaka*, Ma's calling you; it's very important.' As if the words had not reached the warrior's ears, the club-on-the-shoulder elephantine walk continued. Then suddenly throwing away the pummel, he picked up Amjad and put him on his shoulders. Amjad loved it when he was young, but now he'd grown up and felt very shy.

'*Kaka*, put me down,' he implored. But the drunk was lost in his own imaginings. The master singer started singing and dancing.

> '*Chacha*, what a time!
> Where shall I find grub
> For you at such an odd time?
> In the pond the ducks are playing,
> Hens have long stopped laying,
> In the bushes and under trees swaying
> There's not even a fox's cub.'

Chandra shook his head, God forbid! Son of a Muslim! Then he noisily spat on the ground and began a new song:

> 'Don't you worry, nephew,
> We won't eat rubbish, phew!
> We've got a fat auntie at home
> Why not slaughter her here?
> Aha, nephew, that's wisdom,
> And I say hear-hear, hear-hear . . .'

Chandra set off in the direction of the Khans to the happy laughter in the yard. Late afternoon colours tinged the land all around and the trembling song left its melody in the fields about them.

> 'There's a fat auntie at home
> Why not slaughter her here?'

Shamefaced, perched on Chandra's shoulders, Amjad started laughing.

Chapter Thirty-three

A year went full circle.

It was not just unchanging nature which revolved round the sun; the strange world of humanity advanced with it, plenty and want, laughter and tears, leaving their mark behind in strange rhythms.

This maelstrom swept Dariabibi along towards bewildering paths. Her husband was no longer in exile. Azhar had returned with only three weeks to live. He had done many things during the last year. Masonry was his age-old skill; guarding brickfields, assisting the imams of mosques and setting up little shops were mirage-bound passions with him. He had returned hoping for a new beginning. He had set up a shop before coming back. There had been an agitation in his placid mind. He was learning to look at himself. No longer absorbed in his prayers, he started falling asleep on his prayer mat when his head touched the ground in *sizda*. Chandra was an infidel, poorer than himself, yet he possessed happiness. Life's blasts had failed to break his wings. But Azhar, with so much thirst for life and happiness, behaved like a trapped mouse scurrying desperately about. How much faith did he have in all-dispensing Allah? Azhar often sought an answer to the question in his leisure hours. On his last day as a shopkeeper, he had argued with a customer over prices. The following day he sold off the shop. He wanted to get back to his village and ask Chandra where he found his joy in life. Chandra hated Hatem Khans. Was hatred the source of his happiness? Hatred was envy, violence. Could lotuses bloom in such mire? Whatever he did, he thought he would merge every moment of his existence with Chandra's. That Chandra drank *toddy*, danced and sang was no concern of his. Azhar had found a new strength of spirit. But he did not return alone. During his rounds of the country, deadly malaria had made a home in his body. He suffered from malarial fever now

176

and then. A new symptom developed on his way back home. Only the final act was to be played out at Moheshdanga.

Being a humble pious soul, Azhar did not lack sympathy from friends of his class during his last few days. Chandra came often and sat around for hours. Exchanges were minimal, but visits were not missed. As the fever increased, Chandra got the root of a tree from the priest of the temple and tied it round Azhar's wrist. At any other time Azhar would have protested and they would probably have fallen out, but on his way to death, Azhar was a different man. After all he had come back to put himself in Chandra's hands. In the past when Chandra dropped in, everybody was infected by his laughter. But these days he looked grave. One day, though drunk on *toddy*, he sat in silence, did not reply to questions, and left without a word, as if the future of this family already stood like a question mark before him. The family received unlimited sympathy, even from Yakoob. He fetched a qualified doctor in a *palki* from a distance of five miles. But by then the disease was in its final stage and the doctor offered no hope.

Dariabibi's usual spirit had all but disappeared. There was no fault in her housework or nursing. Between household chores, she went and sat by the patient but, unconscious of any need, Azhar lay expressionless. He did not even raise his eyes to look at Dariabibi. His open eyes, lifeless as stone, were as if no longer meant to see: they had become weapons of thought. If Dariabibi asked questions, they were answered with yes or no. His silence upset her and she frequently sent the children to her husband. Conversation took place only with Naima as if only she understood what he had to say. If Dariabibi sometimes appeared during the conversation between father and daughter, Azhar fell silent. Dariabibi would sit by his bed quietly wiping her tears. Did he never realise what responsibilities he was leaving behind? She often thought she would ask him but never did.

There was a kind of rattling sound in Azhar's throat. These days a lamp was kept lit throughout the night. Dariabibi sat up and said, 'Are you in pain?'

'No.' Then staring at her, Azhar said, 'Amu's Ma, I – ' He stopped speaking.

Dariabibi then asked him, 'Do you want to tell me anything?'

Azhar nodded agreement and looked up at his wife with unblinking eyes. Some time passed.

Eager, Dariabibi affectionately ran her fingers through his hair and said, 'Do you want to say something?'

Azhar did not say anything. He stretched out his emaciated hand towards Dariabibib and then made it into a fist, his eyes still unblinking. Apart from the sound of the patient's breathing, nothing competed with the silence in the room. Words would fall from those lips now, Dariabibi tremblingly expected. But no further words were uttered. The life-warrior had already received his passport from this world. Dariabibi did not realise that only his eyes were still alive. Laying her own eyes on her dead husband's, she looked on and on.

Chapter Thirty-four

Amiran advised, 'Raise more ducks and chickens and goats; the days will somehow pass. When my husband died, I too saw the dark. You've got to pluck up courage; worrying won't make the days pass.'

Dariabibi agreed, but there were difficulties. She observed the purdah. There weren't any fields around. Though Amjad had given up school, he was reluctant to take the cattle to graze, such was the influence of education. He feared his father and did not talk back, but now he was defiant. He did not like farming. The first year, he worked with Chandra *Kaka*, but the harvest was poor. He had no love of the land and had neglected weeding. The following year Chandra suggested selling three *bighas* of land. The buyer was Yakoob. They still had a *bigha* and a half left, but that too had to go because Amjad no longer enjoyed the company of Chandra *Kaka*; he couldn't work so hard. Though annoyed with Amjad, Dariabibi had no grievance against him. For a thirteen-year-old, farming was a joking matter.

Amiran's family was small, but it wasn't easy to feed so many mouths in Dariabibi's family. In the beginning sympathy was not lacking, but there was a limit to that. Poor Chandra was much too busy. He farmed, fished and sang, and didn't always make money from these. Yet his sympathy was genuine. If he himself could not come, he would send Elokeshi to visit them. Elokeshi did not come empty-handed. She observed the formalities, bringing with her fish, vegetables or at least a slice of a pumpkin.

Things were crumbling all around. Naima could not see well; she would probably go blind.

Yakoob sometimes came with the usual pomp and circumstance and helped them with money. Borrowing money did not embarrass Dariabibi, but how long could one allow this state of affairs to continue? The cow, which of late yielded little milk, had to be sold, so there was no milk for Shari. She had to eat the food for grown-ups and sometimes had stomach trouble which did not mend easily.

In these hard times, Monadir's letter arrived to fill their cup of sorrow. He wrote:

Ma, please take my salaam. I have been to many places and am now going to school. If you can send me five rupees a month, it will help me to survive. If it is inconvenient, do not send it. I will still somehow survive. With my affection to Amu and Naima.

Yours affectionately
Muni.

The letter had come in an envelope. Amjad read it to his mother who, holding the envelope in her fist with a mixture of happiness and despair, started brooding. How big had Muni grown after these years? She buried her thoughts with a sigh. Five rupees were not the wealth of seven rajas, yet that was what had to be thought about first.

Amjad, who was sitting beside her, said, 'Ma, aren't you going to send money to Munibhai?'

'Can you do it?'

'Why not? You give me the money, I'll send it off by money order. There's a post office in the neighbouring village.'

A mocking smile formed on Dariabibi's lips. Amjad was still so innocent.

A little while ago Amjad had brought the news that Yakoob had filled a boat with the year's harvest and taken it away. The land had been sold to Yakoob some time back but, thanks to his generosity, the family received half the harvest after the sharecroppers had been paid off with the other half. Now that had come to an end. Yakoob owned the land, he'd take the harvest – there was nothing unusual about it, yet Dariabibi was silent with rage. She had felt no need to make any further queries. Holding Muni's letter in her hand, she first thought of Yakoob and muttered 'only five rupees', which Amjad could not hear.

When Yakoob came a couple of days later, Dariabibi sought his help.

'I want you to do me a favour.'

'Tell me, tell me,' Yakoob said eagerly. 'You're so quiet.'

'Not for nothing. You can see how "happy" we are.'

'Why should you be unhappy? Your smile fetches a hundred thousand rupees.'

At any other time Dariabibi would have found such unsolicited compliments insulting, but today she took it in good grace, though Yakoob, having said it, looked at Dariabibi from the corner of his eye.

'It's not an appeal for a hundred thousand; just five rupees.'

'Only?' Yakoob curled his lips.

'Yes.'

'Just?'

'Yes, but you'll have to pay it monthly.'

'Are you giving it to someone?'

'Yes.'

'Who?'

'Please don't ever ask me that.'

'Whatever you say,' Yakoob smiled and nodded. 'You tell me what else you want. You're like a rock, aren't you, never open your mouth. I took away the harvest and you didn't say anything.'

'You took the harvest of your land,' Dariabibi said, with smooth sarcasm in her voice. 'What have I got to say?'

'Why not? You're my kin. I bought the land; must I take the harvest as well?'

'You must.'

'One can't be cruel to one's own folk.'

'What's cruel about it?'

'You could have asked me why I'd taken away the harvest. You didn't. Well then I'll have to tell you. You know I've got two mounds of flesh at home. Their eyes ache because I've bought the land and yet there's no harvest coming in. So I took it home this time. Here's the money for the harvest.'

Yakoob took out twenty-five rupees from his pocket.

'The market price is two and a half rupees a *maund* and we had ten *maunds* of paddy.'

Dariabibi looked at Yakoob; nobody had ever seen such gratitude in her eyes.

Yakoob took out another five-rupee note from his wallet.

'Here. I'll pay this every month.'

Dariabibi put out her hand to take the money.

'Think of me as your own family, Dariabhabi.'

Dariabibi didn't reply, only looked straight at him. He lowered his eyes in fear.

In bed at night, Dariabibi agonised over Yakoob's behaviour. The note was still lying under her pillow.

Groping in the dark, Dariabibi found the note and pressed it against her eyes. She was bursting with tears. It was as if she needed such scraps of paper to soak them up.

Chapter Thirty-five

Amjad had bought an envelope from the post office.

Dariabibi said, 'Write to your Munibhai, Amu, telling him to come home soon.'

Amjad was sitting down to write the letter when Hashu arrived.

Dariabibi said, 'Hashu, you haven't been to see us for the last ten or twelve days.'

Hashu looked around carefully and then whispered, 'Don't you know my mother-in-law's temper, *Bubu*? She gets annoyed if I come here. I haven't borne a child, so starting with that she'd say a thousand things. When can I come?'

'Where's Sakerbhai?'

'I was worried about him as well. He went to fight over some *zamindar*'s land.'

'Can't you stop him?'

'Who listens? He got hurt in the leg this time. I made some lime and turmeric poultices for him. He's better today. He'd been gone for seven or eight days. I was worried sick. You don't feel like going visiting if your mind is not at rest, do you?'

Hashu looked at Dariabibi with questioning eyes.

'That's true,' Dariabibi sympathised. 'If you aren't happy, there's no pleasure in sleeping in a four-poster bed.'

Then turning to Amjad, she said, 'Don't bother to write anything else. Write about me and that we're well.'

'All right, Ma,' said Amjad, plying his pencil.

Hashu said, 'Who are you writing to, *Bubu*?'

'To my Muni.'

'Have you had news about him?'

'Yes.'

'Thanks to Allah! Amu, write my blessings.' Transported with joy, she added, 'There's a handsome boy to soothe a mother's heart.'

183

'My heart keeps burning, Hashubou,' Dariabibi said, sighing.

'Your treasure will return to you. You'll see, my words'll prove right. I've got this hunch.'

'Gold-fated Hashu, if that happens, I'll find a shore to this shoreless sea.'

'I'm sure your rightful treasure will come back to you.'

'He's fifteen now. How he's grown! I haven't seen him all these years.'

Dariabibi's distressed eyes touched Hashu as the two looked at each other.

Amjad, who had finished the letter, was now listening to the women. When they were silent, Amjad said, 'Can I write one more thing, Ma?'

'Have you written everything?'

'Yes.'

'What else then?'

'That *Abba*'s dead.'

'No, you don't have to write that,' Dariabibi said in a tone of reprimand.

'All right.'

It sounded as if the placid boy had gone cold.

Hashu got up to go.

'Amu, come see me off,' she said.

A very willing Amjad followed Hashu. They stood on the path below the compound. The world around them had turned sad in the twilight. Moheshdanga was virtually a jungle. Hashu had goose-pimples in the middle of the dense overgrowth. The outlines of the footpath were very faint. Cicadas on both sides had long started screeching. Hashu followed Amjad. After they had gone some distance, she held Amjad by the hand and said, 'Have you written my blessing, son?'

'I did, Hashu *Chachi*.'

'Really? Swear it. Touch me and tell.'

'I did, I did, I did, there, truth three times,' Amjad said, touching Hashu on the shoulder.

Happily, Hashu said, 'Come tomorrow. I'll cook some rice pudding for you.'

'Right. I'll be there.'

'And when you receive Muni's letter, let me know, don't delay.'

Hashu's gesture of request looked a little strange to Amjad.
'Now you can go, I'll find my way. Look out for snakes, son.'
It was Amjad's turn to be frightened. He did not wait to respond.
For snakes were what he was most scared of.

Chapter Thirty-six

Three or four months later another letter came from Monadir. He had changed address. He had been staying with a family who for some reason could no longer afford to support a student, so he had to go somewhere else and would need no less than fifteen rupees a month. What needed considering was what he should do now.

Dariabibi kept worrying. Fifteen rupees would see the family through a whole month without a hitch. Whatever paddy was received lasted four months; Allah ran the rest of the year. Sometimes Amjad went with Chandra to work as a labourer. People were reluctant to hire young people, but they paid three or four annas to please Chandra. Selling poultry and eggs somehow saw them through. Now, to top it all, there was this request from Muni. Dariabibi kept thinking. A way would have to be found. Throw herself again at Yakoob's feet? No, that wasn't possible. Yet all currents of thought finally converged at the same centre. Dariabibi decided she would have to tell Yakoob.

Yakoob laughed and said, 'Dariabhabi, why don't you just tell me what you need?'

'You've already done so much for us, I feel embarrassed.'

'Don't be embarrassed. I want to see a smile on your face.'

'Smiling doesn't come easy, does it?'

'It comes easy when the heart softens,' Yakoob smiled. There hadn't been any appreciable change in Dariabibi's body since her widowhood except a touch of ruggedness which endowed her with greater dignity. One might think she was haughty. But that was not how she saw herself. She thought she was becoming more like Ashekjan and turned pale in fear.

'No, that's how I look from outside,' Dariabibi said very softly.

'You suffer for nothing. All you have to do is to tell me. I'll pay this

186

fifteen rupees every month. Please ask for three months' advance before I leave.'

'May Allah do good to you. May he make you even richer,' Dariabibi said, her voice heavy with emotion.

'With your blessings,' said Yakoob. Then looking at her shamelessly, he said, 'Your smile fetches a hundred thousand rupees.'

'You shame me. We're poor, miserable. To think of our smile and its value!' Dariabibi concluded with a smile of sarcasm.

Yakoob was probably getting ready to assess the price of something beyond her smile, but she did not give him the opportunity.

'Left the pot on the stove; it's burning, I can smell it.' Dariabibi ran towards the the kitchen.

Yakoob from behind stared at the rhythm of Dariabibi's body and smiled.

Starvation was not unknown to Dariabibi. Sometimes the children would not stop eating until the pot was empty and she would happily serve, but there were times when she was found out and Amjad felt ashamed. Naima and Sharifa were too young to understand. When Amiran found out, Dariabibi got told off. Once she left, sulking, 'You wouldn't tell us, would you? We're not your own folk, are we? Would I be in trouble if you'd sent Amjad to get a fistful of rice or a vegetable?' But asking for something cut Dariabibi to the quick. Looking at her own past, she could no longer trust herself. Her self-confidence had crumbled away. In the past the days of starvation did not seem to be such a sad burden.

That night Dariabibi had nothing to eat after Naima and Amjad had finished. In the morning, when she was feeling fragile, Yakoob came, with no lack of ostentatious hospitality. Fine rice, fish, vegetables, ghee – nothing had been left out of his grand show.

So Dariabibi had to get down to cooking. When everybody had finished eating, Dariabibi ate on an empty stomach and ate well. In the past, sitting in front of the food provided by others had reminded her of Ashekjan and her feasts of the fortieth day of someone's death. Today she did not lack appetite and her hungry stomach made up for the rest.

After midday Amjad went to Chandra's looking for work and Naima, with Shari on her hip, went to Hashu's. Hashu had invited them the previous day. They had plucked a gourd; she would make a pudding with it.

There was a lot to do. Pots and pans had not been washed, the domestic animals needed attention, yet with her full stomach Dariabibi felt like nodding off. She thought she would put her head down for a bit, but as soon as she lay down, she felt very sleepy. There was nothing strange in a starved body wanting a holiday.

It was a hot day of *Vaishakh*, but the heat could not penetrate the thick vegetation around the house, so it felt cool in the room. From the jackfruit tree outside the window a dove kept cooing away. Today no anxiety invaded Dariabibi's fatigued body. She fell fast asleep.

But then she was suddenly awakened. Dariabibi felt she was being crushed in a close embrace. Opening her eyes, she saw Yakoob. She looked at the door. She had left the bamboo door ajar, but now it was shut. Dariabibi's whole body seemed to be getting cold. All she felt was someone else's hot breath on her nose. She tried to get up, but the other person was tying her down with a fierce firmness. In her feeble infirmity, she kept quiet and did not open her eyes again, as if she had gone blind and the whole world was covered in unbroken darkness.

Outside the bereaved dove-mother kept cooing inconsolably.

Chapter Thirty-seven

At meal time that evening, Amjad said, 'Ma, Yakoob *Chacha* left suddenly. I thought he was going to go tomorrow.'

Dariabibi at first didn't respond; then suddenly flaring up, she said, 'You're eating – go on eating. You talk too much.'

Amjad looked up at his mother, then concentrated on his meal. He got told off again the following morning. In the dumping ground behind the house, he found not just cooked food, but also uncooked vegetables. He knew Yakoob *Chacha* had brought these yesterday, so he ran to his mother.

'Ma, come and look. Who's thrown away so much food?'

Dariabibi was feeding ducks and hens; she pretended she hadn't heard. So her son urged her again.

'Can't you see I'm working?' Dariabibi snapped. 'Have you got holes for eyes?'

Looking at his mother's severe face, Amjad arrived at the firm conclusion that it was not wise to stay around much longer.

For the next three or four days Amjad moped about the house. He had never seen his mother in this state. Who knows how long this state of affairs would have continued? But things settled down with Yakoob's arrival. He did not come alone; he brought his son with him, as well as provisions. His son was nine or ten. Why had he brought his son? Dariabibi greeted the child normally and asked Yakoob the usual questions. Her brother-in-law's moves were beyond her comprehension.

Monadir had written again. Dariabibi got the fifteen rupees from Yakoob before he left with his son.

Amjad realised his mother's mood had not settled. He often got scolded; Naima, even Shari, got thrashed if they cried. Ma had never been like this. One day he went and complained to Amiran *Chachi*.

Amiran had not visited them for some time because of pressure of work. One day she came and said, '*Bubu*, is it true that you beat the children?'

'What if I beat them in my agony? My bones will rest when they die.'

'Fie, *Bubi*,' Amiran interrupted her. 'One doesn't say such inauspicious things. I've got only one; she doesn't burn me any less.'

'It's not the numbers. They're here to burn us whatever the number. One of them doesn't even show his face. I'm burning for him. Those who are here aren't burning me any less. Can't Allah take them away?'

Dariabibi had lost her reason. Amiran did not continue the conversation; she left on the excuse of having to get back to work.

Some hens, who hadn't had their feed at midday, were clucking away tormenting her ear. Dariabibi grabbed one close at hand and hurled it down on the ground. The wounded bird tossed about in agony.

Naima, who couldn't see well, was sitting on the veranda; she said, 'Ma, are you slaughtering chicken for dinner?' Dariabibi cried, 'Just you wait, *haramzadi*, I'll slaughter you.'

Amjad was returning home after playing; at the sound of his mother's roar, he crept away towards the outhouse. He would return when the atmosphere cleared.

Chapter Thirty-eight

Predators are skilled in setting up an ambush. Yakoob lacked no wiles. He haunted the house like a predatory animal who had tasted blood, but he did not take advantage of unguarded or helpless moments any more.

Amjad found the atmosphere at home unbearable. *Ma* seemed to be always immersed in some thought. Reprimand and scolding followed every little slip. He had never felt so uneasy and it was he who brought the news.

'Ma, Munibhai's written. He's coming tomorrow.'

'Tomorrow?'

'Yes.'

'Good.'

Amjad looked up at his mother's face, where there was no trace of happiness, as if he had brought day-to-day news.

'Ma!' Amjad called.

'What?'

'I wrote saying *Abba*'s dead and there's want in the family, come and see us one day.'

'Who told you to write all that?' Dariabibi glowered at her son. Amjad could not look back straight at her, but replied softly, 'Ma, Munibhai wouldn't come here because *Abba* beat him. That's why I wrote it without telling you.'

'All right.' Dariabibi went to attend to some job.

The following day Amjad alone stood waiting by the country road. The railway station was quite far. Munibhai would arrive exhausted. He wouldn't be at ease without at least this much welcome.

Monadir really came. When the two brothers got home in the evening, Naima started shouting, 'Ma, *Dada*'s here, *Dada*'s here.'

Dariabibi was in the kitchen at the time. There was no trace of her for five minutes. Monadir stood waiting quietly.

'Where's Ma, Naima?' Monadir asked as he cuddled her.

'In the kitchen.'

'Amu, let's go in.' He walked into the kitchen. The fire was crackling away. Leaning against a bamboo post, Dariabibi was fast asleep.

The brothers were surprised. Amjad called out, 'Ma, look who's here.'

Suddenly opening her eyes, Dariabibi looked on as if thunder-struck. She did not stretch out her arms in eagerness.

There had been great change in Monadir's body. He was fifteen, quite a big boy. A line of moustache had covered the fairness of his upper lip. It was as if that was what Dariabibi was looking at.

Amjad said, 'Can't you recognise Munibhai, Ma? Look how big he's grown.'

Like those of a paralytic, Dariabibi's eyes did not blink.

Monadir called out, 'Ma.'

She did not respond, only blinked once and looked on again.

Amjad was surprised; Naima came in and stood around.

Monadir had forgotten to give his mother the customary salu-tation; he now sat down and stretched out his hands to touch her feet, and Dariabibi held her son in her arms and burst into tears, crying loudly. Monadir felt his mother's breath on his body, and the beating of her breast, and he too wept silently.

Chapter Thirty-nine

'Look, *Bubu*, look how he's grown up!' Amiran said, addressing Dariabibi.

'He's grown up a bit, these three to four years.'

'Not just a bit. Look at his face. When he grows even more, he'll be strong like me, you'll see.'

'Let him live to match your toenail.'

'May he live as many years as I have hair on my head.'

There was the regular crowd on Amiran's veranda. Dariabibi had come to visit her soon after midday. Even Hashu had insisted on coming, defying her mother-in-law.

Monadir started sweating. Though a smart lad, he turned lack-lustre in a strange milieu like this. Ambia gaped open-mouthed at Monadir; she recalled how five years before on a cow-dust evening she had made a fool of him. Ambia's whole body seemed covered in shame.

Amiran reprimanded her daughter: 'What are you gawping at, unlucky one, he's your Munibhai. Go and play.'

But, seeking refuge, she slowly went and sat beside Dariabibi and did not show any willingness to move any further. Apart from the obligatory yes and no, Monadir hardly opened his mouth before Hashu. Hashu said, 'Speak up. You've changed, haven't you?'

Monadir bowed his head. Obeying his mother's instructions, he had touched Hashu's feet in customary salutation, but had not opened his mouth since.

'Why are you so shy?' Amiran asked Monadir.

His mother answered for him: 'He's grown up now; he knows it's bad manners to talk too much in front of elders.'

'Go and play. Go, go, Ambia, go.' Amiran gave the girl a push.

Amjad, who wanted nothing more than Munibhai's company, said, 'Let's go, *Dada*.'

That was an acceptable proposal; Monadir did not delay in responding. Ambia too started advancing with diffident feet and then after a moment or two vanished in the direction of the boys.

The women laughed out loud. Hashu said, 'What a girl! Lively, isn't she? Did you see how she ran?'

'Let her go,' said Amiran, who could not bear her daughter being praised. 'She's a torment.'

'*Bubu*, hasn't your son come back to you? I told you, didn't I?'

'I haven't got much hope in him.'

'Don't say such inauspicious things.'

Dariabibi did not reply; she just sighed. Amiran asked, 'How long is he going to stay?'

'He's going back the day after tomorrow.'

'Oh,' said Amiran and looked a little worried.

'You tell him *Bubu*. If he goes away again, I'll not survive.'

Together Hashu and Amiran said, 'Sure, I'll tell him.'

Ambia ran back laughing and everybody looked at her.

Amiran said, 'Ey, burnt-face, what are you laughing at?'

Ambia stopped laughing, responding to her mother's honeyed address. Then she said, 'Munibhai climbed up a tree and started singing. Then a monkey came along and he hurried down the tree and a red ant bit him.'

'So you laugh. Who knows where those damned monkeys have come from,' Amiran said, looking around at the plants in the courtyard. 'It's hard to protect the plants. They ate up my beans the other day.'

When Monadir got back, Amiran gave him much advice. Ambia had completely overcome her diffidence; she noisily munched puffed rice balls and coconut balls with the rest of them.

Dariabibi said, 'The time's passed happily.'

'Come back, Muni, son. You'll go away the day after tomorrow and I'll have to live with this unlucky one,' said Amiran, laughingly pointing at her daughter.

Chapter Forty

Monadir liked Chandra's proposal very much. He had learnt to read and write, so he would be the leader of their theatre group and write up the songs. These days *babus* didn't like simple country songs. Monadir would polish up the language.

Yet Monadir left on the due date. For some reason his mind did not settle here. He felt a certain lack of warmth in his mother's heart. During these three days he realised that his mother did not crave him as before. Dariabibi's abrupt manners pained Amjad and surprised Monadir. On the day he left, Dariabibi repeatedly requested him to come whenever he had a holiday.

Of late Hashu had been visiting frequently. There weren't any sympathetic souls around her; she had to suffer the torment of her infertile life. Here at least she could unburden her mind. Dariabibi was very affectionate to this inoffensive, simple country wife. Her mother-in-law grumbled, but did not quite say anything to her face about her visits, because Saker himself would defer to Dariabibi's wishes and would even argue in her favour with his mother.

On the day Monadir left, Hashu had come quite early and was not talking of going home even when it was quite late. She kept nattering on to Dariabibi as she helped her with her little household chores.

'Don't be sad, *Bubu*. Such a gem of a child, whose is he except yours?'

It was as if such consoling words were stuck to her lips.

Despondent, Dariabibi kept herself busy, but her mind was not on their small talk. A wicker basket had come apart; she sat down to repair it with Hashu's help.

'*Bubu*, by the grace of Allah, your health is fine, you're putting on weight,' said Hashu.

With a quick look to see if she was well covered, Dariabibi said,

'They say he's fine but nobody sees his teeth gone black eating water-lily seeds.'

Hashu clammed up. There wasn't a trace of friendliness in Dariabibi's voice; she sounded as if she was arguing.

Hashu released a sigh of relief when she heard her mother-in-law calling out for her – it was as if Dariabibi was so very annoyed with her. Frightened, she said softly, '*Bubu*, I'll go now.'

Dariabibi kept splitting a bamboo cane; she did not respond. Perhaps she hadn't heard Hashu, she was so absorbed in her work. Hashu guiltily took leave.

That same afternoon Yakoob came with his son. He left the boy with Dariabibi; he would return in a couple of days.

Yakoob had brought provisions for the whole family; there was no problem on that count. Her own child had left today; now she was burdened with someone else's. But Dariabibi did not neglect the child. The boy was well-spoken and smart. To ease the burden of her mind, Dariabibi asked him many questions about Yakoob's family life.

'You've got two mothers, haven't you?'

'Yes, *Chachi*. I'm the son of my older ma. We're two brothers.'

'How's your younger mother?'

'She quarrels with my mother and with my father.'

'Does she quarrel with you?'

'Yes. There was an argument today. That's why *Abba*'s brought me along with him.'

'There was a quarrel?'

'There's a quarrel every day. That's why *Abba* doesn't stay at home these days.'

'Where does he stay then?'

'He sleeps in the outhouse. And he's sick, he's poorly.'

With the boy lying beside her, Dariabibi gathered more information from him. Yakoob's home was a hell. They were well off by rural standards so, apart from cooking and eating, the women didn't have much to do. In their pride of possessing money and clothes they were forever quarrelling with each other.

After a couple of days, Yakoob said, 'Dariabhabi, I'd like to leave the boy here. There at home he'll never grow up to be a man.'

Amjad was standing in front of him; Dariabibi had to reply.

'Why here in a bamboo shack when you've got a brick building?'

'They'll be spoilt by their mothers. There's only squabbles and arguments.'

Dariabibi did not give any reply.

Yakoob set off with his son. Amjad, who had become friendly with the boy, followed them. A little later he returned and said, 'Ma, he's given you these fifteen rupees. He said he'd forgotten.'

Muni had left with two rupees only. The money would have to be sent off by tomorrow, Dariabibi brooded.

Chapter Forty-one

The immovable days had to be pushed with all one's might. No rest or laxity would be allowed even if one's veins and arteries rebelled. At the bends of the ascent a burden, becoming transfixed, taunted the struggling limbs. If then a storm brewed up in the valley, helplessness and despondency came rushing in like great echoes of the roaring clouds.

Dariabibi had arrived at the cliff face where, among forests teeming with predators and full of ravines, water did not slake thirst nor breeze take away fatigue.

'Ma.'

With her back to the yard, Dariabibi was sifting rice, so she hadn't seen the stranger. Turning round, she was surprised; Monadir had come. He was carrying a sack on his shoulder, his body dripping with sweat. The wayfarer's fatigue was evident from the shortness of his breath.

'What a surprise!'

'Three months to go before the summer holiday. There's an exam on, we've got a week's holiday. So I came along.'

'You've done well.'

Dariabibi took Monadir's shirt off and wiped away the sweat. Hearing the noise, Amjad came along and offered Monadir a cane stool.

Dariabibi was happy; she put the rice pot on. They had finished their midday meal a little while ago and the pot was empty. Amjad sometimes hid an egg or two for pocket money; he brought an egg.

'Where did you find the egg?' Dariabibi asked.

'The red hen lays wherever it likes. Yesterday it was on the *machang* in the cowshed. I forgot to tell you.'

Dariabibi was pleased with her son's skill in discovering things.

She was thinking of doing fried potatoes and dhal. Now that an egg had been found, there would be a complete meal.

Monadir went and bathed in the pond. Elated, he bragged to his brother and sister. He took out a few clay dolls and gave them to Naima and Shari, who were transported with delight. He took out a pair of good tops for Amjad, who jumped at the suggestion that the two brothers would play with those under the jackfruit tree.

To Dariabibi the whole afternoon played like a melody. She had not found such happiness with the children for a long time. With great enthusiasm, she sat down to cook for the evening meal. Amjad had gone to Amiran to ask for a gourd; she gave him a chicken to go with it. Dariabibi brought out all her skill to cook chicken curry with gourd.

After the meal they sat on the veranda, talking. Monadir was at ease; the environment was no longer unfamiliar to him. Dariabibi too unreservedly joined in the rumpus with the children. The next day Amjad and Monadir wandered about by the river, across the fields, in the bushes and jungle off the track. This was the sort of freedom Amjad loved, but left to himself he was rather timid and diffident. He overcame it only when Munibhai was with him.

Amjad was happier because Ma was in a light-hearted mood.

It was Monadir who asked his younger brother, 'Amu, I think Ma's getting a bit fat.'

'Yes, Munibhai, I think she's poorly.'

'No, she's built like me.'

'That's true. You'll be stout like Chandra *Kaka* when you grow up.'

'Well, that's why I'm still alive. With what they feed you at the school hostel, I'd have been ill.'

Enjoying the glory of his brother's heroics, Amjad proposed, 'You want to learn to wield the *latthi* from Saker *Chacha*.'

'I will, when I get back to the village. I'll be good at it.' Monadir showed him his biceps.

They were standing at a spot by the river. It was the month of *Chaitra* and the river was dry. Reeds had grown on the sandbanks on both sides of the river. They had spent much time looking for kingfisher nests in vain. Now leaning against the thick trunk of a *chalta* tree, they were looking far into the cloudless sky. The fields were shimmering under the fountain of a liquid sun. A lonely palm tree blended its trembling body in the sighing wind. In between their words, the two village boys felt the vastness of the world.

Only hunger put an end to the enjoyment of leisure. Back home they found Yakoob had come visiting. Ma hadn't (but Amjad had) told Monadir that this man had given them much help during the last three or four years. Monadir was shy with strangers; he could not initiate a conversation on his own.

When the children sat down to their evening meal, Dariabibi did her duty like a submissive slave. Trying to liven up the atmosphere, Amjad made a joke about Muni and got told off. Eating then became their sole object of meditation.

They had only two rooms. Arrangements were made for Amjad and Yakoob to sleep in one room while Monadir was to sleep in the other room with Ma, Naima and Shari.

Monadir didn't have much conversation with his mother. Thinking how hard she'd worked all day, he fell asleep.

Dariabibi lay sleepless for a long time. It was summer, yet a quilt covered her legs up to her knees. Beyond the window, moonlight had filled the sky.

She couldn't sleep. Finding everybody else asleep, Dariabibi gently opened the door and walked out into the courtyard. Near the window, moonlight filtered down through the leaves of the jackfruit tree. Only a few dull stars shone in the sky. Dariabibi stood there for quite a while. Only occasional bird-calls and the distant barking of dogs broke the silence of the sleeping village.

Perhaps Dariabibi would happily have stood there in that condition for ever, but suddenly a shadow fell across the moonlight. Shivering, she made a move towards the open yard and saw Yakoob advancing towards her. As if under a spell, Dariabibi stood transfixed on the spot.

After a few moments when she had regained her composure, Dariabibi whispered, 'Why are you here?'

'Don't you know why, Daria?'

By then he was holding her by the hand.

Perhaps a tussle would have ensued but, putting his head out of the window, Monadir called out, 'Ma, you're out on your own so late. Why didn't you call me?'

'I'm coming, son. You were asleep, so I didn't call you.'

Like a thief Yakoob moved to slip into the dark, but his long shadow could not escape the moonlight.

When with trembling breast Dariabibi rushed back into the room and shut the door, Monadir was still standing at the window. He said, 'Ma, it was probably a thief. I saw a shadow by the jackfruit tree.'

'No,' Dariabibi said in the dark. 'Now go to bed.'

'Right. But, Ma, don't go out at night on your own.'

'What have we got to attract thieves?' Dariabibi said.

Monadir watched the moonlit night for a few minutes and then went back to bed.

What with the day's fatigue and sleeplessness caused by anxiety, Dariabibi fell asleep before dawn and for the first time in her life missed the crow-cawing morning.

Who knows how much longer she would have slept, but Amjad suddenly rushed into the room and called, 'Ma! Ma!'

With sleepy eyes, Dariabibi snapped, 'What is it?'

'Where are Munibhai's clothes?'

'On the bamboo rack.'

'They aren't there.'

Dariabibi opened her eyes to look at him.

'Aren't they in your room?'

'No. Yakoob *Chacha* left early in the morning.'

Wrapping the quilt round her, Dariabibi sat up and rubbed her eyes. Monadir's bag and his clothes were not on the rack.

Dariabibi went out, her body trembling.

'Go and have a look round the pond; he may be there.'

As Amjad went away, Dariabibi entered the adjoining room and found that Monadir's books were not there either.

Dariabibi would probably have fainted, but she summoned her strength of mind. No, fainting would not suit her.

To ward off the blow, she firmly held her buzzing head in her hands and sank down on the veranda. She only needed a little while to get her breath back.

Chapter Forty-two

One night Chandramani left the village with Rajendra. Chandra hadn't come visiting for about a month. Amjad went to see him, but he had changed much. He still drank, but drank quietly; didn't make a racket, didn't sing. Chandramani's two children lived with their maternal uncle.

Dariabibi heard the news from Hashu and Amiran, but did not make any remark. It was futile sending Amjad to Chandra when he was maddened by his own head-sores. Dariabibi felt sad about Chandra, his misfortune. But then what could one do? Rather than living forever dependent on her brother, Chandramani had passed into somone else's refuge. What harm would that do to the world?

One evening Dariabibi wanted to go to Chandra's house for a visit. Amjad was willing too. But she appeared to have lost her enthusiasm. Who wouldn't be curious about crazy Chandra's home? Even religious bigots like Azhar had got to appreciate Chandra. But she hadn't proposed this when Azhar was alive. She'd never go again, she said to herself. In a village community one person's scandal weighed heavily on the whole family.

A month later, Amjad went to his mother and said, 'Ma, Munibhai's money has come back. Here.'

He counted out the fifteen rupees.

'Why did the money come back?'

'The postman says Munibhai's gone away from there.'

'Gone away,' Dariabibi muttered to herself but did not exchange any further words with her son. Holding the money in her hand, she sat like a graven image. Why should an honest son accept gifts from his fallen mother?

Amjad had already told Hashu, near whose house the postman stood distributing letters. Hashu came, but seeing Dariabibi's tearful face, did not say anything, just quietly sat down beside her.

Gradually Dariabibi's face turned sullen; tears ran down her fair rounded cheeks. Hashu said to Amjad, 'Get me a little water, son.'

Amjad promptly obeyed her orders.

Wiping away Dariabibi's tears, Hashu said, '*Bubu*, the boy's a wanderer; he'll come back again. One doesn't worry so much about a male child.'

Dariabibi did not reply. Hashu tried to lighten the atmosphere.

'It's getting late,' she said. 'You've got a lot to do, come on, get up.'

Some ducks and hens, awaiting their evening feed, were raising a din in the courtyard.

'If you don't get up, I won't be able to go home,' Hashu insisted. 'Your son is still yours.'

Now there weren't any tears in Dariabibi's eyes, but she was absorbed in her thoughts; her chin resting on her knee, she sat like a female image of immobility.

'Get up,' Hashu said, holding her hand. 'You aren't very well yourself; your face looks all puffed up. How's your body going to hold up if you behave like this?'

'I'll get up. You go home now,' Dariabibi said softly.

'You first.'

'I'm getting up. You go now.'

'Well, I'll look back from the far end of the courtyard; if you haven't got up by then, I'll walk back.'

Hashu did as she said. But Dariabibi really got up and attended to the ducks and hens.

Chapter Forty-three

Saker had taken Naima to the district town hospital. Her vision was becoming dim. Her eyes secreted pus so profusely that she could not open them in the morning. So Dariabibi sought Saker's help; Chandra hadn't set foot here for a long time. The hospital doctor had prescribed medicine, but a cure was uncertain. Dariabibi heard the doctor's opinion, but she did not take it too seriously. A blind one's day didn't stop, did it?

Over the last couple of months, Dariabibi had become very calm and composed. She did not neglect her work, but went about it slowly, as if her mind had fled elsewhere in the foreground of which her work was no more than the performance of a duty. She was not annoyed with the children. Shari pestered her but she ignored it. Amjad feared for her present state as much as he had feared her bad temper in the past. The other day his old *lungi* and shirt had disappeared, but when he told her, she simply said, 'So what?' She did not reprimand him, as if she had forgotten how to. Amjad sensed something unnatural in the atmosphere. If Amiran came visiting, Dariabibi became a little lively, but Hashu was hardly noticed. She did exchange a word or two with Hashu, who hung about until it was time to leave. Dariabibi was never chatty; now it was as if her store of words was exhausted.

One morning Yakoob came carrying regal gifts. Dariabibi hated making scenes in front of the children; she quietly put them away.

Yakoob promptly went and lay down in Amjad's room. His eyes sunken, he looked drawn. Dariabibi hadn't made any enquiries beyond the formal ones.

A little later Dariabibi entered Amjad's room.

'Are you asleep?'

That was her first real question to Yakoob, who was lying, his face covered by a sheet, as if he was afraid of showing his face in the light of day.

Uncovering his face, Yakoob looked at Dariabibi. Her eyes were turned away from him.

'Did you say something?'

Without a reply, Dariabibi put down the fifteen silver coins. 'You won't have to give me those fifteen rupees any more.'

'Why not?'

Yakoob's face was lacklustre, his bones boiling with fever.

As Dariabibi turned to leave the room, Yakoob called out in the cracked voice of a dying patient, 'Listen.'

Turning round a little, still facing the direction in which she was going, she said, 'What is it?'

'I've had this fever for a whole week. I've come here for a little peace.'

'We're not setting your clothes on fire, are we?' Dariabibi replied heartlessly.

'No. It's no small matter that you've given me shelter in my misery. There's no place for me at home and I'm not well. If you take back these coins I'll be relieved of pain.'

'There's no need for the money.'

'No?'

'No,' Dariabibi said. 'Would you like some sago?'

'Yes.' Yakoob's voice sounded like a cry of misery.

Dariabibi walked out quickly without waiting to find out if the patient needed anything else.

Amjad was surprised by his mother's enthusiasm today. There was a variety of fish. Yakoob had brought ghee as well as a couple of *seers* of mutton and vegetables. With great eagerness Dariabibi poured out her cooking skill as if exulting victoriously at an enemy being laid low somewhere. There was no ebbing of enthusiasm at the meal. Amjad had never seen Dariabibi eating with such appetite. The food was excellent.

After a rest following the feast, when Dariabibi entered Yakoob's room with a pot of sago, she found him asleep. Putting down the bowl on one side of the bed, Dariabibi looked at him. She had not looked him full in the face before. He was emaciated like a withering plant and the darkened corners of his eyes bore witness to the burden of misery under which he lay.

Standing there, Dariabibi scrutinised the face. The poor man

205

looked miserable. He had suffered from fever these last seven days and was exiled from home in that condition. He had a high fever, perhaps his last. The final days of Azhar's life flashed through her mind.

Yakoob was sleeping quietly – or lying with closed eyes, who knows? Dariabibi felt pity welling up in her breast. The man had travelled all the way by boat, had walked for a mile in his condition and was still starving. Could Dariabibi remain unmoved any longer? She wished he would wake up and eat the sago. But as she was about to wake him, she stopped, as if someone had suddenly put a hand round her throat to choke her.

A man in misery had come to her door for refuge. All the hate was wiped from Dariabibi's mind. She looked at Yakoob; his body was not covered properly; one side of his chest was exposed; his legs below the knees were not covered. If he remained exposed, his fever could rise.

Dariabibi advanced slowly and very carefully touched him to take his temperature. There was no doubt that he had a high fever. She slowly covered his body with the sheet. Before she had taken her hand off the sheet, Yakoob opened his eyes to look. Dariabibi shivered in fright, as if, putting her hand into a hole for *ban* fish she had touched a snake, and quickly made her way out of the room.

'The sago's on the bed, get up and eat it,' she said.

Yakoob closed his eyes, perhaps to sleep again.

Chapter Forty-four

The fever did not abate. People from Yakoob's home came to make enquiries. The nearest doctor lived ten miles away, but Yakoob had no interest in treatment. So they went back.

But three days later news came from the river ghat that, filling two boats, Yakoob's wives had arrived. Now there was no getting away from returning home. And that was what happened. That was his final trip. He did not die of fever, but he did not come back to Moheshdanga again.

Two or three months later along the road of grinding poverty and starvation and anxiety came the night, the playground of which was darkness itself. Dariabibi needed the darkness. She put up her hand to Allah in thanksgiving. What if it had come in the light of the day, in front of the people, the children? How kind you are, Allah! A thousand thanks to you for this much kindness!

The black wings of the night were spread over Moheshdanga. Sleep ruled all around. Perhaps the night birds were awake. And so was Dariabibi.

Dariabibi was awake; she got to her feet and, lamp in hand, stood on the veranda. The flame of the lamp trembled in a gentle wind. A little while before she had shut the door from outside. Amjad, Shari and the near-blind Naima were all asleep. Her ears pricked up, she listened to the breathing of the young ones. It was not possible for her to wait there much longer.

Holding her breath, Dariabibi entered the kitchen and put the bar on the door from the inside. She gave the door a pull to see if it was firmly shut. Then, putting down the lamp, she spread out the mat.

Her whole body was shaking but she had not yet betrayed the slightest twinge of pain. The whole burden was upon her; nobody else would come to her assistance.

As soon as she spread out the mat and took off the tattered *kurta*, a great shaking seized her whole body. She quickly loosened her sari at the waist and a pile of clothes, rags, Naima's loincloth and Amjad's shirt among them, fell out. The swollen abdomen of the expectant mother was not brightened by the light of the lamp. In an even darker place lay the nest of the wonder of all wonders, the human child. Dariabibi ran her hand over her abdomen and remembered what Amiran had said – '*Bubu*'s body seems to be bursting.' Ah, if only it would burst! What a pleasure that would be. Dariabibi took a breath of relief. There was much to do. However much the human child in the darkness of the womb screamed in its eagerness to get out, there would be no let up in Dariabibi's lifelong devotion to duty. She took down a number of small quilts from the shelf and put them on a corner of the mat.

Then lying on her stomach, she grabbed the mat. Ah, if only she had the freedom to cry out a little! To make sure that the children did not wake up, she had not allowed them to sleep during daytime and had kept Amjad working all day. Dariabibi knew that the sleep induced by fatigue was deep. Now, for the first time, Dariabibi puckered up her face in pain. As her grip on the mat slipped, she stretched out and held on to the mud floor. Where else but in the refuge of her mother would the daughter of the soil find strength?

The unbearable pain did not make Dariabibi lose consciousness. She couldn't bear any insult to the stranger–guest. With a hand behind her she had to make sure that it did not slip on to the ground.

There were no more questions in Dariabibi's eyes. Let your coming, O primeval child, be hastened! In the midst of so much pain, your mother looks forward to your coming. So much shame, such humiliation and the scorn of the world out there await me while I wait for you. In her struggle with her mind, this dignified woman had often been beaten – now like a victor she turned simultaneously into mother and midwife. She shook her own body heavily. Unlike the dear wife of a householder, she had no time to stay in confinement for long. Mother and midwife, she had much to do.

Perhaps only God knows how one hour and a half passed.

A helpless cry of the baby sounded the alert through the small kitchen.

The earthenware bowl and water were kept ready.

Dariabibi held the baby to her breast. Perhaps she would have stayed in that position had not the baby's cry brought her to her senses. At this warning, Dariabibi looked at the baby through tears of gratitude and then concluded the details of washing in the bowl. For a bed, she spread out some thin quilts, wrapped the baby in two more, and laid it down. Her own clothes were awry. Promptly cleaning herself, she exposed her breast to the newest guest. What an exquisite suckling noise! What a healthy and fair-complexioned baby! Dariabibi gave it warmth. As she gazed at the baby, suddenly a few drops of tears fell without Dariabibi noticing.

Out there somewhere foxes called out the time. Two owls argued and then hooted in unison.

Was there any pain in the body, or any disability? Perhaps not, Dariabibi sat, expressionless. Warmed by the mother, the baby fell asleep; he too was expressionless. Outside the world lay asleep; inside the kitchen what a profound peace! The child and the mother, in each other's closeness, had forgotten the world.

For humans, was it so easy to forget? A cock crowed; it was nearly dawn. Dariabibi thought to herself, It's nearly dawn; good, it'll soon be morning.

Another cock crowed. She heard it coming from the direction of Saker's house.

As the baby was laid down, he shivered a little, shaking his hands and legs at the interruption to his early sleep. Then he became calm again.

Dariabibi gazed unblinkingly at the baby and then kissed it a few times.

Then she quickly got to her feet. Who could ever blame her for laxity in matters of duty?

Early morning wind blew in through an opening near the support-ing beam of the roof. It was still dark outside.

Standing on the *machang*, Dariabibi tied the cow-rope to the roof-beam. She wasn't just a mother and midwife, she was an executioner too.

She got back to the baby and found him asleep. A male child. Lightly kissing him a few times, Dariabibi rose to her feet. How very affectionate and loyal were the cocks and hens whom Dariabibi fed with her own hands every day. The grateful birds played the morning *sehnai*.

It wouldn't do to delay any longer, Dariabibi said to herself. Suddenly she recalled Ashekjan: the old woman was walking, leaning on a stick, returning from a fortieth-day feast, carrying a bundle of food.

Dariabibi looked at the noose. There she wanted to hang the worries and weariness brought on by the struggle of a lifetime and then rest.

Before that she blew out the lamp and darkened the room.

Chapter Forty-five

The sun had risen on the trees, filling the sky.

Ma didn't hurry them, so Amjad, Naima and Shari slept long.

But when they got up to find that they could not get out of the room, they started shouting and screaming. Saker's mother sent Hashu to look. She opened the door for them.

It was she again who had to devise a trick to open the kitchen from the outside. Her eyes first fell on the newborn baby lying in a forest of colourful quilts. `

Then, looking up, she screamed. In the midst of the fearful situation that followed she picked up the baby in his quilt to hold him close to her breast and did not put him down.

Within a short time this little-known courtyard in this sparsely populated village filled up with a small crowd. Along came Rahim Bakhsh, Rohini Choudhury, the *chowkidar*, Saker, Amiran and many others. The rich ones, the dust from whose feet had never fallen in poor Azhar's courtyard, came too. Those who kept the gates of death decorated were the ones who were more curious about death. They had come to satisfy their curiosity.

A certificate from the president of the local Union Board was enough for everything, so the matter did not got to the police.

Holding the baby to her breast, Hashu went home. Saker raised his objections, but Hashu was desperate. All opposition was swept away in the face of Hashu's indomitable spirit and insistence that the baby was by no means guilty.

Amiran offered refuge to Amjad, Naima and Shari.

Monadir came a couple of months later. He was a young man now. He had taken a job in a jute factory and had a defiant look about him.

Amiran held him by the hands and cried loud and long. Monadir said that while he would work in town, his home would forever be Moheshdanga.

With Amjad, Monadir went to Chandra's. Monadir had come with seven days' leave, but his heart was reluctant to leave the village.

Monadir asked Chandra if it was possible to set up a folk theatre group.

Chandra said, 'People don't want to listen to songs any more. It's hard to fill one's belly singing.'

Monadir was disappointed. Chandra told him that regular jobs were not available in the village.

Monadir said, 'Then let's go to town. You can work hard. They'd love to have you.'

'Really?'

'Yes, *Kaka*, I'll get my mate to find a job for you.'

'Right. When are you going?'

'The day after tomorrow. I'll find something for Amjad as well.'

'I'll go.'

Chandra had a great love of the unknown; yet he was silent for a while as he looked at the palm trees and the fields that stretched to the horizon. Flocks of home-seeking birds were flying towards the dark. Chandra was absorbed in the pastoral atmosphere. There was a certain sadness in his heart.

He said, 'What time are you setting off? We'll go to the station together.'

As if he was prepared to go to the other side of the world with Amjad and Muni.

It was the cow-dust hour of the evening.

A faint darkness spread out in all directions as the colours of the sunset west were being extinguished.

Three silhouettes stood by Dariabibi's grave. They could be recognised as Monadir, Amjad and Chandra.

Monadir stood, his head lowered, his eyes flooded with tears. He was a town-dweller now; over the last six months he had met people at the jute factory who had given him a new vision. He knew much about the world. Yet he could not suppress his tears. A crescendo of agonised ragas surged in his heart. Finally he said, 'Save me a little place in your heart, Ma.' And burst out crying.

Chandra went over to him and said, 'A man doesn't cry so much for his mother, son. I haven't got my mother either. Let's go. It's getting late.'

But Chandra himself was overwhelmed. In a tear-choked voice, he said, 'Dariabibi, salaam, salaam . . .'

He put his arms round the two brothers standing on either side. The three of them walked down the known–unknown highway.

Glossary

Aghran   the eighth month of the Bengali year; late autumn
babu   Bengali Hindu gentleman; equivalent of Mr
baiji   professional singing and dancing woman
batasha   biscuit made of molasses
baul   mendicant singers of Bengal with songs of great spirituality that cross religious boundaries
bidi   country cigarettes; simply made out of rolled up tobacco leaves
bigha   land measure; about a third of an acre
bokul   name of a tree or its small scented flowers
chador   wrapper for the upper part of the body; like a shawl
Chaitra   the last month of the Bengali year; a dry, hot month
chowkidar   a watchman
dhoti   a long piece of cloth wrapped round the waist in a special way. Generally worn by Hindu men in northern India
Eid-gah   open field where Muslims meet for *Eid* prayers
fateha   prayer for the dead or the saints
ferishta   angel
gamtcha   a handloom-woven towel sometimes used as a scarf
ghomta   covering a woman's head, usually with the end of a sari
Hadith   the body of traditions relating to Mohammed
haji   a Muslim man who has made a pilgrimage (*haj*) to Mecca
haram   impure; forbidden by Islam
haramzada   the son of a violator of a prohibition; a word of abuse
haramzadi   the daughter of a violator; a word of abuse
jatra   folk theatre of Bengal
jhinga   vegetable of the cucumber family
kahan   measure of bulk of agricultural produce
karanja   wild plant yielding oil-rich seeds
katha   land measure; a twentieth of a *bigha*
kaviraj   traditional Hindu physician
khichuri   dish of rice cooked with *dal* (pulses)
koyet-bel   variety of wood-apple

kurta collarless shirt worn by men

Lakhshmi Hindu goddess of fortune; a woman who has her qualities

latthi strong, slim bamboo staff; a weapon of martial art

luchi small round flat bread, deep-fried in oil or butter

lungi piece of ankle-length cloth usually worn by Muslims; tied around the waist like a sarong

machang built-in wide bamboo shelf

maktab Islamic school

maund weight measure; about 38 kg

moulana title given to a Muslim respected for his learning

moulvi learned Muslim; a teacher

neem tree with bitter leaves of medicinal value

paan betel leaf filled with various spices, chewed as a digestive

paanwallah seller of *paan*

pakur large tree, usually planted by roadside for its shade

palki Bengali palanquin or sedan chair

parata flat fried bread

pidi very low wooden seat

pir Muslim spiritual guide

pirhan long, loose shirt

potol vegetable of the cucumber family

puja Hindu worship

sala mild swear word; literally, wife's brother

sandesh Bengali sweetmeat

seer Weight measure; about a kilogram

sehnai wind instrument, like the oboe, played at diverse events: weddings, farewells

shapla variety of water lily

Sharia the laws of Islam which govern the religious and secular lives of Muslims

shika pot holder, made of jute string; hung from beams

sizda the gesture of kneeling and touching the ground with the forehead while praying

toddy fermented palm wine

Vaishakh the first month of the Bengali year; a summer month

zakat wealth tax a Muslim is required by his religion to pay towards charity for the poor; the charity thus received

zamindar landowner/landlord

Translator's note

Bengali words for family relationships are not confined to the actual family members. A woman may call a friend 'sister', a child may call unrelated adults 'auntie' and 'uncle', a man may call a distantly related woman 'sister-in-law', and so on. The choice of epithets reflects the perceived standing of the person so called. Furthermore, within actual family relationships, a Bengali word would amplify that relationship while the English word would not: for example, the English word 'aunt' may be qualified to specify 'husband's aunt'. The Bengali terms have mostly been retained in this book, especially in conversation. The following list gives English equivalents, distinguishing between Muslim and Hindu use.

Kinship titles

abba father
babaji father
bhabi brother's wife
bhai brother
bou wife
bubu elder sister (Muslim)
chacha uncle, father's brother (Muslim)
chachi aunt, father's brother's wife (Muslim)
dada elder brother
dadi father's mother (Muslim)
didi elder sister
kaka father's brother (usually Hindu)
kaki father's brother's wife (usually Hindu)
khala aunt, mother's sister
ma mother
pishi father's sister (Hindu)